DOWN A BAD ROAD

REGINA BUTTNER

Black Rose Writing | Texas

©2023 by Regina Buttner
All rights reserved. No part of this book may be reproduced, stored in a retrieval system or
transmitted in any form or by any means without the prior written permission of the
publishers, except by a reviewer who may quote brief passages in a review to be printed in a
newspaper, magazine or journal.

The author grants the final approval for this literary material.

First printing

This is a work of fiction. Names, characters, businesses, places, events, and incidents are
either the products of the author's imagination or used in a fictitious manner. Any
resemblance to actual persons, living or dead, or actual events is purely coincidental.

ISBN: 978-1-68513-188-3
PUBLISHED BY BLACK ROSE WRITING
www.blackrosewriting.com

Printed in the United States of America
Suggested Retail Price (SRP) $21.95

Down a Bad Road is printed in Minion Pro

*As a planet-friendly publisher, Black Rose Writing does its best to eliminate unnecessary waste to
reduce paper usage and energy costs, while never compromising the reading experience. As a result,
the final word count vs. page count may not meet common expectations.

For R & B

To Meredith,

Best wishes!

Regina Buttner

DOWN A
BAD ROAD

CHAPTER 1

Lavender took a bottle of white wine out of the fridge, poured herself a big glass over ice, and dialed the psychic's number. "Thanks for agreeing to do this over the phone," she said when Penelope answered. "I was afraid to go out with that snowstorm coming."

"Phone readings aren't ideal, but I'll do my best," Penelope said. "I see you texted me some photos. Is that the new boyfriend you told me about the last time you were here?"

"Yes!" Lavender's voice bubbled with happiness. "That's Ron Burley. He's actually my fiancé now, he proposed to me this morning. Got down on one knee and everything." Holding her left hand up to catch the fading afternoon light, she admired her sparkly new engagement ring. The princess cut diamond was gorgeous. Burley must have blown the last of his savings on it, hoping to impress her with his devotion. Well, it had certainly worked.

"You've filed for divorce then, I take it?" Penelope said, like the prim old granny that she was.

"Of course I did. Clint and I split up months ago. Anyway, I sent you those photos because—"

"Hold on, don't tell me anything else," Penelope said. "I'm feeling something coming through from his image. Give me a few seconds to concentrate."

Lavender drank more wine and tapped her periwinkle fingernails on her glass, wondering what kind of flowers to put in her wedding bouquet. Tulips would be nice, or maybe a big bunch of peonies in different shades of pink.

"Hmmm," Penelope said after a moment.

Lavender shook herself from her flowery daydream. "What is it?"

"You told me once before that your ex-husband had a temper," Penelope said, "but this man may be even worse."

Lavender giggled, already buzzed from the wine. "That's ridiculous! Burley's the sweetest, most laidback guy you'll ever meet. I've never even heard him raise his voice."

"Just you wait," Penelope said darkly. "He's going to explode one of these days."

"Yeah, right." Lavender twisted a lock of her long blonde hair around her forefinger. "I seriously doubt it. Never mind that, anyway. I have an important question about him and the woman in the second photo I sent. Her name is Marta."

Penelope made a grumbling sound in her throat. "This is why I try to avoid phone readings, especially when it's a complicated situation like this one."

Lavender frowned. "What do you mean, complicated?"

Penelope hesitated before answering. "There's a lot more to this than you realize. I'd much rather sit down with you in person, it would be easier to explain things that way."

Lavender huffed in annoyance. *Why couldn't the damn woman spit it out?* "What's there to explain? Marta was a childhood friend of Burley's, they grew up together. All I want to know is if there was ever anything romantic between them."

"Wait a second while I study her picture." There was a moment of silence, then Penelope spoke again: "He's definitely not in love with her."

"Obviously not, since he wants to marry *me*. Besides, Marta's dead now."

"Dead?" Penelope said. "I don't think so."

Lavender choked on her wine. "Yes, she is!" she sputtered. "She literally died of cancer a few days ago." *And not a moment too soon.*

Penelope chuckled. "Who told you that?"

"Burley did."

"I'm not so sure his information is accurate. There's an aura surrounding Marta's image, and the color is a vivid green. Green symbolizes life and strength."

Lavender gasped. "But wait, how is that even possible?"

"I don't know, I'm just telling you what I see. There's also a gray area within her inner aura, which is often a sign of fear or paranoia. My sense is that she's alive and her body is perfectly healthy. It's her mind that's sick."

The wine glass clanged against the coffee table as Lavender sat up straight. *Was Penelope out of her freaking mind?* "But I'm *certain* Marta's dead!" she said. "Burley told me so this morning. You must be confusing her with someone else."

"When a spirit crosses over to the afterworld, messages do occasionally get mixed up," Penelope said. "This is an art, you know, not a science. But the vibrations coming from this woman's photo are very strong, which means her soul is still dwelling on the earth plane, and I believe it's entwined in some way with your fiancé's."

Auras? Vibrations? Earth plane? Lavender screwed up her face in bafflement. Maybe consulting a psychic hadn't been the best idea after all, and she should have listened to her friend Shayna, who had told her to trust her gut. Despite what Penelope seemed to be implying about Burley's trustworthiness, Lavender had no doubt that he was a good, honest man who would never, ever lie to her. Raising her hand, she gazed at her ring again. Judging by the size of the glittering rock, her darling, hardworking Burley was absolutely gaga for her.

Enough of this nonsense! The purpose of the consultation with Penelope was to put her concerns about Burley and Marta to rest, not to go off on this preposterous Marta's-got-a-green-aura tangent.

"All right, whatever," Lavender said. "Let's *assume* Marta's dead, okay? Since that's what Burley told me. So what I'm really asking you is if they were ever involved in a sexual relationship."

"Let me look at that last picture you sent," Penelope said.

The third photo was a candid shot of Burley and Marta, slow dancing at their high school prom. When Lavender had found it in a box of Burley's mementos while snooping through his trailer while he was at work one day, the intimacy of the embrace had ignited a burst of jealousy in her. She knew a stupid twenty-year-old prom pic shouldn't have any bearing on their wedding plans—but what if Burley still had feelings for Marta? Sometimes old flames were the hardest to extinguish.

"Well?" Lavender said impatiently. "What do you think?"

Penelope seemed to be choosing her words with care. "Uh, yes, their relationship did become sexual on a few occasions in the past."

"How far in the past? When did it start?"

"Oh, it *started* back when they were teenagers, but it didn't go anywhere at that time. He wasn't into her the way she was into him. It was a classic case of unrequited love. But—"

"Oh, thank goodness!" Lavender exclaimed with a gush of relief. "I just *knew* she didn't mean anything to him." A high school crush, whoopee. No more worries there. As far as Burley's feelings for Marta went, it was only about the money she'd dangled in front of him for so long, like a treat held out to an eager dog. Lavender pinched the phone between her ear and shoulder, topped off her wine, and took a triumphant gulp.

There was one other thing, though. "Penelope," she said. "What did you mean about Marta's mind being sick?"

Penelope made the grumbling sound again. "That's what I was talking about when I said it was complicated. Whether this woman is dead or not, you need to understand that she may be dangerous."

Lavender snorted. "How can a *dead* person be dangerous?"

Penelope sighed. "It's hard to explain, the message I'm getting isn't quite clear. This storm that's about to dump on us has thrown my chakras out of balance. It happens sometimes, when the atmospheric pressure is in flux."

What in the hell were chakras? Lavender chewed the remnants of her peach-flavored gloss from her lower lip. This was a whole lot of crazy talk.

"The best I can make of it," Penelope went on, "is that Ron's safety is at risk somehow, and this woman may have something to do with it."

Fear jolted Lavender. At this very moment, Burley was driving down to Pennsylvania, to pay his final respects to Marta.

"When was the last time you spoke to him?" Penelope said.

"This morning. After he asked me to marry him, he said he needed to get on the road—" Lavender's voice rose, on the verge of hysteria. "Are you serious, Penelope? You really think he's in danger?"

"Yes, I believe so, and you may be, too. You need to be careful."

Holy crap! Lavender's insides twisted with fear. Had Burley lied about Marta's death? But why would he do that when he was smitten with *her?* She'd divorced her husband to be with him! She wanted to believe that Penelope's strange ramblings were completely mistaken, but what if they weren't, and something bad was about to happen? Either way, she had to get hold of Burley. *Now.*

"I have to go, Penelope," Lavender said. She hung up without saying goodbye and dialed Burley's number, but the call wouldn't go through. Clutching the phone in her trembling hands, she stared out the living room window as the wind picked up and the swirling snow began to come down harder.

CHAPTER 2

One year earlier

Married women were strictly off limits and Burley normally wouldn't have looked twice, but this one had caught his attention. He was pretty sure he recognized her—Lavender LeClair, the youngest daughter of the lone chiropractor in Helmsburg. A girly chick with wild blonde hair, doe-like eyes, and a body that could melt the wax off a grocery store cucumber.

There were three minutes left in his nephew Cody's soccer game and their team was getting creamed as usual, ten to zip. Lavender was standing a short way down the sideline from Burley, trying to hang onto a hyperactive boy wearing a bright blue soccer jersey and matching knee socks, while beyond them, a cluster of blue-clad teammates were milling around, waiting for their game to start.

The boy flipped his water bottle into the air and let it fall to the ground, and Burley caught the glint of a wedding ring as the kid's mother reached her hand out to pick it up. Cute ass, he observed. Nice legs too, although the spiky-heeled boots seemed sort of impractical for a soccer game, especially when the fields were so wet; but he supposed a girl could wear whatever she wanted to, especially when it looked this good on her.

Something happened on the field and Jack Nielsen, who was Cody's coach and Burley's Thursday night drinking buddy, shouted over to him: "Yo, Burl! *Burl!* Go give the goalkeeper a hand." Burley shook himself out of his fantasy—he hadn't even heard the ref's whistle. Tearing his eyes from Lavender, he noticed all the players on the field had taken a knee except for Cody, who was standing in front of the net yanking on his helmet, which was jammed over one ear. Darn kid was always monkeying with his chin strap. Burley hustled across the muddy grass, got Cody squared away, and the game resumed. Two minutes later, the ref blew the triple whistle, wrapping up another sorry loss for the Red Avengers.

Burley continued watching Lavender from the corner of his eye as he collected the team's muddy practice balls and stuffed them into his big mesh bag. She and her spazzy son had drifted closer, and he could hear them talking now. The boy was around ten years old and was jumping all over the place, attempting to dribble his orange neon ball with his knees.

"That's enough, Logan," Lavender said as she dodged an elbow. "Wait till you're on the field, honey." Ignoring his mother, Logan hiked a knee up and connected with the ball. It ricocheted toward Burley, who threw his arm out and caught it.

Lavender gave an apologetic wave. "Sorry about that!"

Burley dropped the ball to the ground and gave it a gentle return kick. "No prob," he called back, then moved closer and looked the boy's mother straight in the face. Yeah, he knew who she was, had heard the stories about her and her girl crew. They'd been big time partiers back in high school; it was several years after he'd graduated, but his kid brother Richard had shared plenty of tales of their antics. They were brazen drinkers and stoners, wanna-be Phishheads from Helmsburg's upper class—what little there was of one in this town.

As Logan's coach summoned his team onto the trampled field to begin their warmup drills, Lavender sidled over to Burley and smiled up at him. One of her front teeth poked out slightly in front of the other, and her lips were a soft, frosty pink. She was giving him the signals for sure. Must be his three-day-stubble beard, which he liked to think made him look like the country singer Jason Aldean. Feeling a pleasant thrill of attraction, he thrust his hand out. "Hi, I'm Ron Burley."

"I'm Lavender." Her hand was sweaty, but it was an unseasonably warm autumn Saturday in the North Country of upstate New York. Instead of the customary parka, wool hat and scarf, she was wearing only skinny jeans and a low cut, long-sleeved T-shirt that was hugging her chest real good. She started chattering about the weather, oblivious to the start of her son's game.

Burley half-watched the soccer action over Lavender's shoulder and sized Logan up as a mediocre player. The kid's ball-handling skills were adequate but he was dragging himself down the field, as though his heart wasn't really in the game.

Coach Nielsen sauntered over to retrieve the bag of practice balls and check out Lavender. Logan's team scored a goal, and his mother squealed and jumped up and down, making her breasts jiggle. Nielsen gave her an appreciative up-and-down assessment, then aimed a sly wink at Burley as he hefted the ball bag over his shoulder.

Jerk, Burley thought. *Thinks all I wanna do is get in her pants.* He glanced back at Lavender. *Well, yeah, maybe I do.* He knew he wouldn't though, because she was married, and he had morals and standards. Burley was a man of integrity, and this was nothing more than an innocent flirtation. Sort of a practice run, since it'd been a while since he'd hooked up with anyone. Now that he was closing in on forty, he'd gotten sort of lazy about it, to be honest. Women were so much work sometimes.

But then Lavender began asking him about tryouts for the Hogan County indoor soccer team, which he knew nothing about but pretended he did, so he could offer to look into it for her. Logan didn't stand a chance of making the team, but Burley wasn't about to tell the boy's smokin' hot mom that. "I'd be happy to put in a good word with the coach for you," he said. Whoever the coach was. He made a mental note to find out.

"Thanks, that would be awesome!" Lavender reached into a voluminous leather handbag and produced an iPhone in a rhinestoned case. She pressed a delicate fingertip to the screen and entered Burley's digits into her contacts. "I'll text you right now," she said, "so you'll have my number."

The back pocket of Burley's Wranglers buzzed, and he was embarrassed because now he had to take out his crappy flip phone with the scuff marks all over it from the time he'd dropped it out the window of his pickup truck at the Wendy's drive-thru. Lavender thanked him again, said he was *such* a sweetheart, and squeezed his forearm, which sparked something deep in his loins. *Leave it alone*, he warned himself. *Don't even think about going there.* In the gravel parking lot next to the soccer field, Nielsen fired up the huge turbo-diesel engine of his Chevy Silverado and pointed a cocky finger at Burley over the top of his half-open window. "Beers at McAvan's on Thursday, bro," he hollered as he backed out of his parking spot. "Your turn to buy."

• • •

Burley pulled his rusting pickup truck alongside the gas pumps at the Mini Mart on Main Street and squinted toward the shop to see who was working the register. He was the store manager there, but this was his weekend off and he didn't feel like going inside, even though he could use another cup of coffee. The girl Amanda was supposed to be on today, but the morning sickness was hitting her pretty hard, so the new guy, Dustin, had offered to cover her shift for her. Dustin was visible through the front window, his maroon Mini Mart visor bobbing as he rang up a customer.

Burley had started working at the Mini Mart when he was fifteen, and climbed his way up to shift leader by the time he finished high school. He'd gone to Hogan Community College where he earned a two-year degree in business administration, and was promoted to manager. Hard to believe he'd put in over two decades with the same company. He guessed he liked it well enough. The pay was fine for a simple bachelor like him, and he'd found he had a knack for building good relationships with his customers, and for employing reliable people.

A hiring decision he was especially proud of was Dustin, who came from a seriously dysfunctional family, with a barfly mother and an old man in the Mohawk Correctional Facility down in Rome. He'd been so quiet at his job interview, Burley had wondered for a minute if he might be mentally deficient; but the kid needed a break, and Burley was willing to give him a chance. Dustin had turned out to be responsible, honest, and loyal, traits Burley prized in his employees.

A blue Buick rolled up on the other side of the gas island, the driver's window inched down, and Burley's mother stuck her hand out and waved. "Hello there, Ronald dear! I missed the soccer game, didn't I?" She waggled her tightly-permed head. "I jotted myself a note on the calendar, but then I forgot to look at it when I got up to feed the cat this morning! Ah, well." Digging in her pocketbook, she located her debit card and handed it out the window to her son. Burley swiped the card, unhooked the nozzle from the gas pump and began filling her tank.

"I was over to the IGA earlier, picking up a few groceries," his mother said, "and I ran into Helen Phipps. She got to talking, you know how she does, and guess what she told me? She says to me, 'Did you hear about Marta Grolsch?' and I said, 'Marta Grolsch? Why, I haven't seen her in years. What about her?' Helen says, 'Her husband died, down there in Pennsylvania. Happened about a month ago. Sudden heart attack.' So, I said to Helen, 'That's a real shame. What's she going to do, move back up here to be closer to her parents?' And Helen says, 'No, I believe she's going to stay put. Wants to make a go of running the husband's business on her own. Roofing and siding, or some such thing.'"

Burley kept his head down. *Marta Grolsch!* It had been ages since she'd crossed his mind, and for good reason. "I'm sorry to hear that, Mom," he said. "I haven't been in touch with Marta in a long time."

"Maybe you should give her a call." His mother was giving him one of her meaningful looks. "I'm sure she'd appreciate hearing from an old friend."

Burley's unmarried state was a source of distress for his mother, who was forever trying to rectify the situation by urging him to get back together with one or another of his former girlfriends. He usually ignored her well-meaning attempts at match making, and she'd eventually give up; but this time he needed to put the squelch on things right quick, before she got carried away. He replaced the gas nozzle in its bracket with a decisive clunk. "No, Mom," he said firmly. "I am not going to call Marta, and don't go getting any of your ideas about us. We haven't spoken in years, and that's how I want to leave it."

"Oh dear, I was only suggesting—"

The hurt expression on his mother's face made Burley feel bad for being so abrupt. "I'll call her when I get a chance, okay?" he said. "Just don't expect anything to come of it." Handing his mother her receipt, he backed away from the car.

"Don't forget, you need to come over and put up my storm windows," his mother said.

Burley looked at her in dismay—he'd put up her storm windows two weeks ago. Boy, her memory was really starting to slip. "Sure, Mom," he said. "I'll take care of you, don't worry." His mother smiled and rolled her window up, and drove off.

After filling his own tank, Burley climbed back into his truck and headed west out of town, past the lumber mill and the county fairgrounds, and thought about his mother's piece of news. Marta Grolsch a widow! In spite of the estrangement that had developed between them, he couldn't help feeling sorry for his old friend. It had to be rough, coping with a tragic loss while trying to raise a child and run a business on her own.

The two of them had been best friends growing up, when their families owned neighboring summer camps on Fourth Lake in the Adirondack Mountains. They'd built forts in the woods and gone swimming or canoeing almost every day, and Burley had taught Marta how to shoot squirrels and fly cast for brook trout. A real tomboy. He'd always liked that about her.

After high school, Marta had gone off to a preppy liberal arts college in Pennsylvania on a scholarship—she was always the smart one—and majored in philosophy or psychology, or some other pointless thing like that. She married a classmate who was from down there, and soon after, her new husband inherited a local roofing company when a distant cousin of his passed away. The husband was swamped with work in the summer months, so Marta used to come up to Helmsburg to visit her parents for a week every August. She'd always let Burley know when she was coming to town, and they'd meet for a drink and get caught up.

When had he seen her last? Must be five years now. He'd grown tired of listening to her prattle about her wonderful married life, and he started making excuses for why he couldn't see her. As an avowed bachelor, he wasn't much interested in other people's conjugal bliss, and he'd been careful to avoid ever having to meet the young daughter she was constantly bragging about.

It wasn't only that, though. Whenever they were together, it felt like there was something off about Marta, and it made Burley uncomfortable. She always looked at him so intently, like she was trying to read his thoughts, and she had this stilted way of talking about her picture-perfect family, as though she was reading lines from a script. It reminded Burley of the studied nonchalance she'd tried so hard to project that fateful summer after their senior year, when he wasn't quite sure if he could trust her anymore. The memory of what she'd done—or hadn't done, he never really knew for sure—still creeped him out. But now Marta was all alone with no family nearby to comfort her or lend a hand, which made him feel awful. His mother was right, he should call her.

The road forked and Burley veered onto Hickey Road, where his doublewide trailer sat a mile down on the right, on a small wooded parcel that butted up to ten thousand acres of state forest. There was a detached aluminum garage out back that housed a 17-foot Bass Tracker, an old Ski-Doo Renegade, and a mud-spattered ATV. In the summertime he grew Beefsteak tomatoes, zucchini and eggplant in a small garden patch that he dug by hand, and in the fall, he donned his forest camo, loaded his deer rifle, and trekked out to his tree stand deep in the woods. If he'd had the vocabulary for this sort of thing, he might have described the setting as bucolic and serene.

Burley parked his truck in the rutted gravel driveway, climbed a set of wooden steps and swung the unlocked front door open, and his two chocolate labs, Bo and Augie, came charging at him from their matted beds in the corner of the living room. He rumpled their ears and flipped on the lights. The carpet was worn and dirty, the paneled walls were warped, and the whole place smelled of dog, but Burley didn't take notice of things like that. He went over to the tiny kitchen table, pushed his socket wrench set out of the way, and sat down in front of the old desktop computer that he was still running Windows XP on.

Emailing Marta was a better idea than calling her, he'd decided, because what if he got her on the phone, and then she started getting all weepy about her dead husband? He wasn't good in those types of situations, never knew how to respond to a woman's tears. Email was a much safer bet. Plus, it would help keep a necessary degree of distance between them.

Burley searched for Marta's email address in his contacts, then clicked the mouse to start a new message. The subject line stumped him, so he put "Hi," and began:

Hey Marta, it's your old friend Ron Burley. Sorry for not writing sooner. My mom told me about

What was the husband's name, anyway? He thought hard but couldn't recall it. Something with a K, like Kevin, maybe? It would really suck if he got it wrong, but the man was dead and gone now, so what did it matter if he used the guy's name or not? He continued typing:

My mom told me about your husband. Must be hard for you being alone down there so I hope you'll come back up to

Helmsburg soon for a visit to your folks. Let me know if you do so we can get together maybe.

That was enough words of condolence, he figured. Short and sweet. Time to sign off and be done with it. He typed:

Your friend,
Burley

Satisfied with the sympathetic and friendly tone of his message, Burley hit Send, then tipped his chair back and thought about the good old times with Marta, before things got weird. They'd smoked their first cigarettes and drunk their first beers together, and on weekends they used to cruise the back roads with the radio blasting in his dad's Dodge, like typical country teenagers. They'd even gone to the prom together, and had a blast.

Anywho. Burley closed his email and went to fix himself a sandwich. His phone buzzed as he was piling slices of ham and cheese onto a submarine roll, and he was surprised to see a text message from Lavender:

Hi! Nice meeting u today.

Okaaay… what was this all about? After a moment's hesitation, he texted back: *Same here.*

Thanks so much for your help, came the immediate response.

What help? After thinking for a second, he realized she was referring to his offer to speak to the coach of the indoor soccer team. *No problem,* he replied.

We should get together some time.

Was she hitting on him, or being friendly? He had to ponder this one for a minute. Another text appeared before he could reply: *Just to talk*, it said, followed by a winking smiley face.

Definitely hitting on him. Nevertheless, he needed to proceed with caution here. Lavender's husband Clint was an inspector in the county Building and Fire Codes department, and he often stopped into the

Mini Mart for the hot dog and soda lunch special. The dude was skinny and geeky, not likely to beat the crap out of anyone for messing around with his wife; but Helmsburg was a small town and gossip traveled fast, especially when hanky-panky was involved.

Burley set his phone on the counter and spread a thick layer of yellow mustard over the ham and cheese, slapped the sub roll together and crammed one end of it into his mouth. The phone buzzed again as he was chewing: *U free tonite?*

An image of Lavender's frosted lips and chest-hugging T-shirt flickered before his eyes. God almighty, the woman was hotter than the devil's house cat. But then his conscience jerked to life and began shouting at him: *Don't do it! Do not take the bait!*

Forget that, Burley thought. Three sexless months had passed since his brief entanglement with the cute but squirrelly veterinary assistant from Boonville, and he was due for some action. He swallowed his mouthful of sandwich and pecked an answer with his thumbs: *Yes, I'm free.*

Lavender texted right back: *Meet me at 7, Walmart parking lot. Silver Impala.*

The Walmart parking lot was a well-known staging ground for illicit hookups, and so many couples had taken to using the place as a rendezvous point that it was commonly referred to as "Trystmart." Burley bit off another hunk of sub. This was a really bad idea, he was asking for trouble. And besides, he wasn't that kind of guy.

But Lavender! Her sweet little butt, and those hips—nice and curvy, the way he liked a girl to be. Oh geez, he was a goner. He sent a quick reply: *See u there.*

CHAPTER 3

Lavender stood in front of her dresser mirror, finger-combing her hair and enjoying the pleasant swirl of butterflies in her stomach. She'd never cheated on her husband before, and the anticipation of a sneaky dalliance was exciting. Brushing her hair forward over her shoulders, she fluffed it so the golden locks framed her face, then applied a touch more violet eyeliner beneath her lower lids and smudged them with her pinkies to produce a smoky effect. The look she was going for tonight was cute rather than downright sexy—better not to come on too strong too quick. She checked her figure in the mirror, and was happy to see the extra pounds didn't show beneath the flowery peasant blouse she'd chosen. *Cool.*

Her wine glass left a damp circle on the dresser top as she raised it to her lips for a final sip. She hooked her fringed purse over her shoulder and went into the kitchen where Clint was seated on a stool at the breakfast bar, eating a bowl of Lucky Charms. She hadn't felt like cooking tonight, so she'd told him he'd have to make do with whatever sort of meal he could scrounge up on his own.

"I'm leaving for Shayna's now," she said to her husband's back. "Make sure Logan goes to bed on time."

Clint rotated his gangly legs around on the stool and regarded his wife. "Where are you going again?"

"I already told you. A bunch of us girls are meeting up at Shayna's house, then going out to eat. Maybe go to the movies later."

Clint rubbed a thumb along his chin. "The movies here in Helmsburg, or over in Watertown?"

"I don't know, it depends what everyone feels like," Lavender replied as she checked to make sure she'd put her lipstick in her purse. "Watertown, probably. There's never anything good playing here in town."

Clint clinked his spoon into his empty cereal bowl, slipped off the stool and came over to give her a hug. "I heard there's a speed trap up on Route 126, so drive carefully if you head out Watertown way."

Lavender sidestepped him, went into the living room and bent over Logan, who was bouncing on his knees in front of the television, a half-eaten corn dog gripped in his fist. She attempted to land a kiss on his cheek but he shrugged her away, which made her sad for about two seconds. Logan had been a difficult child since babyhood. First it was colic, then croup and intractable ear aches, and now this maddening ADHD that was enough to make you want to tear your own hair out of your head. "All righty then," Lavender said, straightening up and smoothing her blouse. "See you boys later."

The parking lot at the Walmart Supercenter was full and the blacktop was sparkling under a cold drizzle when she cruised in at ten minutes past seven. Swinging her car around to the farthest corner of the lot, she parked and turned off her headlights, then scanned the area for Burley's truck, which was a bit of a challenge, since half the male population in Hogan County drove pickups that looked exactly like his.

The Impala had tinted windows, which would provide concealment when Burley got in beside her, and the rainy weather would help, too. But what were they going to do once they were in the car together? She hadn't thought that far yet. Probably just talk awhile and feel each other out. Burley came across as the upright citizen type who might be reluctant to get involved with her, and he'd likely require a good deal of coaxing. At least he was single, so a jealous wife wouldn't be an issue, but it was too soon for them to get intimate, anyway. Lavender wanted to stretch this out, make sure the hook was set good and deep before they got down and dirty. Much wiser to start things off slow.

There was an airplane-sized bottle of vodka in the bottom of her purse, leftover from Shayna's divorce party last month. Lavender dug it out and took a swig for bravery, then cracked the window a few inches and lit a cigarette. Clint hated it when she smoked in the car, but too bad for him. She took a drag and craned her neck until she spotted an older-model Ford Ranger parked a few rows over, with a husky man silhouetted in the driver's seat. *Yessss, he'd shown up!* Lavender raised her hand and waggled her first two fingers, and when Burley waved back, she motioned for him to come over.

Burley jumped out of his truck and began walking toward the car, then stopped and looked over his shoulder as someone shouted to him from across the parking lot. Lavender slunk down in her seat and peeked over the dashboard as an overweight young man lumbered near. The guy had a Mini Mart visor on his head, and a collared maroon shirt showed beneath his jean jacket. As he drew closer, his face broke into a grin. "Hey, Mr. Burley!" he called. "I thought that was you. How's it going?"

"Hey, Dustin." Burley clapped a hand on Dustin's shoulder and turned him around so their backs were to Lavender's car, and their voices faded as he steered his employee toward the store entrance.

"Damn!" Lavender rapped the steering wheel with her fists as the two men disappeared into the maw of the Walmart. Five minutes passed, and when Burley didn't reappear, she texted him: *where r u?* When no reply came, she tried calling, but he didn't pick up.

She wondered if the blubbery guy had spotted her and suspected something was up, and Burley had decided it was too risky to meet up with her. Or maybe he wasn't interested enough to take the chance. Well, screw him then. Lavender cranked the ignition and peeled out of her parking space. Might as well go home if Burley couldn't be bothered to call her back.

Clint was slouched on the unmade bed with the television tuned to Fox News when Lavender walked into their bedroom twenty minutes later. He looked up in surprise. "You're home early."

"Yes, Clint, I'm home early." Lavender threw her purse onto the pile of dirty clothes heaped on the armchair in the corner. Besides not wanting to cook, she hadn't felt like doing the laundry today, either. Her glass of wine was still sitting on the dresser. She snatched it up and drained the warm dregs, and realized she wasn't nearly buzzed enough to get through another dull Saturday night in this miserable little house. On the way home from Walmart, she'd stopped by Shayna's place, hoping to mooch another drink and bolster her cover story; but Shayna had been in a rotten mood about her recent divorce, and told Lavender to go home and drink her own wine. So here she was once again, stuck at home with her loser husband, watching a damned cable news program that she couldn't care less about. At least Logan was in bed already, so she didn't have to deal with another one of his bedtime tantrums.

Clint pointed the remote and lowered the volume on Laura Ingraham. "Did you girls have fun tonight?"

Lavender glared at him. "Yes, we had a fricking blast. The nightlife in Helmsburg is so awesome."

Clint clicked the station over to CNN, and his mouth set in a thin line. Pissed or hurt, she couldn't tell. Didn't care either. She stomped into the bathroom and slammed the door, slapped the toilet seat cover closed and sat down with her head in her hands.

Her life sucked and she was sick of it. She and Clint had gotten married straight out of high school because she was pregnant, and she'd been slender enough back then that no one guessed she was knocked up until a month after the wedding. College hadn't been an option for her anyway, since she'd never been a good student. But what kind of life was this for her now, married to a lowly county employee, living in a shoddy box of a house, dealing day in and day out with a hyperactive little brat? She was a *doctor's* daughter, for heaven's sake! A woman like her deserved way better than this.

Lavender got up to wash her face, then put on the shortie nightgown that had failed to entice her husband for the past six months. This night was no exception. When she came out of the bathroom, Clint didn't even look at her. He rolled off the bed in his rumpled undershirt and flannel pajama pants, and shuffled his skinny self out to the living room couch, where she knew he'd veg until long after midnight, dozing through the late-night shows, and would only come back to the bedroom when he was sure she was fast asleep. No cuddling, no sex. This was their life now.

Lavender stretched out in the empty bed and thought about Burley. Funny how he went by his last name, but she thought it suited him better than plain old Ron did. He wasn't that great looks-wise—more Luke Combs than Jason Aldean—but he seemed to be a nice, friendly guy, and he apparently knew how to be discreet. Around town, he was known as a respectable businessman who could be counted on for regular contributions to the local sports programs and the food pantry at the Presbyterian church. He'd be a good distraction from the tedium of her marriage. The sex might not turn out to be all that exciting, but anything was better than Clint's halfhearted efforts in bed. Tonight had been a bust, but she was determined to hook up with Burley eventually. It would just require some planning.

● ● ●

The clatter of shopping carts drowned out the sound of Burley's phone ringing as he and Dustin entered the busy Walmart. He needed to ditch the guy, but he had to be careful in case Dustin had seen Lavender, and put two and two together. No need to take any chances. "I was just running in here for batteries," he told Dustin, pointing to a display near the registers. "Then I gotta go check on my mom. See you at work on Monday, buddy."

"Sure thing, boss," Dustin replied, and plodded off toward the grocery section.

Burley felt a twinge of disappointment when he walked out of the store a few minutes later and saw the Impala was gone. Checking his phone, he saw Lavender's text and missed call, and debated a moment before shoving the phone back into his pocket. It was probably a good thing they hadn't gotten together after all. Fooling around with a married woman was a dicey move, and he couldn't afford to get himself into hot water. People looked up to him around here, he had a reputation to uphold. Better to go home, watch some television and forget about her.

He climbed into his truck and gunned the engine. Lavender was going to be a difficult one to put out of his thoughts, though—all that long, loose hair and those dark, smoky eyes he'd caught a glimpse of through her car window. *Dang*. He might have to down a beer or three tonight, to keep his mind off her.

The drizzle turned to sleet as he drove home. When he was back inside the trailer, he logged onto his desktop to check the weather forecast, and saw a new email notification. He clicked it open and found a reply from Marta:

Hi Burley, it was so good to hear from you! Yes, it's been tough since Ken passed away, especially for our daughter.

Ken! That was the husband's name! The message continued:

I'm trying to keep it together but every day is a struggle. Running Ken's company by myself is way harder than I thought. Now that he's gone, I'm afraid I'm going to lose customers and won't be able to support myself. You always had such a good head for business. I wish you lived closer so you could come help me figure out what to do.

Hoo boy, a frigging sob story. It almost made him wish he hadn't contacted her after all. Instead of replying right away, Burley got up and took a bag of Tater Tots out of the freezer—a little snack would help him think of the right words.

He shook the bag of Tots out onto a baking sheet, popped them in the oven, and turned the TV to *Extreme Angler*. Thirty minutes later, as he was squirting gobs of ketchup onto his overflowing plate of food, a text from Lavender buzzed: *U still up?*

Took her long enough, after she'd ditched him at the Walmart. He wasn't sure if he really wanted to encourage her, so he answered with a simple *Yes.*

Sorry I missed u earlier. Had to go home unexpectedly.

That was probably true—she had a young son who seemed like a handful. *That's ok*, he replied.

Maybe we could get together another time. Talk about soccer.

Soccer? Yeah, sure.

Or just hang out.

Okay, she was undoubtedly trying to tell him something. Burley munched a handful of Tots and wondered how he ought to respond. Was it really worth it? As he was thinking it over, a vision of Lavender's spiky-heeled boots waltzed through his brain. The phone buzzed again, and grabbing for it with a greasy hand, he read: *I'd really like to see u.*

She wanted him, no doubt about it. He felt his resistance crumbling. Typing swiftly, he replied: *Same here.*

The phone buzzed again: *How about tomoro nite?*

Burley's private parts tingled with excitement. *Sure*, he texted back. *Sounds great.*

CHAPTER 4

Lavender spent her Sunday afternoon at home, catching up on the neglected laundry. In between loads of Logan's school clothes and Clint's work shirts and pants, she texted Burley: *U still up for tonite?*

His response came directly: *I sure am.*

Super, she replied. *Will call u later*.

Later that afternoon as she was finishing up the monotonous tasks of folding and putting away the clean laundry, it occurred to Lavender that it might be a fine idea to exert herself a little more than usual in the kitchen and prepare a pot roast for their Sunday dinner. Logan would be happy enough with his customary plate of microwaved chicken nuggets, but Clint liked his meat and potatoes. A hearty home-cooked meal would set him up in a good mood for when she told him she was going out later that evening. Not that he ever made an issue about her comings and goings, wimp that he was; but still, it would be prudent to avoid arousing his suspicions.

Lavender hadn't paid attention when her mother had attempted to teach her and her sisters how to cook years ago, and it showed: the hunk of fatty meat she'd bought on special at the IGA shrank down to a stringy lump after simmering in the oven too long, and the carrots and potatoes were reduced to hardened nubs stuck to the bottom of the pot.

Clint was nice about it though, and praised her efforts anyway. He was like that—infinitely patient and understanding, to the point where his placid manner was sometimes enough to drive her up the frigging wall.

When they were through eating, Clint carried his plate and silverware to the sink and was about to rinse them, but Lavender waved him away. "I've got it," she said. "You can go relax and watch TV with Logan."

"Thanks," Clint said. "Dinner was good." The exchange was typical of their interactions these days—fake-considerate, fake-polite. At least they rarely argued anymore.

Lavender cleared the table, loaded the dishwasher and left the charred baking pan to soak, then slipped into the bedroom to touch up her makeup and fluff her hair. When she went back out to the living room, Clint and Logan were watching college basketball highlights on ESPN. "I think I'll run out to the store for a few things," she said. "It'll save me the trouble of trying to fit it in tomorrow."

Clint replied without looking away from the television. "Can you get me some more Lucky Charms?"

"Sure. *Lucky Charms! God, he was such a child.*" Be back in a bit," she called as she grabbed her coat and purse, and hurried out the back door.

It felt good to be going somewhere on a Sunday evening instead of parking herself on the couch with Clint and watching another tiresome episode of *60 Minutes*, with Logan bouncing off the walls and complaining the whole time. At the stop sign at the end of their street, Lavender paused to call Burley, and he answered on the first ring. "Hi," she said. "What're you doing?"

"Nothing much," he said. "Just watching TV, waiting to see you."

Lavender smiled—he was itching to see her! *Perfect.* "It took me a while to get out of the house," she said. "I had *so* much housework to do today, and now I have to go to Walmart. Can you meet me there?"

"Walmart?" Burley said. "I was thinking maybe we could go someplace else, like—"

Aha, he was making plans for them already! Not so fast, buddy—she was the one driving here. Before Burley could finish his thought, Lavender cut him off: "Yes, Walmart. I need to pick up some groceries, so I used that as my excuse for going out tonight. I have to be careful what I tell my husband, you know."

"Of course," Burley said. "Walmart's fine. Should I look for your car in the parking lot again?"

It was freezing out and Lavender didn't feel like sitting in the car with the heater blasting at them the whole time, making her hair frizz out. "No," she said. "Why don't you meet me inside? There shouldn't be too many people out shopping on a Sunday night. Text me when you get there so I can tell you where to find me."

At the Walmart, Lavender grabbed a shopping cart from the corral at the store entrance and whizzed through the grocery section, snatching her usual array of items from the shelves: grape jelly for Logan, Clint's goddamn Lucky Charms, frozen Weight Watchers meals for herself. The humdrum of grocery shopping irritated her. It wasn't fair either, that the task always fell to her. Clint might be the breadwinner of the family, with his steady salary and county employee benefits, but she had a job, too. Okay, so it was only a part-time salesclerk position at a chintzy little boutique in town, but it did cut into her free time quite a bit. She was constantly on the run, shuttling Logan to and from his after-school activities, or driving him to the behavioral specialist in Utica. It was a lot for a working mother to juggle.

Her phone jingled with a text from Burley: *I'm here.*

Aisle 10, she replied. Burley soon appeared at the top of the aisle, looking manly in a brown Carhartt chore coat, jeans and work boots. He casually made his way toward Lavender until they were standing a few feet apart, and they each pretended to be scrutinizing the Buy-One-Get-One-Free specials in the canned soup section.

"Thanks for coming," Lavender whispered. "Sorry for the short notice. It can be tricky for me to get away sometimes."

"I understand," Burley whispered back. "No problem."

Lavender moved closer to him and caught an invigorating whiff of Old Spice. "I thought of a way for us to meet up," she continued in a low voice. "My son has Cub Scouts on Thursday nights and my husband's the den leader. I'll have about two hours free between six and eight o'clock. We could go to that little pizza place out in Martinsville, you know the one that's right before you get to the railroad crossing?"

An elderly man came puttering along on a motorized scooter, and Lavender and Burley pretended to examine the shelves again. The man placed several cans of soup in his wire basket, then rolled away.

Burley nodded. "That could work," he said. "I don't know anybody who lives out that way, do you?"

Lavender made a face. "Why would I know anyone in a place like Martinsville?"

"I just want to make sure we don't run into anyone who knows us."

"Why?" Lavender said with a sideways smile. "We're only having pizza, right?"

"Right," Burley replied with a grin. "It's only pizza."

Lavender made a show of checking the time on her phone. "Oops, I've got to get back now. I'll see you Thursday." She smiled conspiratorially at Burley, and trailed her fingertips lightly down his arm as she brushed past him.

•   •   •

The pizzeria was a small flyblown place sandwiched between a barber shop and a State Farm office. Burley showed up right on time in a navy-blue shirt and jeans that looked freshly washed, and his hair was neatly combed, with no evidence of hat head. He cleaned up nicely, Lavender observed. Not too bad at all.

They ordered a veggie pizza—Lavender's choice—from the girl behind the counter, took their sodas and sat down at a table for two in the corner. Lavender smiled sweetly so Burley could admire her dimples. "I'm so happy we could finally get together," she said. "Someplace where we can have a normal conversation." She peeled the paper cover off her straw and poked it into her Diet Pepsi. "I was wondering, do you know my husband, Clint?"

"Sort of," Burley said. "I see him around town once in a while, and he comes into the Mini Mart for lunch now and then."

"Do you guys ever talk?"

"No, not really. We say hi, how's it going, that's about it."

"What do you think of him?"

Burley shrugged. "He seems like an okay guy, I guess."

"Mmm." Lavender swirled the ice in her drink. "Have you ever been married?" She knew very well that he hadn't, having made some indirect inquiries, but she was trying to make a point here. It was all part of her strategy.

"No," Burley said. "Never took the plunge."

"Ever come close?"

"Nope."

Lavender gave him a slight smile which was meant to look rueful. "Sometimes I wonder if I made the right decision in marrying Clint when we were both so young. But then we wouldn't have our darling son. I can't *imagine* my life without Logan." She looked at Burley for affirmation, and he dutifully nodded his head.

"This might sound funny to you," she went on, "but even though I'm married, I feel so lonely sometimes. It's kind of hard to explain. I guess it's because Clint isn't really my soul mate. We got married because we had to, if you know what I mean. I was only eighteen."

Burley began to play with his fork. "Uh huh."

"He's just—he's not a good fit for me, personality-wise."

"I guess I can see that," Burley said. "You guys do seem to be very different."

Lavender leaned forward so her boobs squished against the edge of the table. "You're right, we *are* very different. I'm a free spirit, I like to laugh and have a good time, but Clint's always so quiet and serious. He likes to follow the rules and keep to himself."

"That must be hard for you."

"Oh, it *is*. Very hard. I'm so glad you understand."

The girl came and set their pizza on the table without a word. They each helped themself to a gooey slice, but it was too hot to eat yet. Lavender rested her chin on her hands. "I just knew you'd be a good listener! That's why I wanted to see you tonight. I need someone I can talk to once in a while, you know? Someone who really gets it." She reached her hand across the table and squeezed Burley's larger, rougher one. "I'm hoping we can become good friends."

Disappointment crossed Burley's face. "Friends?"

Lavender squeezed his hand harder and fluttered her eyelashes at him. "Maybe more than friends." She held his gaze until his expression brightened into comprehension, then released his hand and took a ladylike bite off the tip of her slice. "Ooo, this is delicious."

Burley folded his slice into a V and stuffed it into his mouth. "Mm, yeah," he said between chews. "Delicious."

Lavender didn't want to come across looking like a pig, so she nibbled at her slice while Burley went to work on the rest of the pizza. When she was done, she dabbed her lips with a napkin. "Tell me some more about yourself. Do you have any brothers or sisters?"

"No sisters," Burley said, still chewing. "I had an older brother, Russ, who got leukemia when he was a kid. The treatments put it into remission, but a second cancer caught up with him as an adult, and he died a few years ago. He left a son behind that I'm pretty close with, his name's Cody. He plays on the soccer team I was coaching that day you and I met at the field."

"How nice for him," Lavender said. "You're a good uncle."

Burley smiled. "Yeah, I try to be. Cody's mom got remarried a while ago, but I still like to do what I can to help out."

"Was Russ your only brother?"

"No, I've got a younger brother, too. Richard. He dropped out of school and left home when he was a teenager, and hasn't been back since, except when he came for Russ's funeral. He lives in Florida now, and I hardly ever hear from him. How about you—do you have any siblings?"

"I've got two older sisters who think they're God's gift to mankind," Lavender said. "One of them is the head of human resources for the school district, and she makes sure everyone knows it. The other one stays at home with her kids. She can afford to because her husband's a physical therapist, he works with my father." Lavender raised her eyebrows in question. "My dad's a chiropractor? LeClair Spinal Care?"

"Yeah," Burley said. "I've heard of it."

"They have a beautiful house and two overachieving children. My mom thinks they're the perfect family." Lavender rolled her eyes. "What about your mom and dad? Are they still around?"

"My father passed away a while back but my mother's still kicking," Burley said. "She's starting to have problems with her memory, though. Puts the milk away in the cupboard and the mail in the refrigerator, stuff like that."

Lavender tipped her glass up and crunched a piece of ice. "My grandmother got all mixed up like that too, after my grandfather died. He'd always taken care of the bills and everything, so she was a total mess after he was gone. My dad had to move her into a home."

"I have an old friend who lost her husband recently, too," Burley said. "She's having a real tough time of it, trying to run the family business by herself, so she can support herself and her daughter."

Lavender set her glass down. "That's too bad. Were the two of you very close?"

Burley fiddled with his fork again. "Um, no, not really. We knew each other when we were kids, is all. It was our mothers who were friends, really."

"Does she live around here?"

"No, she moved away years ago." Burley pulled the laminated menu out of its metal holder at the end of the table and ran his eye over the dessert selections.

"Did you, like, ever date her or anything?"

Burley continued studying the menu. "We never dated, we were just friends. Do you want dessert?"

"No thanks, I'm full." Lavender regarded him thoughtfully—he was trying to change the subject. Keeping her eyes on him, she put her lips to her straw and sucked the last inch of watery soda from the bottom of her glass. "I guess I'd better go soon," she said as she pushed the glass away. "I don't want Clint to catch me driving back into town from the wrong direction."

Lavender stood up and put on the new black puffer jacket that she'd deliberately purchased one size too small, so it would hug her curves better, and saw Burley watching her as she tugged the gold zipper up to her chin and smoothed the faux fur trim on the jacket's collar. "I'll walk you to your car," he said, and she shivered with pleasure as she felt the soft pressure of his hand on her back.

Their vehicles were parked in adjoining spaces, covered with a thin layer of wet snow. Burley retrieved his snow brush from his truck and expertly wiped off Lavender's windows and headlights. "There you go," he said. "Ready to roll." Lavender's stomach fluttered—Clint never bothered to brush off her car anymore. He was usually long gone when she got up on the cold winter mornings, leaving her to contend with the heavy blankets of snow on her car, since their house didn't have a garage.

Lavender placed her gloved hand on Burley's arm, taking care not to get too close to him. She didn't intend to let him kiss her yet—he needed to earn it first. "This was fun," she said. "Maybe we can do it again next Thursday?"

"That'd be great. Call me anytime." Burley opened her car door for her, then climbed into his truck and waved as he drove off.

Lavender sat in the cold Impala for a few minutes, waiting for it to warm up. Overall, she was pleased with how the evening had turned out. After chatting with Burley for an hour, she had concluded that he was better looking than she'd first thought, his table manners were acceptable, and he hadn't mentioned any shady family members who might be whack jobs. Things were moving along smoothly.

However, there was that "old friend" he'd mentioned, then tried to cover up. Childhood friends were the worst—they were always popping up on Facebook or Instagram, looking to rekindle old romances. She'd need to keep this one on her radar.

CHAPTER 5

Burley chewed himself out the whole way home as his wipers smeared streaks of wet snow across the windshield. Why had he stupidly brought up Marta, when the conversation with Lavender had been going so well? She'd started to open up to him, but then he had to go and sidetrack things by mentioning his old friend.

He shouldn't have lied. The truth was, he and Marta *had* dated, although only for a very brief period, way back at the end of their senior year. It'd been sort of a test drive, to see if there might be a romantic spark hidden within their friendship, after their "just as friends" prom date unexpectedly morphed into a hot-and-heavy hookup in the backseat of his car.

Afterward, Marta had confessed to harboring a crush on Burley since their adolescence, and she apparently assumed their fevered moment of intimacy was a sign that he returned the sentiment. He'd felt so guilty for having unwittingly taken advantage of her fragile feelings, he agreed to try giving it a go as a couple. Just for a while, he thought, until the thing played itself out. The trouble was, it didn't—at least not for Marta.

But what would've been the point of sharing all that information with Lavender? It was ancient history that no one even remembered anymore, and it had no bearing on the present. If he took care not to mention anything further about Marta, Lavender would forget all about it. He needed to make sure she knew he was fully available and interested. *Very* interested.

Thinking about Marta reminded him that he hadn't replied to her email yet. The oversight had been nagging at him all week, but he'd been busy at work and kept putting it off, which was a lousy way to treat someone who was hurting so badly.

Back at home, Burley sat right down at the computer and reread Marta's message, then composed a brief response:

Dear Marta,
Sorry things are so tough for you right now. You're strong and you'll get through this. If there's anything I can do to help please let me know.

Barely a minute passed after he'd sent the email when his phone rang, and the Caller ID showed Marta's name. *Damn.* She'd probably gotten herself worked up with another sob story for him, and he really, really didn't feel like talking to her right now, when he had so many alluring images of Lavender dancing around in his head. He was about to let the call go to voicemail, but at the last second, he felt guilty for blowing her off, so he picked up.

"Burley?" Marta said. "I hope I'm not disturbing you in the middle of something?"

Hearing her voice for the first time in years triggered a feeling of unease, but her tone was gentle, almost tentative. "It's fine," he said. "You're not disturbing me."

"I just got your email, so I thought I'd call you instead of writing back. Gosh, how long has it been since we've talked?"

"I'm not sure, it's been a while. How're you doing? Everything going all right there?" Burley said, then kicked himself. *Duh!* Obviously, things were far from being all right in her world. He heard Marta winding up with a deep intake of breath, and realized he was in for it now. Pulling another kitchen chair over, he propped his feet on it and braced himself.

"Oh, Burley, it's been so hard," Marta started in. "I miss Ken so much it hurts, and my daughter is heartbroken about losing her father. We're all alone down here, did you know that? Both of Ken's parents passed away a long time ago. His sister's family lives in Maryland, but besides them, there aren't any other relatives." Marta's voice broke into a sob. "I get so lonesome sometimes, it's awful."

Cripes, he was afraid this would happen. Burley groped for a suitable response. "Must be hard for you," he said at last. He needed to steer the conversation away from all this uncomfortable emotional stuff. "How's the company doing?" he said. "You mentioned you were having difficulties."

"It's doing terribly, Burley! I don't know a thing about the roofing business, or about business in general. Ken was in charge of everything and I was only there to help with answering the phone or doing some filing once in a while. I never got to know any of his employees except for the foreman, and he threatened to quit last week because he was sick of me screwing up all the work orders." Her voice quavered again. "I'm worried the company's going to go under, and then what am I going to do? I haven't held a real job in years. I don't even have a resume."

"I'm sorry," Burley said. "I wish I could help."

"You *can* help."

Uh oh. Burley moved the phone to his other ear. "How?"

"You studied business at HCC, right? And now you're a store manager, so you know all about accounting and taxes and stuff. That's the part I don't get. I've learned a lot about roofing products and installation over the past couple months, but the paperwork side of the business is what trips me up. If you came down here for a week or so, you could look over the books and teach me how to do it. It wouldn't take that long for me to catch on, you know I'm a quick learner."

Burley's thoughts jumped to Lavender. What would she think if he went out of town for a whole week, to see another woman? Probably not a smooth move, when their relationship was just getting going. "I don't know, Marta," he said. "I've got a lot going on at work at the moment. Isn't there someone you know down there who can help you out, instead of me traveling all that way?"

"Hold on a sec." Burley heard Marta sniffling and blowing her nose. When she came back on, she sounded somewhat more composed than before. "You can't imagine what I've been through since my husband died, Burley. You wouldn't believe how many people have tried to take advantage of me, or pushed me aside because I'm a woman trying to run a man's business. It's really hard to take, and it's wearing me down. I don't have anybody else to turn to. Please, please say you'll come! You're my oldest friend and I trust you more than anyone I know."

Sure, she trusted him, but could he trust her? Burley could feel himself sliding into dangerous territory here. Tangling himself up in Marta's problems was about the last thing he wanted to do right now, but her crying and plaintive begging were starting to soften him up. "I wish I could help you," he said, "but—"

"Don't forget," Marta cut in. "You owe me one, Burley."

The memories flooded in. She was right, he did owe her. Owed her big time, in fact. He'd always intended to repay the favor somehow, but the opportunity had never really presented itself—until now.

Burley covered the phone with his hand and let out a long sigh. He could certainly spare a couple of days to give her a hand, it was the least he could do for the sorrowing friend who'd saved his neck so many years ago. As he thought it over, he saw how it could work: he'd drive down to Pennsylvania on his next Saturday off from the Mini Mart, assess Marta's business situation, and do whatever he could to help her get things back on track. The long drive would necessitate an overnight stay, but he was sure she wouldn't mind putting him up at her house for one night. And if Lavender wanted to see him that weekend, he'd make up a reason why he wasn't available, without mentioning anything about the trip.

He uncovered the phone. "Okay, Marta," he said. "I'll come."

"Oh, Burley! I knew I could count on you! You have no idea what this means to me. Thank you, thank you!"

"No problem. I'll see you soon." Burley ended the call and sat with his forehead propped on his hand, his thoughts drifting back to a rainy summer night twenty years ago.

CHAPTER 6

The incident occurred about a month after their high school graduation. Burley's town league softball game was rained out, so he and a bunch of the guys had gone to someone's house to hang out and watch TV. After pounding a few beers, he telephoned the girl he'd started seeing recently, and invited her to go bowling with him and two of his buddies.

The new girlfriend—whatever her name was, he couldn't recall anymore—met him at Helmsburg Lanes, and their group got set up to bowl. As Burley was waiting his turn between frames, a shout of laughter rose from the snack bar, and glancing up, he caught a glimpse of Hunter Stanwell, the county attorney's spoiled dick of a son, who played third base on Burley's ball team. Hunter was sitting sideways at the end of a booth, with a group of girls fluttering around him, vying for his attention.

Standing on the fringe of the group was Marta, looking cute in a blousy white top and jean shorts. She was pretending not to see Burley, but he could tell she was aware of his presence by the way she kept peeking sideways through her overgrown bangs, bobbing her head to a Shania Twain song he knew she didn't even like. He tried to ignore her and keep his attention focused on the game, but that was hard to do with Marta's eyes boring into him from across the room.

Marta had popped up in his path several times since he'd broken up with her, after realizing his feelings for her were never going to blossom into love. There were plenty of guys he knew who had sort-of girlfriends that they dated for the convenience of sex, but Burley wasn't like that. In his opinion, if two people didn't truly care about each other, they had no business being a couple. It was better to be honest and end the relationship, rather than drag it along under false pretenses.

Unfortunately, Marta didn't seen things the same way, and had a difficult time letting go. Hard as Burley tried to avoid her, the frequency of them running into each other was clearly accidentally-on-purpose on her part. She stopped for gas at the Mini Mart more often than she could possibly need to, and always came inside to pay cash; she'd even turned up at Wendy's one night when he was there with a date. Burley tried to be friendly and casual each time, in consideration of her feelings, but their meetings were always awkward, with Marta blushing and stammering, then rushing off, leaving him shaking his head.

He did miss their friendship, though. That was a genuine loss. But in the end, he was thankful he'd extricated himself from a clingy romance that wasn't meant to be.

"You're up, man," one of his buddies called. Burley shot another quick look at Marta, hoping she wouldn't try to pull anything in front of his new girlfriend, then turned his back. The beers he'd consumed earlier had loosened him up and he was bowling pretty well that night, picking up plenty of spares and strikes, and in the eighth frame, he rolled a double.

The girlfriend cheered and flung herself at him, and as Burley turned to kiss her, he saw a blur of white near the snack bar as Marta detached herself from Hunter's gaggle of girls and bolted out the side exit. He felt a flicker of sympathy—the poor girl was probably jealous, seeing him out with someone else, but what was he supposed to do about it? You had to cut your losses and move on, not waste your time dwelling on the past.

As the game progressed, Burley continued to watch Hunter, who now appeared to be hitting on Donna Schulze, one of Burley's younger co-workers at the Mini Mart. Donna-Do-Ya-Wanna, they called her at school, on account of her poor judgment where boys were concerned. Donna was giggling drunkenly in response to Hunter's obvious come-ons, which wasn't good—the guy was notorious for the pump and dump. And he didn't even hunt.

The beef between Burley and Hunter was basically a class thing. Burley's family was third generation North Country and solidly working class. In contrast, the white collar Stanwells had moved to Hogan County only four years ago, when Hunter's hotshot lawyer parents decided to trade the New York City rat race for the slower-paced upstate life. His father embarked on a career in public service, and the family settled into a comfortable home in a pricey private development on the Black River.

For all the privileges of his upbringing and his father's prominent position in the community, Hunter's attitude toward the locals was one of disdain. At Helmsburg High, he'd been a good student and a talented ballplayer, but his arrogance made him incapable of getting along with his teammates, and especially with Burley, who was the team captain. There were several occasions when the hostility between the two boys came close to erupting into a full-blown fistfight, requiring the swift intervention of their respective friends.

Burley hefted his bowling ball, stepped up to the line and rolled another spare. Glancing over his shoulder once more, he saw that Hunter had his arm around Donna now, his hand snugged up tight beneath her breasts. As Hunter steered the girl toward the side exit, he had to stop and catch her as she stumbled. She was wasted, Burley could see. This wasn't going to end well.

"You got one more roll, Burl," his buddy called. "Tenth frame."

Four years of pent-up resentment were about to boil over. "Skip it," Burley told his friends. "I gotta go take care of something." He dropped his ball onto the rack and hurried to follow Hunter and Donna out the side door.

The floodlight outside had been shot out by some yahoo, so the parking lot on that side of the building was dark, and Burley could barely make out the couple's shadowy forms as they veered towards a rain-slicked Volvo. As he splashed through the puddles after them, he saw Hunter pull Donna around to the passenger's side of the car and open the door.

The rear door.

Asshole.

Burley's reaction was swift. "*Stanwell*," he shouted, as he sprinted across the asphalt. "*Leave her alone*."

Hunter looked over his shoulder, then released his grip on Donna, who slumped against the side of the car. He backed away from Burley, his hands up in gesture of feigned innocence. "What the hell, man? She's too drunk to drive so I'm going to take her home."

"No, you're not." Hunter backed up another step as Burley advanced. He was dying to take a swing at the prick, but his common sense warned him not to throw the first punch. Donna swayed and tried to catch hold of Hunter's arm, but he batted her off. As she grabbed for him again, Hunter jerked his arm away, clocking her full in the face with his elbow. The girl shrieked and crumpled to the ground.

Burley lost it. As he lit into Hunter with his fists, shouts rose from across the parking lot and a moment later, a bunch of Hunter's friends swarmed in and pulled Burley off. They weren't really fighters, so as soon as he stopped swinging, they released their hold on him and retreated to a safe distance.

Hands still clenched, Burley surveyed the semi-circle of young men with disgust, then knelt down to check on Donna. Her hair was plastered to her bloody face and she was blubbering hysterically. He tried to wipe the blood away with the tail of his shirt, but her nose wouldn't stop bleeding. "You're okay," he said. "I got you." The girl was too agitated to understand that he was trying to help her, and shrank away from him in fear.

The crowd grew larger. Donna's girlfriends pushed their way to the front, where they stopped and stared at their injured friend, then at

Burley. "Oh my God!" one of them screamed. "*What did you do to her?*"

A sheriff's deputy pulled up and climbed out of his car. After observing the girl's condition and the blood on Burley's hands and shirt, he took a step closer and noted the alcohol on Burley's breath. The deputy scanned the faces in the crowd, and paused when he recognized Hunter standing a few feet away. "Stanwell," he called, his hands gripping his belt. "Come here and tell me what happened."

Hunter stepped forward and pointed at Burley. "It was him, sir. He did that to her. I tried to stop him, but he's drunk and he went ballistic on me."

"You lying piece of shit." Burley lunged at Hunter but a couple of boys caught him by the arms and held him back. When he tried to explain to the deputy what had really happened, a chorus of angry shouting rose from Hunter's friends, drowning him out. The crowd quieted down after a moment and he again attempted to speak, but was silenced by a raised hand. "Turn around," the deputy said. "Put your hands on the hood of the car." Burley was patted down, placed under arrest, and pushed into the back seat. As the police vehicle exited the parking lot, Burley caught the flash of a white blouse at the periphery of the milling crowd, then saw Marta running to her car.

Chaos ensued at the tiny police station on the corner of Main and Second Street. Hunter and Donna were brought in separately, and an unruly throng of teenagers attempted to follow them inside. It all came down to Hunter's word against Burley's, since no one else had witnessed the injury to Donna's face. Even though Burley had never had a run-in with the law before, the questioning officer's bias appeared to fall squarely in favor of Hunter Stanwell, whose father held considerable sway around town.

Burley was eighteen, so his parents hadn't been called down to the station, and he wasn't about to call home and drag them out of bed so late at night, to deal with the mess he'd gotten himself into. He was sitting alone in a locked room weighing his options when a commotion arose in the hallway outside, and he heard Marta's voice. "I was there!"

she shouted. "I saw what happened. Ron Burley didn't do anything wrong, he was just trying to protect Donna from that asshole Hunter Stanwell!"

Marta's eyewitness testimony and a large cup of black coffee were all it took for Donna to sober up enough to get her account of the event straightened out. Marta signed an affidavit attesting to Burley's innocence, and he was eventually allowed to go. When he walked out of the building sometime after midnight, he found her sitting cross-legged on the wooden bench out front, patiently waiting to offer him a ride home.

After all he'd been through that night, the sight of his old friend touched a soft spot in Burley's heart. But when he asked Marta if she'd take him to get his truck from the bowling alley instead, she resisted for some reason. It was late, she said. The truck could wait till morning. Burley pressed her, saying there was no sense in waiting when they could go get the truck right now, and Marta reluctantly agreed.

Back at Helmsburg Lanes, which had closed at twelve, the place was deserted except for Burley's pickup, which was parked in the middle of the lot. As Marta pulled up next to it, he noticed the front end was canted at an odd angle. "What the hell?" he said. "Looks like I've got a flat."

He got out of the car and squatted beside the wheel on the driver's side to take a closer look. "Someone slashed my tire!" he said. "Unfuckingbelievable." There was a puddle of fluid around the base of the tire as well; he touched his fingers to it and sniffed them, and detected a fishy odor. "I think this is brake fluid. How the hell did that happen?"

Burley reached into the truck to retrieve a flashlight from the glove box, then got down on the ground on his back and shined the light behind the left front wheel, then the right one. "Those pussies cut my brake lines!" he exclaimed. "On both sides." He slid himself out from beneath the truck and looked at Marta, who was nervously gnawing on a thumbnail. "It looks like they used a utility knife or something, to hack through the cables." He gestured angrily with the flashlight. "What total idiots! It's not like I was gonna drive off without noticing something was wrong, and crash somewhere down the road. That stuff only happens in the movies."

"Oh," Marta said. "I didn't know that. Good." She tapped her thumbnail on her teeth. "Are you going to report it to the police?"

"What's the point? If I get the police involved again, it'll only aggravate that dumb bunch of townies even more. Next thing I know, I'll have Stanwell's father up my ass, making a stink about me stirring up trouble for his son."

"That's true," Marta said. "You don't want to make things worse."

Burley yanked the truck door open, threw the flashlight back into the glove box and slammed it shut. "Screw it," he said. "I can take care of the tire myself, but I'll have to call Weber at the garage tomorrow morning, and have him tow the truck in to fix the brakes. At least he's a friend of the family, so he won't charge me too much for the labor." Burley went around to the back of the truck and opened the tailgate. "If you don't mind waiting around for a few more minutes, I'll get this tire changed and then you can drive me home."

"That's fine," Marta said. "I can wait."

Once the spare was in place, they got back into Marta's car. After riding in silence for a minute or two, Burley turned to her. "Thanks for what you did tonight," he said. "If you hadn't gone down to the police station and spoken up for me, I'm not sure what would've happened."

Marta kept looking straight ahead. "You don't have to thank me," she murmured.

Burley tapped his palms nervously on his thighs. "Listen," he said after a moment. "I know we never really talked about it, but I wanted to say that I'm sorry for how things turned out between us. I hope there aren't any hard feelings, and we can still be friends."

Marta looked at him sideways as she coasted to a stop at the traffic light at the far end of Main Street. "Really," Burley said. "I mean it. We've known each other a long time and I value your friendship. I'd hate for things to not be cool with us."

The light turned green and Marta drove on. "Don't worry," she replied in a quiet voice. "You know I'll always be your friend, Burley."

The Burleys lived in an old farmhouse on the outskirts of town. Marta turned down the unlit driveway and parked beside the ramshackle barn. When Burley opened his door, the car's dome light blinked on, illuminating a rusty smear of dirt on the sleeve of Marta's white blouse. She noticed it at the same time he did, and quickly reached to brush it off. "Goodnight," she said. "Hope you get your truck fixed quick." Burley thanked her for the ride and got out.

•   •   •

Late that night as he was still trying to fall asleep, the elusive detail that had been nagging at Burley's thoughts finally crystallized in his mind: when he was getting into Marta's car at the police station earlier, he'd seen her reach into the passenger's side, then fling her hand over the back of the seat, where something had fallen to the floor with a metallic clunk. Something about the size and shape of a utility knife.

CHAPTER 7

Marta lived in a town called Granger, a five-hour drive from Helmsburg. Burley rose before dawn on Saturday morning and was underway within minutes, having packed his overnight bag and stowed it in the truck the night before. He liked getting an early start to his days, and he enjoyed a good road trip. This time of year, he usually drove up to the High Peaks region of the Adirondacks for muzzleloader season, so the trip south into central PA would be an interesting change of scenery for him.

As the miles rolled by, he daydreamed about Lavender. They'd seen each other again that past Thursday evening at the same dumpy pizzeria, and she'd let him kiss her for the first time when they said goodbye. He'd been so excited about the way things were heating up between them that he'd lain wide awake for hours that night, fantasizing about her.

Burley's thoughts turned to Marta as he crossed the state line into Pennsylvania. She'd sent him a steady stream of email over the past week, and the state of her dead husband's company had sounded worse with each new message: employees quitting, equipment going missing, customers canceling orders. He wondered what sort of shape Marta herself would be in when he got there, and he was pretty sure it wouldn't be good.

When Burley arrived at last in Granger, he discovered it was a much bigger town than Helmsburg. Following the directions Marta had emailed, he navigated his way through the unaccustomed traffic. He finally pulled over to the curb in front of a diner on the main thoroughfare that ran through the center of town, and immediately spotted Marta sitting at a table by the window. She was watching for him, and returned his wave with an eager smile.

Marta was already on her feet when he walked up to her table. She looked almost exactly the same as when he'd last seen her—tall and angular like a teenaged boy, with thick dark hair that brushed her shoulders. Her face was still very pretty, and she had the same intelligent eyes and shy smile he remembered, but there was a tinge of sadness in her expression now.

"Thank you so much for coming, Burley," Marta said, moving in for a hug. Burley circled his arms around her. Her body felt the same as he remembered, only thinner now, and her hair gave off a light shampooey scent. She pushed away from him to dab at her eyes for a second. "It's great to see you again," she said, hugging him tightly one more time, then invited him to sit down.

It was lunchtime, so they both ordered soup and sandwiches. Marta crumbled Saltines into her cup of minestrone but hardly touched it. "This week has been crazy," she said. "All kinds of stuff is going wrong at work, and then, out of the blue, Kenny's niece Lyla calls me up. She's nineteen and lives with her mother in Baltimore. She offered to come work for me, said she wanted to help." Marta sighed. "I told her thanks, but no thanks. If she was a little older and had some real experience, I might have taken her up on it, but I think she's just looking for an excuse to get out of the house."

Burley slurped a spoonful of soup. "Is there anyone else in your husband's family who could help you out?"

"No, there's no one else. I've been beating myself up for not taking more of an interest in the company when Ken was alive, and learning how to do things. It was so stupid of me. It was never a partnership, it was all his deal. I was a psych major, remember? I don't really have any practical job skills. I felt more comfortable staying at home being a mom." Marta let out a laugh that sounded like a cough. "You know me, Burl—I'm not exactly a people person."

Burley munched his grilled cheese. Marta was definitely not a people person. She'd always been quiet and self-conscious, wary of people she didn't know very well. Besides Burley, her comfort zone when they were kids hadn't extended further than an equally shy girlfriend or two.

He wanted to turn the subject away from all this chit-chat and back to the business at hand. "How about we go over to your office after this?" he said. "You can show me the whole set-up, and then I can spend the afternoon looking over your files and account books."

"Yeah," Marta said. "Sounds good." When they'd finished eating, Burley reached for the check but Marta grabbed it first and held it out of his reach. "Uh uh," she said. "You came all this way for me, so you're not paying for a thing this weekend." She left a few bills on the table and Burley followed her outside, where she pointed across the street. "My car's over there. You can ride with me."

The roofing business was situated in a brick storefront in a run-down industrial section of town. Marta drew a keyring from her pocket, unlocked the heavy glass door and pushed it open. A plywood counter bisected the room, with a banged-up metal desk and filing cabinet arranged behind it. "My office is in here," Marta said, unlocking another door. "Sorry it's so messy." She showed Burley into a smaller room which contained another dented desk, a swivel chair with stuffing poking out of its seat, and a wooden drafting table piled with roofing samples and product manuals.

Marta checked the time on her iPhone. "The trucks and equipment are in the garage around back," she said, and showed him which key to use. "I don't mean to run off and leave you, but I've got to pick up my daughter from a birthday party. I'll log you into the computer before I go." She bent over the desk and clicked at the keyboard. "Here you are—

building permits, contracts, schedules, specs. It's all alphabetical. Ken used a pretty simple filing system that should make it easy for you to find things."

There was a Keurig machine on a square folding table in the corner, and Marta waved her hand in its direction. "Help yourself to coffee," she said with a smile. "I know you need your caffeine fix." She set a Styrofoam cup out for him, then paused and tapped a thumbnail against her teeth, a nervous gesture he remembered well. "Do you want me to come back and go through everything with you, or would you rather look it over on your own?"

Burley preferred to wade through everything on his own. "I'll figure it out," he said. "You go on and take care of whatever you need to with your daughter. I'll call you if I have any questions."

Burley worked steadily all afternoon, reading files and making notes. By his estimation, the company didn't appear to be in quite the degree of distress that Marta had made it out to be, which he chalked up to her lack of experience and the stress she was under. When she returned to pick him up at five o'clock, he replaced the files in the cabinet and stuffed his notes into a folder, feeling optimistic about the state of things. With some coaching from him and an improved business strategy that he was planning to outline for her, he felt confident she could get the company back on solid footing in a month or two.

"Why don't we get my truck and drop my bag off at your house," he said as Marta locked up. "Then we can go out to eat and talk things over."

Marta did the thing with her thumbnail again. "Well, um…you see, Burley, I can't really let you stay at my house."

"You can't? Why not?"

"It's my daughter. It's too soon after her father died for there to be another man staying overnight."

Burley looked at her in surprise. "Seriously? I'm a friend who's visiting for the weekend. It's not like I'm some strange man who wants to move in with you."

"Yeah, no. I know. I just don't want her to get confused." Marta's lower lip started to tremble. "She's still so…sensitive."

Don't set her off crying now! "No prob," Burley said quickly. "I'll get a motel room."

"No, I'll get it for you. This weekend is on me, remember?"

Marta drove Burley back to the diner, and then he followed her to a Super 8 Motel near the interstate. As they got out of their vehicles, she gestured toward a Chinese restaurant right next door to the motel. "Want to get takeout instead of going out someplace?" she said. "It'd be easier for us to talk in private instead of in a restaurant."

"Okay by me. What about your daughter, though? Don't you need to go home for supper?"

"She's fine, she's with a sitter." Marta popped her trunk open. "I brought a few beers for us. Would you mind getting the cooler out while I go check you in?" She went into the motel office, then came back out and handed him a yellow plastic tab with a key attached to it.

The room held a queen-sized bed with a chenille spread that looked like someone's grandmother's, a small desk, and a chest of drawers with a tube TV bolted to the wall above it. They turned on a movie, climbed onto the bed, and ate chow mein and drank beer like they were teenagers again. After downing two cans, Burley felt a good buzz coming on. He tugged his flannel shirt out of his jeans, stretched his legs out, and balanced a carton of fried rice on his chest. The movie was about a 1970s rock band with a bunch of libidinous groupies following them around, and he kind of wanted to watch it instead of talking shop with Marta. "I'm awful beat after that long drive this morning," he said. "Do you mind if we go over my notes tomorrow?"

"Tomorrow's fine. I'm pretty tired too." As Marta got up to fetch two more cans of beer from the cooler, Burley's cellphone buzzed. He pulled it out of his pocket and glanced at the screen: *Lavender.* She was going to have to wait. He'd told her he was going to a mandatory Mini

Mart in-service training in Buffalo this weekend, and wouldn't be back till Sunday evening. He turned the phone off without reading her text and set it on the nightstand.

Marta went over to the closet. "It's so nice of you to come help me out like this, Burley," she said as she pulled an extra pillow off the shelf. "You've always been such a good friend." Returning to the bed, she handed him one of the beers. Burley popped the tab and it foamed over, and he had to take a quick slug to prevent beer from dribbling onto his undershirt. As he wiped his lips on the edge of his pillowcase, he felt Marta move her leg closer to his. "Burley," she said. "I've been wanting to ask you something. How much do you make as a manager at that convenience store? I mean, if you don't mind my asking?"

"I don't mind." Burley took great pride in his position and the responsibility it entailed. It had taken a lot of effort for him to get where he was—he'd finished near the top of his class at HCC, and had worked hard to impress his supervisors as he climbed his way up in the Mini Mart organization. "I make thirty-eight thousand a year," he said proudly. "And I'm up for a raise in January."

Marta's eyebrows went up. "Really?"

Burley was puzzled—did she think it was a lot of money, or not? He thought it was a darned good salary, especially compared to what his hunting buddies made, working as roustabouts for the paper mills, or laborers for the bigger farming operations in the county. "Yeah, really," he said. "It's plenty enough for me."

"I suppose it is, since you don't have a family to support." Marta edged closer and flipped the back of her hand against his arm. "Hey, remember how we got your dad's truck stuck on the way out to camp that time, after it rained all week? My gosh, that was such a disaster." She wiggled her foot until her pinky toe was touching his through their socks.

Burley tapped his foot against hers in return, in time to the soundtrack of the movie that neither of them was paying attention to anymore. "Yeah, I remember. Ripped the muffler clean off when I backed out of the ditch. Never even saw it laying there in the mud. My father was so mad when he saw it was missing. He knew right away it was my fault."

Marta laughed. "I remember how he made you pay for it."

"Took me all summer," Burley said, slurring his words a little. "Had to work my tail off, taking all the extra shifts I could get." He drained his third beer in one long pull. They were going down awful easy and he was getting drunk quicker than usual, which was fine with him. He was surprised by how much he was enjoying himself, lying there reminiscing about old times with Marta. The visit was turning out to be not nearly as bad as he'd thought.

Burley crushed the beer can in his fist and pitched it across the room, missing the wastebasket by a foot. He squinted at the TV, admiring the lead actress who was a sexy little thing with a wild head of blonde hair like Lavender's. *Mmm, Lavender.* His imagination got his blood flowing into a region where it had no business going under the present circumstances. He rolled onto his side toward Marta, and she turned to face him. She was freshly widowed, he reminded himself, still mourning her loss. It wouldn't be fair to make a move on her in her vulnerable state.

But Marta's legs were entwined with his now, and it felt so pleasant to be lying there together in this comfortable, buzzy way, laughing about old times. Her face had lightened up, erasing the sad worry lines. She poked her fingertips into his belly and gave him a playful tickle like she used to do, and it reminded Burley of his prom date Marta, way back when. He leaned in and kissed her.

• • •

When Burley woke the next morning, his head was pounding from the beers and Marta was snuggled against his bare chest, snoring softly. *Uh oh*, he thought. *What did we do?* A lot, apparently, judging by the fact that they were both bare-ass naked. It was an odd feeling, knowing they'd done the deed, considering how badly it had turned out the last time. He was about to slip out of bed and head for the shower, but then

Marta opened her eyes and smiled at him. Burley gave her a friendly squeeze with one arm as he reached his other hand out, feeling around on the nightstand for the remote. He clicked the TV on and they lay quietly for a while, watching a rerun of Bonanza.

The show went to a commercial. Marta leaned up on one elbow and began tracing a pattern in Burley's chest hair with her forefinger. "That was really nice last night."

Oh man, he thought, *is she gonna get all sappy on me now?* He wasn't sure what to say in response, so he simply nodded.

"We make a good team, don't we?" Marta said.

"Uh, yeah. We sure do."

Marta continued to caress his chest. "We've been friends a long time, haven't we, Burley? And we still get along great, even though we haven't seen each other in years." Her fingers wandered lower, to his sensitive midriff. It didn't tickle this time. It felt good.

"I've been thinking," she went on. "I'm a widow now, and you're still single. We're not kids anymore, Burley. What about us giving it another shot?" Her hand dipped south and Burley's vision went cross-eyed. His manhood jerked to attention, and within seconds they were going at it again. He had his standards, sure, but how could you expect a guy to turn down sex when a woman offered it up on a silver platter like this? Widow or not.

Afterward, Burley hopped off the bed, pulled on his jeans, and told Marta she could use the shower first. She picked up a quilted tote bag that he hadn't noticed she'd brought with her the night before, and went into the bathroom. While she was showering, he cleaned up the remains of the Chinese food and the empty beer cans, and tried to decide what to do. He was in a tricky situation here, one that needed to be handled carefully, without hurting Marta's feelings.

When it was Burley's turn in the bathroom, he set the shower on full blast and plotted his escape. First off, he needed to direct the convo back to business and away from all that lovey-dovey nonsense Marta had brought up; and second, he needed to get the heck out of here before he got himself in any deeper.

When Burley went back out to the bedroom, Marta was seated at the little desk, tapping a pen on a Super 8 notepad, the sad worry lines etched on her face again. She reached into her tote bag for a spiral notebook, and the shirt she'd worn the day before spilled out, along with the bra and undies she'd peeled off herself in such a hurry last night. As Burley bent down to help her gather the clothing, an orange prescription bottle fell out of the bag and rolled across the rug. He picked it up and glanced at the label: *Zyprexa*. The name meant nothing to him.

"Give me that," Marta said, snatching the bottle from him. "It's just something I've been taking to help me sleep." She zipped the pills into an inner pocket of her tote bag and turned back to Burley. "Sit down," she said, gesturing toward the bed. "We need to talk business."

Thank goodness, things were back on track. Burley sat on the edge of the bed and Marta clicked her pen. "I've got to be straight with you, Burley," she said. "I'm in over my head with this company. I know it's a mess, you don't need to tell me."

She looked so darn discouraged, it tugged at Burley's heart. "It's not as bad as you think," he said. "When I went through your books yesterday, I saw that you're in better shape than I expected." He got his folder out and showed the notes to her. "I made a rough outline of some important steps you need to take to get your operation back in order, and I'll act as your business consultant as you begin to implement the plan. You can call me whenever you—"

Marta flapped her notebook at him. "Hang on, I haven't finished what I'm trying to say. I've got this idea I'd like to run past you." She took a deep breath. "Here's what I propose: you move down here and become my general manager, and I'll pay you a salary of fifty thousand dollars a year. That's ten thousand higher than the national average in the convenience store industry."

Burley's mouth dropped open. Fifty grand to run a small-time roofing business? It sounded too easy. She had to be playing with him.

Marta's tone turned pleading. "I know I've screwed things up, Burley. That's why I need you. I've done the research—there's huge potential for growth in the construction industry right now. I could make you a partner in the company and we could work together to expand it. We could maybe even get married someday, to make it all official."

Married? Burley flinched as though she'd revealed she had an STD. *Married!* Good God. He'd learned from his mother and father's quarrelsome example that marriage required superhuman amounts of patience and restraint, and it wasn't something he'd ever sign on for with a woman he wasn't madly in love with. Last night in bed with Marta had felt comfortable and satisfying—but seriously? No. He would never marry her.

"It's a real nice offer, Marta," he said. "Very generous. But I'd need some time to think about it. Got a lot going on at the Mini Mart, several issues that need my attention…" His voice trailed off as Marta's face fell, and he was afraid she was about to burst into tears. He blundered on: "I mean, yeah, like you said—you and me, we get along great and all that, but I think you may have gotten the wrong idea about us."

Tears welled in Marta's eyes. She blinked them away and waved at Burley dismissively. "Never mind. Forget it. I didn't really mean it. It was just a thought I had, that's all." She slapped the notebook onto the desk and stood up. "I'm grasping at straws here."

Burley stood there gaping at her with his arms hanging at his sides. Marta looked so terribly sad and disappointed. Should he try to hug her or something? He took a step toward her but she avoided him. "You'd better get moving," she said, waving him off. "You've got a long drive ahead of you."

"But we haven't had a chance to talk about your business plan, or go over the books or anything."

"Never mind. I'll be fine. You know I always figure out what to do."

That was true—Marta had always been a resourceful person. Burley felt a bit annoyed for having come all this way to help her, then ending up doing pretty much nothing. What a waste of his time. Then it occurred to him that maybe all she'd really needed was the moral support of having a friend nearby, which made him feel better about making the trip. "I can always come back down here," he said. "Another weekend, if you need me to."

Marta kept her face averted as she pushed the straps of her tote bag over her shoulder. "I've got to go now. The room's paid for, all you need to do is return the key to the office." She gave Burley a swift kiss on the cheek. "Thanks for coming. It was nice seeing you again." The door closed behind her with a thump.

Burley remained rooted to the spot for a minute, wondering what the hell had just happened. Marta had gone from a job offer to wedding bells in about two seconds flat, and then she'd ditched him. Shaking his head in bewilderment, he gathered his things and crammed them into his duffel bag, then waited a full ten minutes before leaving the room, to make sure Marta was gone.

Out in the truck, he turned his cellphone back on. There was a missed call from Lavender at eight last night, round about the time Marta had been vigorously straddling him on that lumpy motel bed. She'd also sent a text: *Yr not mad at me r u? Plz call me back.*

Why would he be mad at her when things were going so good with them? *Women,* he thought, and dropped the phone into the cup holder. He'd return Lavender's call as soon as he got back to Helmsburg, to avoid the roaming charges on his Tracfone plan.

Burley smiled as he started the truck's cold engine. Marta was chock-full of emotional issues and he didn't need that sort of turmoil in his life, but this thing with Lavender was different. Lovely Lavender. She was so easy. Not *easy* easy, but refreshingly straightforward about what she wanted, which was a no-strings-attached affair. He could hardly wait to see her again, and he was even getting a little worked up now, thinking about her. He adjusted himself to make things more comfortable, and set off on the long drive home.

CHAPTER 8

The Mega Millions jackpot was up to $200 million, so Lavender figured that was as good an excuse as any to pay a visit to Burley at the Mini Mart. She donned a pair of tall suede boots and the new puffer jacket, and drove over there on a morning when she knew he was working.

Lavender pushed the door open and took a quick look around. A heavyset employee was hunched over in the snack section, making a crinkly racket as he replenished the supply of Lay's and Doritos. The guy raised his head as Lavender's boot heels clicked across the floor toward him, and a bag of chips slipped through his fingers. When he straightened up to greet her, she saw *Dustin* printed on his nametag, which was pinned to a snug uniform shirt that emphasized his man boobs. Ah yes, she remembered him now—this was the guy who'd derailed her liaison with Burley in the Walmart parking lot.

"Good morning, ma'am," Dustin said. "Can I help you find something?"

When had the boys switched from calling her "miss" to "ma'am"? She wasn't even thirty yet, so this doofus ought to be showing her more respect! Lavender smiled at him anyway. "I'd like to play the lottery, please."

"Right this way." Dustin abandoned the snack foods and shuffled over to the lottery machine. Stepping behind the counter, he leaned on his meaty forearms, breathing audibly through his nose. "What'll it be today?"

Lavender twirled a tendril of hair between her fingers. "I've never done it before. Can you show me how to do it?"

Dustin's face went red. "Um, yeah. Do you want to play Mega Millions or the Powerball?"

"Mega Millions."

"You sure? Powerball odds are better."

Lavender fixed an eye on him. "I want the Mega Millions."

"Quick Pick or self pick?"

"What's the difference?"

"With Quick Pick, the computer generates numbers for you. With self pick, you decide what to play."

Lavender liked being in control. "Self pick."

"You want the Megaplier option? It's an additional dollar per ticket and it'll increase your winnings."

Why in the hell was this so damn complicated? "Sure," Lavender said. "I'll take it." Dustin took her money, then showed her how to fill in her playslip. The numbers she chose were her lucky ones: the date when she'd won the swimming race at summer camp, and the date on which she'd lost her virginity to the captain of the lacrosse team. She handed the completed slip to Dustin, stepped back from the counter so he'd have a full-length view of her, and unzipped her jacket. "Is the manager in today?"

Dustin's face went red again. "Yeah, Mr. Burley's here. Do you want me to get him for you?"

"Yes, please," Lavender said, then spied Burley striding towards them from the back of the store, shaking his head and pointing out the window at the large Sysco truck that had pulled up out front. "Hey, Dustin," he called. "Go out there and tell the driver to bring it around to the back like he's supposed to, then double-check the invoice and make sure he stacks the pallets in the right place this time."

"Okay, boss." Dustin grabbed a coat and hustled out the door.

Burley didn't acknowledge Lavender until the truck had rumbled past the windows with Dustin jogging heavily behind it. "You shouldn't come here," he said to her in a low voice. "Someone might see us and rumors'll start flying."

"Baby, you worry too much." Lavender tried to stroke Burley's sleeve but he nudged her away. "I only stopped in for a sec," she said, withdrawing her hand, "to tell you something."

At that moment, a car drove up and parked in the handicap spot out front. The driver's door eased open and the tip of a quad cane poked out, followed by the humped form of an elderly woman. Burley glanced toward the window, then back at Lavender. "What's up?" he said. "Tell me quick, before this customer comes in."

Lavender crossed her arms and pretended to pout. "Clint's taking Logan to an away basketball game on Friday night, so I'll be free for the whole evening. I wanted to see if we could get together."

The old woman began inching her way toward the entrance. "Wait a minute," Burley said, squinting. "I think that's Mrs. Phipps." He rushed to open the door for the woman.

"Hello there, Ronald," his mother's friend said as she tottered over the threshold. "What a pleasure to see you. Would you mind directing me to the digestive care products?" Burley led her to the correct section, and was promptly drawn into a prolonged conversation about the merits of MiraLAX versus Metamucil. When Lavender poked her head impatiently around the end of the aisle, Burley signaled for her to go away, which pissed her off. She shot him a dirty look and stalked out of the store.

She got into her car but didn't want to leave yet, in case Burley decided to chase after her once he'd taken care of the constipated crone. Through the store window, she could see the woman inching her way toward the cash register. Burley rang up the purchase, then held onto the old bat's elbow as he walked her outside and helped her into her vehicle.

Burley held up a furtive finger to Lavender as he passed, went back into the store, then came out a moment later with a sack of de-icing salt. He cast a quick glance at her, but a minivan had stopped at the gas pumps, so he kept his head down and sprinkled salt pellets across the handicap spot until the customer had gassed up and left. He tossed a few extra handfuls of salt onto the sidewalk, then walked over to Lavender's car.

She lowered her window partway and waited for the apology. Burley hooked his fingers over the top of the glass. "Sorry I couldn't talk to you in there," he said. "I'm worried your husband'll find out about us. I don't want to get you into any trouble at home."

Burley didn't have a coat on and the wind was whipping across the icy blacktop. Lavender could see he was freezing. She pursed her lips. He was right, they needed to keep their budding affair a secret. They hadn't slept together yet, but that was part of her plan. She dipped her head and kissed Burley's cold fingers. "Don't worry, I'll be careful."

"Friday's good for me," Burley said. "I'm up for anything you want to do."

"I was thinking we could meet for dinner in Utica. Then maybe… I don't know." Lavender widened her eyes and shrugged her shoulders.

Burley picked up her coquettish vibe and nodded eagerly. "Sure," he said. "Dinner would be great."

"I'll call you Friday, then." Lavender said. "So we can make plans."

A shiny black Silverado with *Nielsen Electric* emblazoned on the side came cruising down Main Street, slowed and put on its directional signal to turn into the Mini Mart. Burley recognized his buddy Jack Nielsen behind the wheel and stepped away from Lavender's car. "Gotta get back to work," he said. "See you Friday." Lavender gave him a cutesy two-fingered wave and drove off.

The high school basketball game didn't start till seven p.m., so Lavender told Clint she was going to the 5:30 hatha yoga class at the

Helmsburg community center with Shayna. She made sure he saw her changing into her tank top and leggings, then sneaked into the bathroom with her tightest pair of jeans and a fuzzy cropped sweater, and packed them into a large zippered shoulder bag. Her plan was to find a McDonald's somewhere along her way to meet Burley, and use their restroom to change into the alternate outfit.

When she was finished with her preparations, Lavender found Clint in the kitchen, reading the directions on a box of frozen burritos. "I'm off to yoga now," she said in a cheery voice. As she bent over to pull on her sequined Ugg boots, the front of her loose tank top gaped open and Clint's eyes connected with the lacy black push-up bra she was wearing underneath her top. His left eyebrow twitched ever so slightly, but he didn't say anything. Lavender took her coat from the coatrack and pulled it on, and picked up the shoulder bag. "Have fun at the game," she said, and banged out the door.

They lived in a quiet neighborhood of modest brick ranches and dormered Capes. When she came to the stop sign, Lavender texted Burley: *Leaving now. Meet me at Lotus Garden.* For their first "real" date, she'd chosen a rendezvous point in Utica, a small city about an hour's drive from Helmsburg—far enough that they wouldn't be likely run into anyone they knew, but close enough that she'd have adequate time to achieve the night's objective. Her phone rang a few seconds after she'd sent the text. "Where's Lotus Garden?" Burley said.

"It's downtown, right behind the Stanley Theatre."

"I don't know where that is, I've never been there."

"You've never been to the Stanley? Oh my gosh, I've seen like a million concerts there. It's on Genesee Street, right in the middle of the business district. You can't miss it, it's got a huge marquee out front."

"What kind of restaurant is it?"

"It's a noodle and sushi house."

"Sushi? I don't think I can eat raw stuff."

He was *so* uncultured! But never mind, she was going to change all that. "It's *Asian*, Burley," Lavender said. "They have regular food too, that's cooked."

"Okay." He sounded doubtful.

A horn honked behind her, making Lavender jump. She checked her rearview to make sure it wasn't Clint and Logan leaving for the game already. "Don't worry, you'll love it," she told Burley as she stepped on the gas. "I'll see you in an hour."

Burley was waiting outside the restaurant when she arrived. For the special occasion, he'd upgraded his look to chinos and a crew neck sweater, which scored him a point on Lavender's mental scorecard. As they were shown to their table, she could feel his eyes burning into her backside. He had manners enough to help her remove her coat and pull her chair out for her (another point!) and she felt his hand brush the bare skin on her lower back as she took her seat. The cropped sweater had been the right call.

A deep furrow appeared on Burley's brow as he perused the menu. "I'm not sure what most of these things are," he said. "Like lemongrass? What's that?"

"Just get the Mongolian Beef," Lavender said. "I promise you'll like it. I'm going to get the shrimp appetizer for us to share, and the Spicy Szechuan with chicken." When they'd given their orders to the waiter, a self-conscious silence fell over them. Burley played with his fork and knife, which appeared to be a favorite habit of his. "So," Lavender said. "Do you have to work tomorrow?"

Burley seemed relieved that she'd taken the conversational lead. "Yeah," he said. "I work a few hours every other weekend, to keep an eye on the operation as a whole, and I rotate my days off during the week."

"How many employees do you have again?"

"Five. Two full-time and three part-time. I'm mentoring one of the full-timers, Dustin, so I can promote him to shift leader. He says he wants to follow in my footsteps and go to HCC to study business."

"How interesting. You're a good role model."

Burley looked pleased with the compliment. Their entrees arrived and he dug into his food. "Hey, this is pretty good," he said.

Lavender winked at him. "I knew you'd love it." As they ate, she continued to ask him questions about his job because she knew how much men loved to talk about themselves, and she took pains to act like she was paying close attention to everything he said. "Are you getting busier with the holidays coming up?"

"Yeah, I'm always busy this time of year. I've got these detailed year-end accounting and inventory reports that I have to fill out for the regional manager. He's a stickler for data, so the reports are a real pain in the neck to complete, very time-consuming."

"I'm sure they are."

"And every Thanksgiving and Christmas, scheduling turns into a huge hassle because everybody wants time off. There's always someone who wants to change their hours, or somebody else who needs to switch their shifts. Drives me nuts."

"I'll bet it does."

"I'm always glad when the holidays are over, and things get back to normal."

"Yes," Lavender said. "That must be a relief."

They finished their meals and Lavender again declined dessert, which disappointed Burley. She patted her midriff, said "Gotta watch my figure," and was delighted to see his eyes brighten as he took in the smooth band of her exposed skin. The check came and Burley picked it up without hesitating, which scored him a hat trick of points for the evening. As they were leaving the restaurant, Lavender decided to press her luck and see if he'd agree to the ultimate sacrifice of the devoted boyfriend: a visit to the mall.

"Sure," Burley said. "Whatever you want."

They took his truck to Sangertown Square and strolled through the mall for a while, then sat on a bench and people-watched. After a few minutes, Burley got up to buy them an order of cinnamon pretzel nuggets, and when he returned, he casually reached for Lavender's hand. "We'll keep it on the down low," he whispered, "in case someone we know happens to walk by."

Lavender scooched a little closer so their thighs were touching, and ate two of the pretzel nuggets, daintily brushing the sugar from her lips between bites. "I forgot to ask you before," she said. "Whereabouts do you live?"

"I'm out in the country, off Hickey Road. Got a half-acre with a doublewide and a detached garage."

Ugh, a trailer. "That sounds nice," Lavender said. "We live in town, on Spring Street. It's a small house, only two bedrooms. It was all we could afford." Burley made no comment; he tipped the empty pretzel cup up to his mouth, and tapped it to dislodge the remaining grains of cinnamon sugar.

Nine o'clock approached, and the clerk at the GameStop across from them came out and lowered his security gate partway. Lavender reached for her purse. "We'd better get going." As she withdrew her hand from Burley's, she gave him a long, suggestive look, and saw his ears go pink. *Yes!* Her plan was in motion.

They returned to Lotus Garden, and Burley pulled his pickup next to the Impala and let the engine idle. "Good restaurant," he said. "I really liked it." He leaned over to kiss Lavender goodnight, and let out a soft *uh!* of surprise when she grabbed his face with both hands and slipped him the tongue.

She was ready to make her play. They kissed for another minute, and then she abruptly pulled away. "Let's go back to your place," she said in a sultry whisper.

Burley gave her a deer-in-the-headlights stare. "Do you have enough time?"

Lavender flashed a coy smile. "I do. The basketball game is at Thousand Islands, so I've got plenty of time before Clint and Logan get back."

Burley stared at her open-mouthed, then shook himself back to life. "Great," he said, settling back into the driver's seat. "Let's go. You can follow me."

Lavender was not impressed with Burley's trailer. "You didn't tell me you had dogs," she said, after the labs tried to maul her the moment she set foot inside the door. She brushed dog hair off her clothes and took a look around. The couch upholstery was a mottled green that made her not want to sit on it, the kitchen appliances were ugly and outdated, and the bathroom was sorely in need of a scrub.

The sex was so-so, but she'd expected that on their first time. The two stinky dogs sat panting beside the bed the whole time, watching their every move and drooling on Lavender's discarded clothing. Burley started off like a ball of fire, but he was overexcited and his fuse burned down in a rush.

Afterward, they spent more time lounging in each other's arms than they'd spent on the entire event, from front door to bed. "That was amazing," Lavender said, stroking Burley's sweaty cheek. "You're incredible."

He toyed with a hank of her golden hair. "So are you, beautiful."

Lavender dropped a lazy trail of kisses along the curve of Burley's chin and down his neck, then rested her head on his chest. "It'd be so nice if we could do this more often," she said. "Maybe make it a regular thing."

"I'd like that too," Burley said. "I'm really enjoying our time together. Only thing is, I feel bad that you're married. I don't want to do anything to mess it up."

Lavender rolled onto one elbow. "My marriage is already messed up, and anything you and I do won't make any difference. My husband and I have been growing apart for years, and to tell you the truth, our relationship sucks. I guess I'll always love him for being the father of my child, but I'm not *in* love with him. There's a big difference."

Burley caressed her arm. "Are you sure this is okay with you?"

"Yes, I'm sure."

"Good," he said, "because I could fall for a girl like you."

Bingo.

Lavender fell back on the pillows and gazed up at the trailer's sagging ceiling. "I've been thinking about leaving him."

She hadn't actually been thinking about that at all. Clint was her bread and butter, and she'd be hugely inconvenienced if they were to split up. She'd only said it to gauge Burley's reaction.

He continued rubbing her arm. "You need to do what's right for you, honey." It was the first time he'd used that endearment with her. A good sign. They kissed again and lay in each other's arms in contented silence for a few minutes, and then Lavender looked at the alarm clock on the nightstand, and jumped up to put her clothes back on.

"We can go to my house next time," she said as she tugged her sweater over her head. One of the sleeves felt strangely damp and she glared at the dogs, who were now sprawled asleep on the threadbare rug. "Clint wants to do this father-and-son bonding thing with Logan, and take him to all the high school basketball games this season. There's this church a couple streets over from mine. You could park there and cut through the backyards."

"I'm not sure that's a good idea," Burley said as he buttoned his fly. "What if they came home early and we got caught?"

Lavender finished dressing, then realized her mistake: she couldn't go home wearing her sweater-and-jeans outfit when she'd left the house in yoga gear. "Shoot," she said. "I left my other clothes in the car. Would you mind getting them for me? They're in a tote bag in the backseat."

Burley readily complied with her request. When he returned, he found Lavender kneeling in the middle of the bed in her underwear; the dogs had woken up and she was trying to stay out of their reach. "Can you keep them away from me while I get dressed?" she said. "They keep trying to lick me."

Burley clamped his hands on the dogs' collars while Lavender pulled her yoga clothes on. "Anyway," she said as she repacked her bag, "we wouldn't get caught at my house. We'd be careful."

"It's too risky," Burley said, shaking his head. "If we got busted, there's no telling what your husband might do."

Lavender cocked her head to one side. "What, are you afraid of him?"

Burley laughed and let go of the dogs. "Afraid of a scrawny guy like him? I don't think so. But I don't want to get you into hot water if we can help it. What's wrong with my place, anyway?"

"It's the dogs. I think I'm allergic." Lavender sniffled and rubbed her nose, then pushed Bo's (or was it Augie's?) fat rump out of her way so she could sit on the edge of the bed and pull her Ugg boots on. She tried to imagine what Clint would do if he found out about them. He was usually pretty chill, and it took quite a lot to get him riled up. He'd lost his patience with her only a handful of times over the years they'd been together—always her fault, for pushing his buttons too hard.

Clint did have an annoying moralistic side to him, though. If he caught Lavender cheating, he might do something high-minded and dramatic like kick her out of the house, and the whole town would end up hating her. She'd have to move into an apartment and go full-time at the boutique to support herself, which would suck. Burley, meanwhile, would go on living the carefree bachelor's life he always had. People didn't care that much about the men—they could do as they pleased without major consequences, while the women were expected to follow the rules.

"I suppose you're right," Lavender said at last. "I know someplace else we could go. My family has a cottage out on the Stillwater Reservoir that we hardly ever use. My mom's afraid of bears and my sisters can't stand the black flies, so they never go there."

The Stillwater Reservoir was a huge man-made lake that lay a few miles inside the western boundary of the "forever wild" Adirondack Park. A forty-five-minute haul from Helmsburg, it was a beautiful and secluded destination for outdoorsmen from all over the North Country.

"I know Stillwater pretty well," Burley said. "It's a popular area for snowmobiling in the winter. But isn't your place already shut up for the season?"

"No, it's fully insulated and it has a fireplace, so it can be used year-round." Lavender got up from the bed, stepped over the dogs, and kissed Burley's cheek. "It's a bit of a drive, but I think it would be a good place for us to go." Especially since the cottage was cleaner and more comfortable than Burley's dump of a trailer, and smelled better, too.

A muffled ringing sound came from beneath the comforter that had tumbled off the end of the bed during their brief lovemaking. Burley reached down and picked up his phone, and saw Marta's name on the screen. He pressed Decline and shoved the phone into his pocket.

Lavender gave him a sharp look. "Who was it, baby?"

"No one," Burley said. "Just another telemarketer. They've been bugging me all day."

CHAPTER 9

Thanksgiving came and went, and Lavender and Burley's affair continued to heat up. Their desire for secrecy remained strong, but they decided the Stillwater cottage was too impractical of a place for them to drive out to in the dead of winter, with the weather and road conditions so unpredictable. Lavender balked at getting naked again in Burley's doggy trailer, so on those occasions when Clint took Logan out for the evening, Burley parked his pickup behind the Presbyterian church and hoofed it through the backyards to Lavender's house.

One Friday about two weeks before Christmas, their plans for a movie date in Utica were complicated by a band of lake effect snow that dipped southward from Lake Ontario and began dumping along the New York State Thruway corridor. Burley called Lavender as he was getting ready to leave the Mini Mart at the end of his workday. "I think we'd be safer going up to Watertown tonight instead," he told her. "Looks like the worst of the snow is going to bypass us up here on Tug Hill, but they're gonna get buried down in Utica."

The basketball game Clint had been planning to take Logan to was postponed because of the weather, so Lavender was forced to employ her usual ruse of yoga class with Shayna. She drove out to Burley's place and changed into her street clothes, and they rode together in his truck to Watertown.

The Regal cinema was in the Salmon Run Mall. Because of the threatening forecast, Lavender and Burley found themselves among only a dozen or so fellow moviegoers, which allowed them to let down their guard. They waited boldly together in the ticket line, and stood with their arms touching at the concession counter, where they ordered sodas and a tub of popcorn to share.

The theater had stadium seating, so they sat way up at the top where they wouldn't be noticed, then whispered and kissed throughout the movie, a forgettable PG-13 chick flick chosen by Lavender. Towards the end of the film there was a bedroom scene that almost put them over the edge, and they ended up making out through the credits, breathing heavily and fumbling at each other in the dark. Burley was a good kisser, Lavender had discovered. With patience and a little coaching, he might not be so bad in the sack after all.

The weather had deteriorated by the time they came out of the theater. They were dying to get at each other, but the roads were slick and it was snowing heavily, so driving all the way to the cottage was out of the question. "I guess we'll have to go to your place," Lavender said with a definite lack of enthusiasm. "Let's stop at a liquor store first."

In the trailer's messy kitchen, they swallowed a few gulps of a sickly sweet Moscato, then began tearing each other's clothes off, stumbling down the narrow hallway to the bedroom. Burley was able to go the distance this time, much to Lavender's delight. *That's what I'm talking about!* she thought as they lay panting on the disheveled sheets afterward. Burley's robust performance was exactly what she'd been waiting for.

●   ●   ●

It was after midnight when Lavender returned home. She eased the back door open and stepped quietly into the kitchen, and was startled to see her husband standing there, fully dressed and wide awake. "Oh, hi!" she said. "What are you still doing up?" Her mind raced as she took off her coat and boots. *Act normal. Don't say anything till he does.*

"I've been waiting for you," Clint said.

"I can see that." Afraid her hair was mussed in a telltale manner, Lavender gathered the loose ends in her hands and coiled it into a thick rope. Looking past Clint toward the living room, she saw the Christmas tree lights still glowing and pieces of Logan's new Lego set scattered across the rug.

Clint folded his arms across his chest. "You didn't go to yoga tonight."

Lavender set her purse on the kitchen table and began to rummage through it as though there was something very important in it that she needed to lay her hands on right away. "Yes, I did," she said, keeping her head down. "What're you talking about?"

Clint reached behind the breakfast bar and held up her rolled-up yoga mat.

Oh, snap! Lavender glanced at it a second, then resumed her rummaging. She could feel her pack of cigarettes and was suddenly dying for a smoke. "Oh, I know," she said casually, "I forgot my mat. Shayna loaned me her extra one."

"Really."

"Yeah, really."

"Bullshit."

Lavender jerked her head up. Milquetoast Clint was *swearing* at her? "What do you mean, bullshit?" she said. "What's your problem?"

"This is my problem." Clint pulled his cellphone from his back pocket and pointed it at his wife like a switchblade. "I got a text from someone I work with. He said he saw you at the movies tonight with some other guy."

Lavender threw up her hands. "You think I'd drive all the way to Watertown on a night like this? It's snowing like crazy out there. Me and Shayna decided to hang out at her house after yoga and watch Netflix instead."

Clint narrowed his eyes. "Watertown."

Oops. Lavender scrambled to cover up her blunder. "Well, yeah, where else would anyone go to the movies? Anyway, I didn't—"

"Shut up!" Clint slammed the yoga mat onto the kitchen table, and a ketchup-smeared dinner plate skittered off and shattered on the tile floor.

Lavender jerked back, her heart thumping her chest. She'd never seen him so angry. "Stop it, Clint!" she said in an urgent whisper. "You'll wake up Logan."

"I know you're lying," Clint said, advancing toward her. "I think you've been lying to me for a while now, and I'm not going to put up with it anymore."

Lavender shrank away from him. "No, Clint, I swear it wasn't me that your friend saw tonight. You can call Shayna and ask her."

Clint got in her face, raising his hand as if he was about to strike her. "You think I'm stupid?" His face was blotchy with fury. "You think I'm gonna believe more of your lies?"

Lavender backed up until she felt the wall pressing her shoulders. Clint's eyes were fierce and there was a strong odor of booze on his breath, which scared her more than anything, since he so rarely drank. He gripped her roughly by the arms. "How could you do this to me, Lavender? How could you be so reckless?"

"I told you, I didn't do anything! I—"

Clint tightened his grip and began to shake her. "*Who is he?*" Lavender's knees gave way and she let out a frightened whimper as she slid down the wall to the floor. Her husband hovered over her, his fingers still digging into her skin. "*Tell me who he is.*"

"Daddy?"

They both turned and saw Logan standing in the hallway in his Minecraft pajamas, his hands clenched to his chest. Clint released Lavender's arms and she scrambled away from him.

"It's okay, buddy," Clint called to his son. "Everything's okay." He held his arms out but the boy backed away, his eyes wide and doubtful. Clint continued speaking in a softer voice: "Mommy slipped on the wet floor and I was trying to help her. Go back to bed. I'll come see you in a minute." Logan ducked his chin to his chest, turned and disappeared into his room.

Lavender picked herself up from the floor and regarded Clint from a safe distance. The fire in his eyes had sputtered out and his shoulders sagged as he rubbed his forehead with trembling hands. He seemed about to say something, then changed his mind. "Forget it," he said with a firm shake of his head. "You're not worth it." He walked heavily down the short hallway, opened the door to the linen closet and pulled a blanket from the shelf. "I'll sleep on the couch tonight," he said with his back to his wife. "Tomorrow, I'm gone."

●　　　　●　　　　●

Burley arrived at the Mini Mart at five the next morning, looking forward to some quiet time to get caught up on his email and finish the annoying year-end paperwork that Tod Travis, the regional manager, had been pestering him about.

He was tired from his late night with Lavender, so he wasn't able to accomplish much before opening the store at six, and then only a handful of customers straggled in over the next hour, to pick up coffee or the newspaper, which irritated him further. When Dustin clocked in promptly at seven, Burley asked him to take over on the register so he could return to his office and continue working on his reports.

He was studying a spreadsheet when his cellphone rang, and he reached for it with an annoyed grunt. "Burley!" Lavender shouted. "We're screwed! Clint knows. He *knows*, Burley! Someone saw us together at the movies last night and they told him."

"Whoa, slow down." Burley got up and closed his office door. "Whaddya mean someone saw us? Who?"

"I don't know, Clint didn't say. Someone he works with, I guess. He's pissed."

"So, what did you say to him?"

"I denied it, of course!"

"Does he know it was me that you were with?"

"No. He would've said if he did. He slept on the couch last night, and this morning he left the house before I was up. I'm not even sure if he's coming back. Most of his clothes are gone."

Burley's bad mood lifted. If Lavender's husband was outta there, it was all cool with him. From the stories she'd shared, it sounded like their marriage had been shaky right from the start, so Clint leaving might turn out to be the best thing for everyone involved. For one thing, it would give Burley easier access to Lavender, without all that inconvenient sneaking around. But on the other hand, if things started moving too fast, he might find himself being sucked deeper into the relationship than he was willing to go.

This was the part where he always lost his nerve—when things started getting serious. Being a lifelong bachelor, Burley shied away from commitment, and felt most comfortable when he was going it on his own. Yes, he was extremely attracted to Lavender, but they'd only been seeing each other for three months, and he wasn't yet sure how real he wanted this affair to get.

"Your husband's upset right now," he said to Lavender, "but it might blow over if you keep denying it, and he doesn't find any other evidence. Did you try calling him?"

"Yeah, but he hung up on me. I tried to make up a story about being with my friend Shayna last night but he wouldn't listen. He thinks I've been lying all this time, about going to yoga on Fridays."

"Well, you have been lying about going to yoga on Fridays."

"I *know* I have! That's not the *point.*"

The business phone on the desk began to ring but Lavender was too fired up for Burley to dare interrupt her. "The point is," she went on, "he doesn't trust me anymore. He says he's sick of my shit. Can you believe he said that? *My* shit, like I haven't been putting up with his crap all these years—"

A knock sounded on the door. Burley reached behind him and swung it open, revealing Dustin standing there with his visor dangling from one finger. Burley covered his cellphone so his employee wouldn't overhear the woman screeching on the other end. "What is it? I'm on with the regional manager here."

"Tod Travis is holding for you on the business line." Dustin looked pointedly at the cell in Burley's hand. "Should I tell him you're busy with a customer?"

The kid wasn't nearly as slow as he sometimes appeared to be. "No, no," Burley said, "I'll talk to him in a second. I meant I was on with the *other* regional, the one from Rochester." Dustin nodded and shut the door, and Burley put the phone back to his ear. Lavender was still ranting. "Hold on a second, honey," he said. "There's an important call coming in that I need to take. Can I call you back later?"

Lavender shrieked and swore, and then the line went dead. Burley massaged his temples, rolled his chair closer to the desk and tapped the damned paperwork into a neat stack. It had finally happened, they'd been found out, and he wasn't sure what to make of it. He felt responsible for the part he'd played in getting Lavender into this fix, but it was also kind of exciting, being involved in a clandestine affair like this—as long as his name stayed out of it. He decided he'd call her back tonight, after she'd calmed down and he'd had time to think about what this turn of events meant for him.

It was snowing hard when Burley left the store late that afternoon. On his drive home, the wind picked up, creating whiteout conditions. His cellphone rang several times but he ignored it, keeping his attention on the road. It was probably Lavender, wanting to gripe about her marital woes some more, and he wasn't ready to deal with her.

When he'd finally made it home, he waded through the fresh snowdrifts in the yard, went inside the trailer and kicked off his work boots. His cell rang again, and with a heavy sigh, he pulled it out of his coat and answered it.

It was Marta and she was crying. "Burley!" she wailed. "I'm so glad I finally got hold of you."

Marta had tried to reach him several times since his trip to Granger, but he'd been so caught up in his romance with Lavender that he hadn't returned her calls. "I just walked in the door," he said. "What's wrong?"

More crying. Burley sat down on a kitchen chair, resigned to his fate as the listening ear for another distraught woman. As he waited for Marta to get on with it, a clump of snow he'd tracked inside melted into a puddle and began to seep through his socks.

Marta gasped for air. "Burley."

"Yeah, I'm here. What's the matter?"

More hiccuping and gasping. He heard her set the phone down and take a few deep breaths, then she came back on and blurted, "I have breast cancer."

A cold feeling washed over Burley and he was momentarily speechless. *Cancer.* He despised the word. It brought back the awful day when his brother Russ got the news that he'd relapsed and had only a few months left to live. "Aw, Marta," he said. "I'm so sorry."

"I'm scared, Burley." Marta's voice was shaking. "Really scared."

"I know you are, hon." He didn't know what else to say, had no words of comfort to offer his friend. "When did you find out?"

"This afternoon. I got back from the oncologist about a half hour ago. She says it doesn't look good."

"You're tough, though. You're gonna beat this."

"No, I'm not. They think it's already spread. I'm doomed. I might as well already be dead."

Burley hated this sort of hopeless attitude. Russ had gotten that way as he neared the end, and it had been a painful thing to witness. "You gotta think positive," he said. "I'll help you. Is there someone I can call and ask them to come stay with you?"

Marta sniffled. "You could come."

Oh hell. Burley stuck one foot out and nudged his wet work boots upright into a nice neat pair. The last thing he had time or the inclination for right now was another road trip to Pennsylvania.

"I need you, Burley." Marta's voice was a choked whisper. "You're my oldest friend. I can't even tell you how much that means to me." She dissolved into tears again and it made Burley want to cry, too. Breast cancer! It was salt rubbed into the open wound of Marta's grief, besides all her other challenges. He couldn't imagine how she was going to cope.

"Please," Marta begged. "Can't you come down here for a day or two, and help me figure out how I'm going to handle this?"

Burley was already feeling bad for not helping her more—he hadn't even sent her the business plan he'd promised. He had to go see her, it was the right thing to do. It wasn't an ideal time for him to be taking time off from work, but he had a few personal days he needed to use up before the end of the year. Use 'em or lose 'em was the Mini Mart policy.

"All right," he said. "I'll drive down this weekend."

CHAPTER 10

Lavender was in a panic. Three days had passed since Clint left, and it looked like he wasn't coming back. He wanted nothing more to do with her, he told her over the phone. She was going to have to face up to the damage she'd done to her marriage, and get used to being a single parent.

Burley was too busy to talk to her for long, so the only one left to vent to was Shayna. Thus far, Lavender had kept her affair with Burley a secret from Shayna because of her friend's notoriously loose lips—the woman had never met a rumor she wasn't willing to embellish, then broadcast far and wide. But now it was time to spill the dirt.

Lavender dropped Logan off at her mother's late one afternoon, and invited Shayna to meet her for drinks at the Come On Inn, a favorite local watering hole. When Shayna arrived, Lavender steered her to a booth rather than a table, so she'd have a degree of privacy as she made her confession, and offered to buy their first round of happy hour margaritas.

Heavy-boned, pot-smoking Shayna had been a marginal member of Lavender's girl crew in high school. They'd drifted apart after graduation, then reconnected in their mid-twenties when they discovered they had sons the same age who liked to play together, which was a godsend for Logan, whose hyperactivity tended to repel other children. "So, what's up?" Shayna said after their drinks arrived in tall, salt-rimmed glasses. "You said you had something important to tell me."

"Remember that guy I mentioned back in the fall?" Lavender began." The one who was going to help get Logan onto the travel soccer team?"

"Yeah, I remember." Shayna sucked at her drink. "How'd that turn out?"

"It's going great, actually. We've become very close."

Shayna raised an eyebrow. "I meant how did soccer turn out. What are *you* talking about?"

Lavender felt her face growing warm. "Well, um... that guy, his name's Ron Burley? He's really nice. He's the manager down at the Mini Mart. Anyway, we started talking, and then one thing led to another..." She touched her fingertip to the edge of her glass, and licked a grain of salt from it. "I guess I'd better come right out and say it. We've been seeing each other since October."

Shayna's mouth fell open. "No way! You've been sleeping with someone and you didn't tell me?" She leaned back and folded her arms across her D-cup breasts. "So all this time that I've been crying to you about how sexually frustrated I've been since my divorce, you were *getting it on* and didn't have the courtesy to share this piece of information with me?"

"Don't get mad about it," Lavender said. "There wasn't anything to tell you at first. We started out as friends, getting together for pizza and stuff. Then a few weeks ago, things started to heat up." Lavender realized she was smiling, which she knew her friend wouldn't appreciate, so she forced a more subdued expression. "I didn't set out planning to get involved with him, it just happened. We couldn't help it."

"Oh, yah," Shayna said, looking peeved. "It just happened. Uh huh." She sucked down the rest of her margarita and waved to the waitress for another. "Anyway, how is he in bed?"

Lavender grinned. "He's fantastic!"

Shayna scowled, obviously jealous. "What about Clint? Does he know what's going on?"

"He does now."

Shayna's scowl deepened. "I can't believe you're cheating on him. Clint was always kind of a doormat, but he's not a bad guy, really."

"Oh, spare me! Who are you to stick up for my husband, when you didn't hesitate to dump yours?"

Shayna pointed a finger. "Excuse me, big difference there. *My* husband was a certified alcoholic. I had to leave him, to preserve my own sanity."

Lavender waved her hand. "Okay, okay, I know. Sorry."

Shayna put her hand down. "How did Clint find out?"

"It's a long story." As Lavender related the events of the past several days, her manner turned serious. "I'm not sure what I should do," she said. "Clint thinks we need some time apart, so he's going to stay with his sister Patty for a while. He even talked about us formally separating, said he might go see a lawyer about it."

"Then hire your own lawyer," Shayna said. "File for divorce before he does."

Lavender groaned. "I'm too chicken. I keep thinking he'll come crawling back to me and life will go on like it was before. We have a lousy relationship but at least we've kept it together this long for Logan's sake." She paused to lick more salt from her glass.

"Yeah," Shayna said. "The single parent life sucks, let me tell you. There's always all this fuss about who's picking up, who's dropping off, where'd he leave his backpack, whose weekend is it. It can make you crazy."

Lavender's face fell. "I know. It's going to be so complicated with all Logan's after-school activities and his counseling appointments and everything."

"A lawyer could help you," Shayna said. "They'll draw up a visitation plan so everything's spelled out. There's no guesswork because you follow the schedule. That's what we did when Garth and I split up. I went to this woman lawyer over by Fort Drum who does no-fault divorces. She's got a reputation for being a badass, and she doesn't even advertise. Doesn't need to, I guess, with the army base right there."

"How am I supposed to pay for a lawyer?" Lavender moaned. "I can't afford it on the piddling amount I'm making at the boutique. Clint's not paying me any support yet, either. He says he's been footing the bills for my 'shopping addiction' all these years, and he's not going to give me a single dime until he's forced to." She paused to dab her eyes. "I don't want to get divorced, Shayna. It's so messy and embarrassing."

"It is," Shayna agreed.

Lavender pushed her heavy glass away. "I honestly don't know if I can stand living with Clint anymore, though. We bicker constantly and we haven't had sex in like a year. Well, *good* sex, anyway." She puffed her cheeks out. "I wish I knew what to do. I can't talk to my mom and dad about this, they'd only get pissed at me for screwing things up. And you know my sisters, they think their shit doesn't stink. I'd never hear the end of it."

Shayna leaned across the table. "You could go to a fortune teller and see what they have to say."

Lavender laughed out loud. "A fortune teller? Are you kidding?"

Shayna gave her a dirty look. "I went to see one before I left Garth. She was very helpful."

A party of four had been seated in the adjoining booth and one of the women was leaning back against the padded seat with her head cocked, listening. Shayna noticed and lowered her voice. "It was this woman up in Carthage, she did a tarot card reading for me. The cards showed me everything Garth was up to, and what I needed to do about it."

Lavender blinked a few times. "Really?"

"Yeah, it was pretty cool. It helped me get my head together and come up with a plan."

Lavender tapped her chin thoughtfully. "That's so wild. Maybe I *should* try it. It might help me figure out if I should try to get back together with Clint or not. Can you give me her contact info?"

"I would, but I think she died."

"Shoot. Do you know of anyone else?"

"There might be someone over in Old Forge. I can't remember her name, though—Priscilla or Penelope, or something. Try checking the bulletin board for her business card next time you're at work."

•   •   •

The boutique where Lavender worked was called Mystic Moon, and it was owned by a fiftyish redhead named Copper who took deep pride in her groovy new-ageiness and her selection of essential oils, sacred crystals, and fake batik scarves made in China. Copper was into astrology and spiritualism, and had compiled a modest library containing informative books about the zodiac and numerology. The place did surprisingly good business, considering its location in quiet, conservative Helmsburg.

Tinkly music conducive to meditation and healing was emanating from the boutique's wireless speakers when Lavender slinked in through the back door at a quarter after nine the next morning. Copper swooped out of her office nook in a purple muumuu and matching cat-eye glasses, and tapped the Fitbit on her wrist. "You're late again."

"No duh," Lavender muttered under her breath as she hung her coat up in the hallway. "I'm *so* sorry, Copper," she said in a louder voice. "Logan's school bus was running behind schedule again. I called the dispatcher and complained for the ten millionth time but I don't think anyone at the transportation office even gives a crap."

Copper tapped an espadrilled foot. "Really, Lavender, you've got to try harder to get here on time. A jewelry shipment came in yesterday and I need you to enter it into inventory and put it on display right away. I'm expecting a lot of holiday shoppers this weekend."

"Gotcha," Lavender said with a phony smile. "I'm on it."

Once the jewelry was arranged to Copper's satisfaction, Lavender went around the shop with a feather duster, cleaning the merchandise she'd been neglecting for weeks. When she got to the rack containing the tarot cards, she paused. She'd never given them a second glance before and she examined them with curiosity. They came in a cardboard box similar to a regular deck of cards, but they were bigger and there were more of them in each pack.

Lavender noticed Copper watching her over the top of her funky eyeglasses, so she replaced the cards on the rack and waved the feather duster around more energetically. "Dusty over here," she said, and stifled a pretend sneeze.

On the stroke of noon, Copper inserted a fresh stick of incense into the brass holder on the counter and lit it with a match, causing Lavender to crinkle her nose in distaste. "Sandalwood," Copper said. "For cleansing."

Cleanse this, Lavender thought, poking her hand into the pocket of her cardigan and flipping her employer the bird. Copper shook the match out, pinched it between her fingers and dropped it into the trash can. "I'm going to lunch now. I'll be back by one." Exchanging her espadrilles for rubber galoshes, she donned her long woolen coat and ugly pom-pom beret, and went out the front door.

Lavender waited till Copper had clomped past the front windows before returning to the tarot card rack. She slipped a pack of cards and a how-to booklet into her sweater pocket, then hustled to the back hallway where she transferred them to her handbag. Back on the shop floor, she licked her thumb and forefinger, and extinguished the smelly stick of incense.

•　•　•

Logan was missing his father and raised hell about going to bed that night. "*I want Dad*," he yelled, glaring daggers at his mother as she attempted to corral him into his bedroom. "Why isn't he *here*?"

"We already talked about this," Lavender said through clenched teeth. "Dad's staying with Aunt Patty for a while." Patty was Clint's dour older sister, even bonier and more reserved than he was. Clint was currently shacked up in her basement.

"But *whyyy?*" Logan whined. "It isn't *fair.*"

Lavender clapped her hands over her ears. For the love of Christ, would he just STOP? "That's enough, Logan!" she shouted. "You're going to bed now, and no PlayStation tomorrow. That's what you get for talking back to me. Go put your pajamas on and brush your teeth." To her surprise, the boy stopped crying and did as he was told.

When Logan was asleep at last, Lavender opened a bottle of chardonnay and spread the pilfered tarot cards out on the kitchen table. Some of them were very pretty, with exquisitely detailed drawings of the sun, moon and stars, magical wands, and raven-haired medieval ladies on horseback. Others were downright scary—swords and flames, a horned devil, an eyeball with death rays shooting out of it. Lavender flipped through the how-to booklet, but was put off by the weird terminology: major and minor arcana, divinatory meaning, archetypes and pentacles. Scooping the cards back into their box, she poured herself another glass of wine.

On her next day of work at Mystic Moon, Lavender returned the stolen goods while Copper and a customer were deep in a discussion about energy work. She had nothing else to do at the moment, so she got out the feather duster again and brushed it over the shelves, working her way toward the bulletin board hanging on the wall by the front entrance. As she scanned the hodgepodge of ads and notices, a business card caught her eye. *Penelope,* it said in bold script. *Psychic Medium & Tarot Card Readings.* Checking to make sure Copper wasn't looking, Lavender unpinned the card and pocketed it, and when she got off work later that afternoon, she called and made an appointment for a tarot reading the next morning.

CHAPTER 11

Lavender dragged Logan out of bed fifteen minutes early the next morning, to make sure he got to the bus stop on time for once. She waited for the school bus doors to slap shut behind her son's Zombie Apocalypse backpack, then jumped into her car and set off for the frigid town of Old Forge in the heart of the Central Adirondack region.

A ticklish ball of nerves rolled around in her stomach as she drove. She'd never dabbled in anything supernatural before, and she wondered if this Penelope person was legit or a total fraud. If the woman turned out to be a fake, there was no way Lavender was going to fork over the seventy-five-dollar fee for the reading. She'd threaten slander, or libel, or whatever it was that you did to dishonest people.

Penelope's house was a weather-beaten A-frame on a winding wooded track called Birdsong Lane. The psychic met Lavender at the front door, which opened directly into the living area. "Get inside quick!" she said. "It's below zero out there this morning." The woman's plump figure and curly white hair suggested a jolly *Saturday Evening Post* grandma. She gestured to a pair of overstuffed armchairs on either side of a wood-burning stove. "Make yourself comfortable," she said. "I'll go fetch the teapot."

The A-frame was rather drafty, so Lavender kept her coat bunched about her waist as she sat down and looked around. The furniture was constructed of sturdy pine and colorful rag rugs were scattered across the unfinished floorboards. A small staircase ran up the rear wall, leading to an open loft where a profusion of spider plants and English ivy spilled over the balustered railing.

Penelope bustled back from the kitchen with a tray holding a teapot, cups and saucers, and a plate of Lorna Doones. She untied her calico apron, sat down in the other armchair, and folded her dimpled hands in her lap. "Let's chat for a few minutes before we get started," she said. "And be sure not to tell me anything too personal—I like to go into a reading fresh. Now drink your tea and have a cookie."

Lavender's hands had begun to tremble, and her teacup clinked against her saucer as she took a sip of tea. Looking up, she noticed a painting of two chubby, naked cherubs smiling down at her from their perch above the stove. For lack of anything more useful to say, she made a generic remark about the weather.

Penelope smiled kindly and pointed out her collection of angel figurines in a curio cabinet beneath the staircase. "Did you know your guardian angels follow you wherever you go? When the roads are bad, you should mentally place an angel on each of the four corners of your vehicle. They'll surround you with the white light of protection and keep you safe on your journey."

WTF? Lavender drank her tea—it was something herbal, which she didn't care for—and took another Lorna Doone.

When they had finished their refreshments, Penelope removed the tea things, produced a pack of tarot cards from a drawer, and tapped the deck on the small wooden table beside her chair. "While I'm shuffling," she said, "I want you to reflect on the particular issue in your life that brought you here today." After passing the cards back and forth between her hands a few times, she paused and looked at Lavender, whose gaze was roving nervously around the room. "It will help if you close your eyes, dear," Penelope said.

Lavender shut her eyes but still couldn't concentrate. *If any weird shit starts to go down,* she thought, *I'm out of here.* Her eyes fluttered open again and she found herself staring up at the damned naked cherubs.

"Why don't we try a relaxation exercise first?" Penelope suggested. "Close your eyes and take a few long, deep breaths." Lavender tried to breathe slowly in and out, but it was hard to do with her heart beating so fast. "Picture yourself in a place of peace and comfort," Penelope said. "Try to tune in to how you feel when you're there."

Lavender squeezed her eyelids tighter and pictured herself in Burley's bed after making love, his strong arms encircling her body. Like magic, warm fuzzies expanded from the center of her chest, and she felt her body begin to relax against the chair cushions.

"Very good," Penelope said. "Now I want you to focus on the people in your life, the ones you're closest to. Think about your interconnectedness."

Burley. Logan. Shayna. Lavender's thoughts stuttered. *Clint? Uck.*

She tried to do as Penelope had instructed, and reflect on the burning question that had brought her here: should she split from Clint, or try to patch things up? She didn't want to be the one to blame for breaking up her son's home, but the longer she stayed in the marriage, the more suffocating it felt. She was so tired of hating her life. A relationship with Burley might be her chance for a fresh start.

Lavender opened her eyes. "I want to know if I should divorce my husband."

Penelope frowned a little. "You've never had a reading before, have you? Let me explain a little more about how this works before we go on. The Tarot isn't intended for straight yes-or-no questions, and it doesn't foretell the future. It shows you a *possible* future, depending on what course of action you choose to take. Think of the cards as a tool that helps you reflect on your decisions, sort of like a compass for your life."

"Okay," Lavender said. "I get it."

"Very good, dear. Now let's rephrase your question, something more like, 'What will happen if I stay with my husband?'" Penelope handed the deck of cards to Lavender. "Shuffle them any way you want to, and meditate on your question as you're doing it. That will infuse your energy into the cards."

Lavender accepted the deck, cut it precisely in two, and executed a flawless bridge shuffle. Penelope took the deck back and laid five cards face down in a cross on the table. Beginning with the card in the center, she turned it over and tapped it with her forefinger. "Five of Swords. This represents your present situation. There's been a loss of trust due to deception of some sort." She flipped the card to its left. "Hmmm. Reckless behavior and denial." Another card. "Oh dear, The Tower. See the flames and the lightning? It means destruction and chaos will result if you continue on your present path."

Lavender drew a sharp breath and her eyes grew big.

"Does that resonate with you in some way?" Penelope said.

"Yes, it does! It must have something to do with my husband. We got into an argument over the weekend and he was SO angry at me. Really lost his temper."

Penelope turned over a fourth card. "Here's The Star. It symbolizes hope and renewal, so that's a good sign."

Lavender tucked her coat more snugly around her waist and leaned forward. "There's another part to my question," she said. "I was wondering when I should do what I was thinking about doing."

"Let's see." Penelope turned over the last card. "Seven Of Swords. This calls for swift and decisive action."

"Oh, my," Lavender said. She sat hunched over in quiet thought for a moment, amazed by the uncanny wisdom of the cards, then all at once she sat up, tugged her coat out from beneath her and pushed her arms into the sleeves.

"Are you leaving already, dear?" Penelope said. "We've only gotten started. There's a whole lot more for us to discuss if you can stay a bit longer."

"No," Lavender said, "I think that covers it. I know exactly what I need to do now. Thank you very much, you've been a huge help."

Penelope swept up the cards and returned them to the drawer. "It will be seventy-five dollars for today, please."

Lavender hastily counted out the money, her thoughts flying every which way. *Destruction and chaos! Holy shit!* She needed to act fast, like that card with all the swords on it had told her to.

She jumped into her car and sped down Birdsong Lane. Everything the tarot cards had revealed fit her situation exactly, starting with Clint's loss of trust in her, and her denial of the affair with Burley. She swallowed hard, imagining the emotional damage her psyche would suffer if she chose to stay in her marriage. But there was that Star card, which meant there was hope. Hope and renewal, Penelope had said—renewal that could only be achieved by transferring her affections from Clint to Burley.

It was all so damned spooky and confusing, though. Shayna, she needed to talk to Shayna! Steering with one hand, Lavender felt around in her handbag for her phone.

"I'm on my way to Walmart to return something," Shayna said when Lavender got hold of her. "I'll wait for you at the service desk."

Twenty minutes later, Lavender went running into the Walmart, grabbed Shayna by the arm and pulled her into the Health & Personal Care section. "I went to see a psychic in Old Forge this morning," she whispered excitedly. "Her name's Penelope. She did a tarot card reading for me."

"Oooh, she's the one I've heard about!" Shayna said. "That's so cool. What'd she tell you?"

"She said my life's a mess and it's basically all Clint's fault for not trusting me. I asked her if I should divorce him, and guess what? The cards said I need to do it right away or everything will end in chaos."

Shayna's hand flew to her mouth. "Oh my gosh, that is *so* amazing!"

"It was an incredible experience. Like she could see into my soul." Lavender's gaze rose dreamily to the store's high ceiling. "You know, I wasn't sure if I really wanted a divorce before, but now I can see it's the right decision. Logan can't go on living with parents who don't love each other. It's a bad example." She turned back to Shayna and lowered her voice to a whisper. "I really, really like Burley, and I know he feels the same way about me. I think we may have a future together."

Shayna looked skeptical. "Are you sure? I mean, you haven't known him that long."

Lavender nodded her head with conviction. "I'm certain of it. There was this article I read the other day in Copper's *Psychic Woman* magazine, about twin flames. That's what I think me and Burley are— one soul split into two bodies."

"Whoa," Shayna said. "That is serious. Are you really going to file for divorce now?"

"Yes. I was afraid to at first, but now I know it's exactly what I need to do."

"Here," Shayna said, taking out her phone. "I'll text you my lawyer's number."

"Thanks," Lavender said. "I'll call her as soon as I get home."

CHAPTER 12

The lawyer's name was Janice Crocker, and she had a time slot available on Thursday morning. After dragging a howling Logan out of bed and onto the waiting school bus once again, Lavender sped out of town in the opposite direction from Old Forge, past low-slung dairy barns and frozen cornfields covered with flocks of squawking black crows.

Crocker's office was located in a place called Calcium, a hamlet consisting of military housing tracts and discount shopping centers, about a mile from the main gate at Fort Drum. The walls of the office were covered with U.S. Army insignia and framed training certificates that bore the lawyer's calligraphied name. Crocker herself was built like a sturdy draft horse, and she was dressed in mannish garb, as though she'd just come in from working the fields. She planted her hands on her broad hips, eyed Lavender from head to toe, and grimaced when she got to the sequined Uggs. "I charge a thousand dollars up front for an uncontested no-fault divorce," she said. "You can get it done cheaper by that shyster over in Watertown, but he's slow as hell and he's bad about returning phone calls."

"A thousand is fine," Lavender said, knowing full well that she didn't have it. "Can I pay by credit card?"

"I only accept cash."

Lavender winced. "I don't have that much money on me at the moment, so can I give you part of it today, and the rest next week?" She'd have to borrow from her parents, who were certain to get their noses out of joint about a divorce. Although they'd never been very impressed with Clint, especially compared with their two other more prosperous sons-in-law, the prospect of Lavender's marriage breaking up was sure to fling them into a righteous tizzy.

"That'll be fine," Crocker said, rubbing her hands on her cargo pants and casting another disgusted glance at the Uggs. "It'll take anywhere from six weeks to six months for the divorce to be finalized, depending on how busy the courts are, and how prompt your spouse is about signing and returning the necessary documents." She handed Lavender a plain white business card. "You can call me on my mobile number any time, day or night. I always pick up, unless I'm in court."

Lavender felt giddy as she drove back to Helmsburg. She tried reaching Burley on his cell so she could share the exciting news that she'd hired a lawyer, but he didn't answer. He'd told her not to call him at work anymore because of the chance of Dustin answering the phone, so she didn't want to try the Mini Mart number. Burley might have taken the day off, she thought, since he'd been putting in so much overtime lately. She decided to swing by his place on her way home and see if he was there.

Burley's truck was parked in front of his trailer, so Lavender turned into the driveway and climbed the wooden steps up to his door. After protracted knocking with no response, she let herself in and found Burley emerging from the bedroom, looking like he'd just woken up. He blinked sleepily at her a few times, then wrapped his arms around her. They kissed for a moment, and then Lavender disengaged herself and peeled off her hat and gloves. "I tried calling you, but you didn't answer," she said.

Burley rubbed his face and yawned. "I worked late last night and I turned my phone off when I got home."

"It's almost noon. What's the matter, are you sick?"

"No, I needed to catch up on my sleep. I've got so many freaking issues to deal with at the store. Amanda's having complications with her pregnancy, so we've been shorthanded all week. I've been trying to hire someone to fill in for her but I can't find anyone who meets my standards. It's sad how little a high school diploma is worth anymore."

"Aw, baby, that's a bummer." Lavender put her arms around Burley and nuzzled his cheek, the stubble prickling her skin. "Guess where I went this morning?"

Burley led her over to the couch and Lavender snuggled up next to him on the grungy upholstery. Burley draped one arm across her shoulders and used his other hand to smooth her staticky hair. "Where'd you go?" he said. "To see some other guy?"

Lavender gave him a playful swat. "Very funny. I went to see a lawyer."

Burley's hand went still. "A lawyer?"

"Yeah, Shayna recommended her. She's a real ball-buster, ex-military. She says I can get a divorce in a few weeks, and it'll cost me only a thousand dollars."

"A few weeks?" Burley removed his hand from Lavender's hair. "I thought it took a lot longer than that."

"That's only if you've got major assets and contested issues, and all that crap to deal with. I looked it up on the internet before I met with her. Can you believe it, though? Only a few more weeks and I'll be free!" Lavender stroked Burley's cheek. "What do you think, baby?"

Burley considered for a moment. "I didn't know you were going to talk to a lawyer," he said. "It seems sort of sudden."

Lavender pulled loose from him and sat up on the edge of the couch. "Burley, I've been trapped in a loveless marriage for ten years. That's an entire *decade* that I've been leading an unfulfilled life. It's time for me to take action and empower myself."

Burley squinted uncertainly at her. "I'm happy for you honey, as long as you're sure it's what you want."

"You know it's what I want, I already told you." Lavender jumped to her feet. "Let's have a drink to celebrate!"

"I can't," Burley said. "I gotta go in to work for a few hours, but you can go ahead and have one. Your wine's still in the fridge."

Lavender poked around in the grimy refrigerator until she found the leftover bottle of Moscato. Unscrewing the top, she poured several inches into a tumbler and took a large slug. *Hooray, she was getting divorced!* As she gulped more wine, she suddenly remembered it was her turn to pick Logan up from school and take him to his counseling appointment. *Forget that.* She took her phone out and texted Clint, saying she'd gotten tied up with something very important and he'd have to take Logan this time.

"I'm gonna go jump in the shower," Burley said, edging toward the bathroom.

"I'll stay until you're ready to leave." Lavender drank more wine, enjoying the tingly sensation coursing through her limbs. Day drinking always felt so wonderfully daring! She hadn't done anything like this in ages.

As she sipped her wine and stared idly out the kitchen window at Burley's snow-filled backyard, she thought how it was odd that he hadn't been more excited about the news of her impending divorce. They'd been sleeping together for months now, so she would have expected him to react with more enthusiasm.

Take Christmas, for example. Burley had given her a really nice sweater, one she'd admired in a store window the first time they'd gone to the mall together. It said a lot that he'd remembered how she liked it—but a really nice sweater was still just a sweater, and didn't signify all that much in the context of their relationship. Was it possible that Burley wasn't as into her as she'd thought he was? That might be the real reason why he'd turned his phone off last night. He might actually be attracted to another woman, someone who was single and readily available, without all the baggage she was dragging around.

Burley's phone was on the kitchen table. Lavender picked it up and turned it back on, and scrolled through his recent calls. Her thumb stopped moving and she stared at the phone, then glanced down the short hallway toward the bathroom, where the shower had just turned off.

The bathroom door opened a minute later, and Burley came out with a towel wrapped around his waist and headed toward the bedroom.

"Burley?" Lavender called sweetly.

He turned around. "Yeah, honey?"

"Who is Marta?"

CHAPTER 13

It took a moment for Burley to respond. "Nobody," he said. "No one important."

Lavender brandished the phone. "Oh really? It looks like she's been calling you all week. Who is she?"

Burley adjusted his towel, which had begun to slide off. "She's an old friend. A friend of the family."

"Old? How old?"

"Not that old. About my age. We grew up together."

Lavender jammed a fist into her hip. "And she feels the need to call you every five minutes, to reminisce about the days when you used to play in the sandbox together?"

Burley ventured a few steps closer. "Hold on a minute, hon, and let me explain. She's a widow, see? I think I might've mentioned her before. Her husband died last year and she's having a hard time keeping his business going. She calls me for advice once in a while, that's all."

"A widow who needs business advice? You expect me to *believe* that?"

Burley arranged his face to look sorrowful. "Yeah, she's really struggling."

"Quit lying!" Lavender cocked her arm as if she was about to wing the phone at him, but Burley stepped in and caught hold of her.

"Take it easy, honey," he said, steering her into a chair, then knelt at her feet and took her hand. "It's not what you're thinking, it really isn't, I promise. She's stressed out from being alone, and she doesn't have anyone else to talk to. She keeps calling me, but I hardly ever call her back. Trust me, I have zero interest in her."

"How sad for her," Lavender said with a sarcastic eye roll.

"It is sad. She's lonely."

"I'm sorry the woman's husband dropped dead," Lavender said, "but you've got to tell her to stop calling you. It isn't right, Burley, when you and I are in a serious relationship here!"

"That's true," he said. "I'll be sure to tell her that."

Burley's ready assent short-circuited Lavender's righteous anger. "Well," she said. "Good." Maybe this wasn't anything for her to be concerned about after all, she thought. She vaguely recalled Burley mentioning something about this Marta woman living out of state, so she couldn't be that much of a threat anyway.

Burley kissed Lavender's hand. "You know you're the only woman I care about, honey. There could never be anyone else."

"Really, baby? You mean it?"

"You bet I do," he said, pulling her to her feet.

Lavender hooked her arms around Burley's waist. "You're happy I'm filing for divorce, aren't you?"

"Yeah," Burley said, burrowing his nose in her hair. "I am."

"Why don't we go out to the cottage this weekend, for a little getaway? Logan's got an overnight Scouting event that Clint's taking him to, so I'm off the hook from Saturday morning till Sunday evening. We could pick up something for dinner and have some alone time."

Burley stiffened. "Um, I don't think I can."

Lavender tipped her chin up to look at him. "Why not?"

"I forgot to tell you, I'm going to see my grampa this weekend. Down in Gloversville. I'm way overdue for a visit."

Lavender thumped his chest with her fist and wriggled out of his embrace. "Geez, Burley," she said. "It's always something with you."

A cold front descended overnight, making for slippery driving conditions as Burley set off for Granger early that Saturday morning. He and Marta had planned on meeting up at the diner before she went to her radiation appointment at one o'clock; but the weather delayed his arrival so he went straight to the Super 8 Motel instead, and passed the afternoon watching TV while he waited for her.

He was determined not to sleep with Marta this time. The long drive had given him plenty of time to mull over Lavender's announcement about getting a divorce, and he'd come to the awareness that his feelings for her were growing deeper and he didn't want to do anything to screw it up. He'd never been one to get bogged down in emotion, particularly in regard to the women he slept with, but something about this affair with Lavender felt different from anything he'd experienced before. In a good way.

It turned out he needn't have worried about being tempted by Marta again, anyway. When she arrived at the motel after her radiation appointment, she looked exhausted and there were purplish half-circles beneath her eyes. Burley folded her into a hug and held her for a long time, stroking her hair and rocking her gently. She felt smaller than the last time, thin and fragile as a bird.

They ordered out for Chinese again but skipped the beer this time, and sat cross-legged on the bed without touching. Burley dug into his Lo Mein. "How're your treatments going?"

Marta picked at the knobby bedspread. "The radiation's going fine, I think. I'm also on chemo and hormone therapy, and a medication that's supposed to make my bones stronger. I feel okay so far, but I know it's going to get a lot worse." She poked a plastic fork into her fried rice and took a small bite, then thrust the carton at Burley. "You can have this. I'm afraid it'll upset my stomach."

Marta swung her legs over the edge of the bed and pulled a bottle of Vitamin Water out of her handbag. After a few sips she seemed to feel better. "I do have some good news," she said, screwing the cap back onto the bottle. "The town of Granger got a grant for a downtown revitalization project. They're going to refurbish all the historical buildings on State Street, and I bid on the roofing component of the job. If my company wins the contract, we'll be guaranteed so much work that I won't have to worry anymore."

"Why don't you just sell it?" Burley said. "You don't need any more stress right now. You've got to focus your energy on getting better."

Marta bristled. "That business is Ken's legacy for our daughter! I've got to keep it going for her. It's all she has left of her father." Her eyes glistened and Burley was afraid a deluge was coming. He closed the flaps on his carton of food and set it over on the desk, then returned to the bed and put his arm around Marta's shoulders. "I get it, hon," he said. "You don't have to say another word about it."

Marta sniffled and wiped her nose but didn't start full-on crying, thank goodness. "I want you to know, Burley," she said with downcast eyes, "that I'm really sorry for what I said before, about us trying to be a couple again. It was my loneliness talking. I didn't mean to make you uncomfortable. I'm really embarrassed that I brought it up and I hope you'll forget I ever said anything."

"Don't worry about it," Burley said. "I understand."

"I also want you to know that my job offer still stands. I'd way rather have you running my company than hire a stranger. You've always been a good person and I trust you more than anyone else I've ever known."

Marta's face was obscured by her hair. After a moment, she pushed her hair back and turned to look Burley straight in the eye, and he was relieved to see there was no sign of tears. "You never really gave me an answer," she said, "about coming to work for me." Burley was about to respond but Marta held up her hand. "Hear me out first. I can give you a five-thousand-dollar signing bonus, in cash and off the books, in addition to the salary I offered you before. That's the best I can do at the moment. But don't say anything right now, okay? Think about it after you get home. When you're ready, you can call me and let me know what you've decided."

Burley was touched by Marta's heartfelt apology and the earnestness of her offer. Pulling her into a hug, he patted her back. Poor kid. Poor lonely, grieving, dying Marta.

"I'm so grateful to you, Burley," Marta murmured into his neck. "You've been such a loyal friend. You might not realize it, but that truly means the world to me." In a sudden movement, she lifted her chin and kissed him full on the mouth. Burley was caught off guard and was about to pull away, but Marta twined her arms around his neck and went on kissing him, and he found to his dismay that he couldn't prevent his body from responding.

NO, his conscience shouted. STOP THIS. He tried to deflect Marta's onslaught but she'd scooted down between his legs and was undoing the buttons of his fly now. As he attempted to push her away, an oddly guilty feeling hit him—he was rejecting a dying woman, which was cruel and heartless! Marta might not be long for this world, so what difference would it make if he gave her what she wanted? Lavender would be none the wiser. No harm, no foul. All good. Burley closed his eyes and let out a groan of pleasure. *What the hell,* he thought. *Might as well enjoy the ride.*

When the action was over and an acceptable interval of cuddling had passed, Burley disentangled himself from Marta's long limbs, got up from the bed and re-buttoned his fly, and went to retrieve the leftover Chinese food.

Marta sat up and pushed her tangled hair out of her face. "I don't feel so good," she said, then clamped a hand to her mouth and ran for the bathroom. Burley heard retching for a minute or two, then the toilet flushed and water ran in the sink. Marta emerged from the bathroom looking pale and apologetic. "Sorry about that," she mumbled. "I was afraid this would happen."

Burley felt somehow responsible for her discomfort. "I shouldn't have ordered takeout," he said. "I should've known the smell would make you nauseous."

"It's not your fault." Marta summoned a brave smile. "I think I'd better go home now. A good night's sleep will help me feel better."

• •

Burley awoke early the next morning with a strong urge to get the hell out of Dodge before Marta came back and aimed her emotional firehose at him again. He waited until seven to text her, claiming that an urgent situation had cropped up at the Mini Mart, requiring him to get back and take care of it. Apologizing for not having time to say goodbye in person, he promised to check in with her after he got home.

He got on the road as fast as he could so Marta wouldn't have time to interfere with his escape. The wooded hillsides along the state highway running north out of Granger were covered with snow, but the roadway was clear. Burley twisted the radio dial until he found a country station with a decent signal, and when Jason Aldean and Kelly Clarkson's *Don't You Want to Stay* came on, he cranked up the volume and sang along, thinking of Lavender. The sun poked through a bank of clouds, lighting up the tumbling waters of the west branch of the Susquehanna River, and Burley felt a lightness in his chest, as if his heart was expanding. All at once, he realized he was in love.

What a fantastic feeling! He'd never dreamed he would ever want to give up his carefree bachelor's life, but lovely Lavender had reeled him in. He was caught and he liked it. Things seemed to be falling into place for them too, with Lavender and Clint splitting up. Logan would be fine, maybe even better off. A child couldn't thrive in a home where his mother and father weren't committed to each other.

The word *marriage* flittered across Burley's consciousness and he was amazed by how different he felt about it with Lavender in mind, rather than Marta. She was such a free spirit, so beautiful and sexy, and she understood him so well. Burley had never felt this way about a woman in his whole life. Overwhelmed with happiness, he rolled his window down and shouted his newfound love for all the world to hear.

Burley rode the lovestruck wave for several miles before reality sank in: Lavender was still in her twenties, so he'd need to consider the possibility that she'd want more children. If he was going to be a father to their future baby and a stepfather to Logan, he needed to be making a lot more money than he was at present. Lavender would want a proper house for them to live in, not a two-bedroom trailer in the country, and their kids would need braces, and bicycles, and all kinds of clothing and sports equipment...

It was a lot to think about. Was he really capable of delivering the lifestyle Lavender would be expecting? As Marta had pointed out, his salary at the Mini Mart was merely average, so he'd need to step up his game significantly. Tod Travis was due to retire soon, so maybe he could apply for a promotion to regional manager. There was downside to that, though—the position required a lot of time on the road. The increase in salary would be significant, but what good was the extra money if he couldn't be at home to enjoy it with his beautiful new wife?

As he steered the truck onto Interstate 81 north toward Syracuse, Burley continued to ruminate. If only Marta lived closer, he'd take the job she'd offered him in a heartbeat! But accepting was impossible— Lavender would never agree to it, even if it was only temporary. Forget it. Out of the question.

Burley's phone rang. "Ronald dear," his mother chirped. "Where on earth are you? I've been waiting for you to come pick me up."

His mind skidded to a confused halt. "What for, Mom?"

"For breakfast, of course! At the pancake house."

Burley searched his memory but nothing he could think of even remotely added up to going out for pancakes with his mother. Boy, oh boy, was she ever getting confused. Not wanting to embarrass her, he tried to make it sound like it was his mistake: "I'm really sorry, Mom," he said. "I forgot that I had to, uh—go to the dentist." Never mind that it was Sunday morning; he was betting his mother wouldn't notice.

She didn't. "Oh, silly me!" she said. "That's right, you had mentioned that."

He'd mentioned nothing of the sort, which was also concerning. For some time now, he'd been worried about his mother living all by herself in the sagging farmhouse that he and his brothers had grown up in. He kept urging her to sell the place and get an apartment in town, but she was a stubborn old girl and refused to give in.

It was getting to where she needed to move into one of those assisted living places, where there were people to look after her around the clock. The big question was how to pay for it when his mother had so little in the way of savings. Selling her house would bring needed cash, but the place had fallen into disrepair over the years, and wouldn't fetch a very good price.

Burley's buoyant mood dropped several notches. He'd never had to worry about money before, but all of sudden it had become an issue. Something had to change.

CHAPTER 14

Because Burley was a salaried employee, the additional hours he had to work while he was short-staffed at the Mini Mart didn't bring him anything but frustration. The headaches continued: Amanda was put on bedrest for the duration of her pregnancy, the three people Burley interviewed to replace her were complete morons, and the stack of applications on his desk was equally unpromising. To get by, he was relying on a steady flow of strong coffee and Dustin's willingness to work overtime until they found someone acceptable to hire.

The sound of a diesel engine jerked him from his glum thoughts as he was filling the coffee dispensers one morning, and he saw Jack Nielsen's giant Silverado idling in the fire lane outside. Nielsen jumped down from the crew cab and came striding into the store. "Yo, Burl!"

"What's up, man?" Burley greeted him. "Haven't seen you in a while."

Nielsen sauntered down the candy aisle. "Was on a big job down in Syracuse all last month," he shouted over the top of the shelves. He tucked a box of Twix bars into the crook of his elbow, then stacked packages of Starbursts and Skittles on top of it. Burley followed him to the register. "Hang on," Nielsen said. "I need something to drink." He dumped the candy on the counter, went to the wall of coolers at the far end of the store, and returned with a 2-liter bottle of Mountain Dew. "You been to Syracuse lately?"

"Nope," Burley said. "No need to."

"Downtown's looking good. The University has expanded into some of those old warehouse buildings, and a cousin of mine opened a Sandwich King franchise near Armory Square. Says business is booming." Nielsen reached for his wallet. "Franchising is the way to go, Burl, if you want to make any money. Forget this convenience store bullshit."

Burley rang up the candy and soda, and threw in a complimentary pack of Big Red chewing gum for his friend. "You really think so?"

"I know so. My cousin's place is making money hand over fist, and he's got plans to open a second location. That's how you bring in the big returns, by scaling up your operations." Nielsen took his receipt and shoved it into his pocket. "You around Friday? We oughtta go out for a beer."

"Yeah," Burley said. "McAvan's around five?"

"Sure thing, man." Nielsen gathered his loot. "Gotta get back at it. See ya 'round, bud."

• • •

Later that afternoon, another job applicant arrived for her interview in ripped jeans and a Buffalo Bills T-shirt, smelling faintly of marijuana. For ten meandering minutes, Burley attempted to assess her qualifications. "What would you say your greatest strengths are?"

"Oooh, let me think." The girl gazed up at the ceiling. "I'm pretty chill," she said after a moment's reflection, "and I'm really good at guitar."

Burley slapped his file folder closed. "Thank you for coming in today," he said, "but I don't think we're a good fit."

He sat morosely at his desk for a while, his earlier conversation with Nielsen playing on a loop in his head. Normally, he enjoyed the daily challenges of managing the Mini Mart, but lately things were getting on his nerves a lot more than usual. Nielsen might be onto something, and Marta, too—maybe this job really was a bunch of bullshit, and he wasn't being adequately compensated for his efforts.

Late Friday afternoon, Burley walked down Main Street to McAvan's Grill and found Nielsen sitting at the bar drinking a Bud Ice. He climbed onto a neighboring stool, pointed to Nielsen's beer and held up two fingers to the bartender.

"Got some news to share with ya," Nielsen said. "My wife's pregnant."

Burley's face broke into a smile. "Hey, that's great. Congrats."

"Yeah, she's due in August. Real excited. With the baby coming, we decided it was time we bought ourselves a house. Ya know that new development going in behind the Walmart? We're gettin' us a nice new three-bedroom colonial with a two-car garage. We close on it next month."

"Cool," Burley said, tamping down a flicker of jealousy. "Good for you."

"The wife's going bananas with all the finishes. She wants granite countertops, stainless steel appliances, the whole nine. Gonna cost me a fortune." Nielsen grinned and guzzled his beer.

Hooray for you. Burley nodded his head and drank his beer in silence.

"So, how's the mini business treatin' ya?" Nielsen asked.

"It sucks."

"Whattsa matter?"

Burley shrugged. "You name it, it's going wrong. The regional manager's been up my ass all week because my year-end report is overdue. I haven't had time to finish it because I'm short-staffed. Can't find anybody suitable to hire."

"That's tough, man. You thought anymore about franchising?"

"Nah. I don't have the dough for something like that."

"It's not as expensive as you might think," Nielsen said. "I was talking to my cousin about it the other day. He says Sandwich King's one of the cheapest franchise options out there. The fee's only fifteen thousand."

"That's not much," Burley said, "considering how big they are."

"You might wanna look into it, bro."

"Maybe I will."

Burley nursed his beer and shot the breeze with Nielsen for another half hour, then returned to the Mini Mart to cover the evening shift. At midnight, he closed up the store, sat down at the office computer and typed *Sandwich King franchise* into the search engine.

What Nielsen had told him was correct—the franchise fee was only $15,000, a sum he could afford if he dipped into his modest savings. He also learned that the total investment necessary to open a restaurant was lower than other fast-food franchises, which was additionally encouraging.

Burley skimmed a list of the advantages of franchising with Sandwich King: global brand recognition, excellent training and support, ease of expansion. It all sounded pretty awesome. Forget about Marta's job offer, with all the strings attached to it—Sandwich King was the way to go.

But then he read a little further and discovered the devil hiding in the details: the start-up costs for equipment, inventory, and advertising could run between fifty and a hundred grand, depending on your location, and he didn't have that kind of money. Not even close.

In his younger years, Burley hadn't been much of a saver, being in the habit of blowing his disposable income on the various outdoor toys he'd accumulated in his garage. It wasn't until he turned thirty that he decided it was time to start exercising fiscal discipline, and had begun socking away a portion of his paycheck every month. Currently, he had only about half the cash he'd need to get a franchise off the ground. A bank loan was a possibility, but he doubted he could get one with his spotty credit history. What he really needed was a partner to invest in the venture with him; otherwise, he might as well forget it.

Burley tilted his chair back, deep in thought. What about Nielsen? The guy seemed to be made of money—he owned his own electrical contracting business, drove a luxury model truck, and was about to purchase a brand-new house. A hardworking family man like him would be a great person for Burley to team up with. The idea was enticing. With Nielsen's financial backing, Burley could be his own man, run his own show! No more reporting to that butthole Travis, no more toeing the Mini Mart line.

Burley shut the computer down and went out into the store to make sure everything was turned off and put away for the night. When he'd completed his closing checklist, he pulled on his Carhartt coat and locked the front door behind him. Lingering on the sidewalk, he gazed across the frozen parking lot to the darkened storefronts along Main Street, and decided he was going to go for it. He'd talk things over with Nielsen and start saving more aggressively, so he'd be in better financial shape when it came time to make his move. He walked around the side of the building to where his truck was parked next to the dumpster, marveling at the thought of becoming the owner of his very own business.

•   •   •

The following Friday, he walked down to McAvan's to meet Nielsen again. His friend was seated at a pub table this time, halfway into a pitcher of beer. "Yo, buddy," Nielsen said. "What's new?"

Burley pulled up a chair. "Not much. Same old, same old."

Nielsen filled a mug and pushed it across to him. "I saw your nephew Cody playing soccer last weekend, down at the sports complex in Whitesboro. He's looking sharp on the field."

"Yeah, he's really improving. I haven't been able to catch any of his games lately, though. Been too busy."

"Busy with what?" Nielsen said with a lecherous grin. "You got yourself a new woman?"

"No," Burley answered quickly. "I've been putting in a lot of overtime so I haven't had any free time." He paused to clear his throat. "Speaking of work, there's something I wanted to talk to you about."

Nielsen poured the remains of the pitcher into his mug. "What is it? You need some wiring done on the place?"

"No, nothing like that. I've been thinking about opening a Sandwich King franchise."

Nielsen's eyebrows shot up. "Oh yeah?"

"Yeah, I am. After hearing about your cousin's place, I did a little research and I'm really interested, except I'd need a little help. I've got the cash to pay the franchise fee but I don't have enough to cover all the startup costs. I was wondering if you'd consider going into business with me as a silent partner. I'd be in charge of the day-to-day operation of the restaurant and all you'd need to do is put up the money for the equipment and inventory. I figure I'd need about 50k." He looked hesitantly at Nielsen. "Is that something you'd be interested in?"

Nielsen leaned back in his chair. "We'd split the profits?"

"Yeah, if that's how you want it."

"Fifty-fifty?"

Burley paused. He was in unknown territory here and didn't know what sort of arrangement was standard. "I guess so," he said. "We could work something out."

"Hmm. Let me think about this for a minute." Nielsen waved down a waitress, then grinned at Burley. "Beer's on you tonight, right, bro?"

A fresh pitcher arrived and they refilled their mugs. As Burley went into greater detail about how the franchise would work, Nielsen interrupted him. "You don't gotta explain it to me, I already know all about it. I thought about getting into the fast-food business myself, as a sideline, but I can't spare the time."

"Well, I can," Burley said. "If I do this, I'm going all in."

As Nielsen raised his mug to his lips, the thin cardboard coaster stuck to the bottom and he knocked it off with his thumb. "You mean you'd leave the Mini Mart after all these years?"

"Yeah," Burley said. "It's getting old and I've had enough. Time to move on to something new, where I can make better money. Once I get my first restaurant established, I'll expand into multiple locations. Then

I'll hire someone to manage them for me, and all I'll have to do is count the money."

Nielsen laced his fingers behind his head and nodded thoughtfully. "I think it sounds real good, Burl. You got your act together. I'll need a little time to think this through, to make sure I can swing it. Gimme a day or two, and I'll get back to ya."

Nielsen called at noon the next day. "I'm on my way to your place to get gas. You free to talk turkey for a few minutes?"

"You bet," Burley said. "I'm in my office. Come right on back when you get here."

Nielsen pulled up to the gas pumps a few minutes later. He filled his tank, then left his truck blocking a waiting vehicle while he went inside to talk to Burley.

"I've been thinking this through," Nielsen said when they were seated in the office with the door closed. "I consider you a good friend, Burl. I know you're gonna make a killing in this new enterprise, but it don't seem right somehow for me to take half your profits when I'm only putting up the money for it. So, here's what I propose—how 'bout I make you a loan instead?"

"Well, yeah, sure," Burley said, "if you think that'd be a better way to do it."

"Great. Now let's clarify a couple points. First off, we need to agree on the terms. What kinda collateral you got?" Nielsen patted the air with his hand. "Not that I think it'll be necessary to our agreement. It's just a formality. Worst-case scenario, and all that."

Burley thought for a moment, picturing the contents of his garage. "I've got a pretty nice Bass Tracker that I bought new a few years back, a used Ski-Doo that's still in good shape, and a four-wheeler that I've had forever."

"Anything else?"

Burley shrugged. "Not really. Some firearms. My truck's so old, I don't guess it's worth too much anymore."

Nielsen hunched forward in his chair. "What about your trailer? You own it or rent?"

"I own it, plus a half-acre of land. My brother left it to me when he died and I assumed the mortgage."

Nielsen clapped his hands together. "Super. Here's what I can do for you. If you put up the trailer and land as collateral, I'll loan you the 50k at fifteen percent. That okay with you?"

Burley thought the interest rate was a bit on the high side, but not unreasonable either, considering the convenience of not having to jump through a bunch of hoops at the bank. "Yeah," he said. "Fifteen percent is good."

Nielsen went on: "We'll set the payback period to begin six months from your first full day of business. The money should be rolling in by then. You good with that?"

"Yes, that seems fair."

"Great, man. You got yourself a deal. Nobody I'd rather do business with than you, Burl. To keep it all nice and legal, I'll have my lawyer, Chuck Stevens, draw up papers. I'll tell him to let you know when they're ready, so you can swing by his office and sign 'em."

Nielsen held out his hand and they shook on it. He got up and was about to open the door, but instead turned back to Burley. "Oh, one more thing. You'll want to buy all your restaurant equipment from my cousin's vendor in Syracuse. Tell them you're a friend of mine and they'll give you a good deal. I'll text you their contact info later."

Burley shut the office door behind Nielsen, pumped his arm and did a little dance in front of his desk. *Yeeesss!* His future was suddenly looking rosy.

There were so many things he had to do now—submit his application to Sandwich King, write up a business plan, find a retail space to rent. Once he was approved as a franchisee, he could turn in his notice to Mini Mart and share his plans with Lavender. She was going to be so proud of him!

CHAPTER 15

Lavender drove over to her parents' house one afternoon to hit up her mother for the rest of the money she needed to pay Janice Crocker for the divorce. Mrs. LeClair was laboring over a pan of homemade lasagna in the spacious kitchen, and as expected, she was upset about the divorce.

"Are you sure you've thought this through?" she said as she grated a ball of mozzarella cheese. "Have you considered how it will impact Logan?"

"Yes, Mom," Lavender replied irritably. "Of course I did. Clint and I have been having problems for years, and I can't take it anymore. My mind is made up, there's nothing you can do to change it."

"Why aren't you using your own money to pay for it, then?" her mother said as she slid the heavy lasagna pan into the oven. "You're the one who wants to blow up a perfectly good marriage."

"I can't do that, Mom. Clint will figure out what I'm up to if I take that much money out of our joint account. My lawyer says I need to keep quiet until the papers are served on him, so I retain the upper hand." Lavender plunked herself onto the floral sofa in the TV room adjacent to the kitchen and raised her voice so her mother could hear her over *The Young and the Restless*. "It's not a 'perfectly good marriage' either, and you know it."

"You're going a down a bad road, Lavender," her mother called back. "You don't realize what you're giving up."

"Oh, right. And by the way, thanks so much for insisting that I get married at eighteen. It worked out really well."

"Fine. Have it your way." Mrs. LeClair threw her Martha Stewart apron aside and stalked off to find her checkbook. When she returned, she scrawled her signature on a check and tore it off, and looked the other way as she held it out to her daughter.

Lavender jumped up and plucked the check from her mother's hand. "Thanks a bunch," she called on her way out the door. "I knew you'd understand."

• • •

A woman named Rochelle who was Sandwich King's business development agent for the Upstate region called Burley on Thursday morning. "Congratulations, Ron," she said. "Your application has been approved. I'll be forwarding the franchise agreement to you via email. Once you've paid your fee, you'll be an official Sandwich King franchisee. Since you've already got your financing in place, your next steps will be to lease a commercial location and register for your training course."

It was Burley's day off, so he immediately hurried down to the Moose River Realty office in town and inquired about space to rent. An agent showed him a vacant unit on First Street, a few blocks from the courthouse and the county office building. The monthly rent was reasonable, and the proximity to the government offices would bring plenty of foot traffic. Burley went straight back to the realty office with the agent and signed a lease.

Back at home, he composed his letter of resignation for Mini Mart. Relief and pride filled him as he clicked Send, and he sat back and folded his hands on his chest, feeling immensely pleased with himself.

It crossed his mind that he really ought to shoot an email to Marta as well, to let her know he was turning down her job offer. However, figuring out how to say it without offending her would take a lot of effort, and he wasn't in the mood for it right now. He'd do it later that week, after he'd had more time to think about it. Another few days wouldn't make any difference.

• • •

Even though they weren't legally separated yet, Clint and Lavender had agreed to an every-other-weekend schedule with Logan. On her next childless Saturday, Lavender invited Burley over for an overdue hookup.

He texted her at six o'clock that evening, saying he'd parked at the nearby church and was about to sneak through the backyards. Lavender was nervous about him coming to the house, since Janice Crocker had warned her not to do anything to antagonize Clint. She drew the blinds and turned off the outside lights, and when Burley knocked on the back door a few minutes later, she grabbed him by the wrist and yanked him inside. His jeans were coated up to the knees with snow, so she made him stand on the doormat and brush himself off, then grabbed his wrist again and tried to pull him down the hall to the bedroom.

She was surprised when he resisted. "Hold on, honey," Burley said. "There's something big I need to tell you first." He backed Lavender into a kitchen chair and sat down opposite her, looking so full of good news that it made her stomach flutter.

"What is it, baby?" she said.

Burley squared his shoulders. "I'm opening my own fast-food franchise," he said proudly.

Lavender stared at him, her face a blank. "You're what?"

"I'm going to open a Sandwich King. I've already been approved and I signed a lease the other day. No more Mini Mart—I'm going to be my own boss!"

Lavender jumped up with a squeal and threw her arms around his neck. "Oh, Burley, that's the best idea *ever*! I'm *so* excited for you!"

They went into the living room so they could discuss it more comfortably. Lavender pushed Burley toward Clint's recliner, climbed into his lap and slipped her hand beneath his shirt. "You'll be making so much more money now, won't you?" she said. "You can get rid of your crappy trailer and buy a house."

"My trailer isn't crappy."

Lavender giggled. "Yes, it is." She nuzzled Burley's neck. "Once my divorce goes through, maybe you and me could start thinking about getting married."

"Maybe we could," he said, and shifted his hips. The nuzzling was getting him heated up.

Lavender kissed his cheek. "Can't you just picture us in one of those big new houses they're building in that tract over by the Walmart?"

The image was appealing but Burley's mind was too full of Sandwich King to be able to think that far. "Let's not rush things, honey," he said. "There's still a lot of work for me to do. I gotta buy all kinds of equipment and get the place set up for business. Let me get things going first, and then we can talk about our next step."

"All right, baby," Lavender said. She didn't want to push him too hard and scare him off. Better to bide her time and allow things to play out at their own pace. Meanwhile, she'd employ her feminine charms to lure him even deeper into her snare. Repositioning herself so that she was straddling his lap, she kissed Burley long and hard, and smiled to herself as she felt him responding beneath her. It was a trick that always worked.

CHAPTER 16

The commercial space that Burley leased had suffered extensive water damage earlier that winter due to a burst pipe (thus the remarkably low rent.) To save money, he tried to do as much of the repair work as he could. He gutted the mildewed kitchen area, hung fresh wallboard, laid new flooring, and painted the entire place a bright but unimaginative white.

He ordered a freezer, a walk-in cooler, and a refrigerated sandwich prep table from Bracco Brothers, the restaurant supply house in Syracuse that Nielsen's cousin had recommended, and scheduled the deliveries so everything would be in place and ready to roll the moment he finished his two-week training course.

Nielsen stopped by now and then to check on Burley's progress, and did more talking than helping. He came in early one morning, when Burley was fooling around with the outlets in the kitchen, in preparation for the appliances that were supposed to be delivered on Monday. "Can you come take a look at this?" Burley called to Nielsen. "I don't know much about electrical stuff."

"Can't," Nielsen said as he unwrapped a stick of chewing gum. "I'm swamped today, got a deadline to meet."

"Just give me a hand for a minute."

"Sorry, bro," Nielsen said, turning to leave. "Catch ya next time."

Meanwhile, the Bracco Brothers were turning out to be extremely unreliable, constantly calling about delivery delays and items being out of stock. The freezer was the only piece of equipment that arrived on time, and Nielsen made himself scarce the day it arrived. "C'mon, man," Burley pleaded with him over the phone. "The guys left it by the back door and took off. It's heavy as hell and I need help getting it inside."

"No can do," Nielsen said. "I'm on the road, starting a big job over in Oswego today. We're not partners in this, remember? I'm only the money man. Find someone else to help you."

Burley ended up asking Dustin to help him. He was planning to poach the young man from the Mini Mart, but couldn't afford to do so until the Sandwich King opened for business. It was Dustin's day off but he was more than willing to come help, even though he wasn't exactly suited for heavy work. It took a good deal of effort for him and Burley to wrestle the new freezer into place, and then the stupid thing didn't work when they plugged it in.

Other things went wrong. The slicer that cost three hundred dollars arrived without its blade guard, and the dishwasher came with a huge dent in its side that prevented the door from closing all the way. The refrigerated compartments in the prep table wouldn't get cold enough, and the toaster oven wouldn't toast. When Burley called to complain, the Braccos got salty with him, and their conversations usually ended with cursing and threats.

• • •

Lavender popped in for a visit one day, when Burley was busy replacing the faulty ignitor on the convection oven. "Hey baby," she said, sashaying across the empty kitchen in a fuzzy pink scarf and vest, skinny jeans and ankle boots. "How's it going?"

Burley wiped his hands on a towel. "Not so good. The restaurant supply company I bought this equipment from sucks. I had to send several defective items back, and now they're being touchy about replacing them. I told Nielsen about it but he says it must be my fault, like I'm some sort of idiot."

Lavender looked around the vacant space and frowned. "You need to get this sorted out. When are you going to be done?"

Burley tried to keep his voice even. "I don't know. I'm working as fast as I can, but I'm only one guy."

Lavender untied her scarf, looped it around his neck and shimmied up to him. "I could help you, baby."

Burley gently pushed her away. "Not now, Lav. I'm really busy."

Lavender stepped back and glared at him. "Do *not* call me that. I'm not the fricking ladies bathroom."

He'd messed up again, saying something stupid without meaning to. Burley mumbled an apology.

Lavender rewound the fuzzy scarf around her neck. "You aren't going to be ready in time if you don't get moving here, Burley."

Burley drew a breath, counted to three and exhaled. "I'll be ready in time if I can keep working without any more interruptions."

Lavender fluffed her hair. "You're coming over to my place tonight, right?"

"I thought you were worried about your neighbors seeing me, so we were going to the cottage."

Lavender crinkled her upper lip. "I changed my mind, I don't feel like driving so far. It's supposed to snow tonight and that road out to Stillwater always gets so slippery." She whisked the tasseled ends of her scarf over her shoulders. "I've already got enough running around to do today, anyway. I've got to go to my lawyer's office to sign something, and then I have Logan's parent-teacher conference at school this afternoon." Giving Burley that infuriating little two-fingered wave of hers, she breezed out the door.

• • •

Three lines were blinking on Janice Crocker's desk telephone, and she wasn't in the mood for chit chat when Lavender arrived at her office. "Where did I put that thing?" she said, shoving documents and legal pads around on her desk. Stomping into the adjoining room, she rifled through stacks of paper on another overflowing desk. "Here it is." She beckoned to Lavender. "Sign here."

Lavender signed the document without reading it and handed it back. "How much longer will it take for the divorce to go through?"

Janice flipped a palm up. "Slight hitch there. Judge Werner had a massive coronary last week, so the court docket's backed up. It could be months before they get to your case. You'll be lucky if it's resolved by the end of summer."

"Are you kidding? You don't understand, I can't wait that long."

Janice glowered. "I am not kidding. You will need to be patient." She gestured toward the door to signal that their meeting was over.

Lavender fumed all the way back to town. Clint had finally retained a lawyer of his own and they were now formally separated. As the non-custodial parent, he was required to pay child support every week, but the money didn't go very far. The bills at the house were eating up Lavender's meager paychecks, forcing her to put off getting her nails done and her highlights touched up.

And Burley! He was certainly taking his sweet time getting the stupid Sandwich King going. It had been weeks since he'd taken her out to dinner or a movie, and he kept harping about how he needed to cut back his expenses so he could pay for the renovations at the restaurant. He'd even grudgingly admitted that it might take up to two years before he saw any return on his investment, which meant it would be ages before they could afford to get married.

Checking the time on her phone, Lavender saw she was going to be late picking Logan up from school. She zoomed into the parking lot of Helmsburg Elementary and pulled into a handicap space, but the sign had been knocked over by the snowplow. She got out of the car and slammed the door hard. She'd invent another after-school activity for Logan and demand more money from Clint, that's what she'd do. Then she'd push Burley to get his ass in gear, and get the darned Sandwich King open for business already. He needed to start making some real money, to help her get out from under the bills and the dreary vibes swirling around her ugly little house.

Lavender ran inside to the main office and signed Logan out, hustled him to the car, dropped him off at taekwondo practice, then raced back to school for the parent-teacher conference. Logan's teacher, Miss Morgan, had set up folding chairs in the hallway outside her classroom. Clint was already there, seated on the chair nearest the door. He rose to his feet as Lavender came rushing down the hall and she gave him a furtive once-over. His face was pale and drawn as though he hadn't been sleeping well, and he looked even more beanpole than he usually did.

Lavender sat two chairs away from him. "Why exactly did I have to run my butt off getting Logan to taekwondo, when you apparently had plenty of time to do it? I'm awfully busy you know, trying to juggle work and childcare every day."

Clint sat down again. "I was afraid my last building inspection might run long and I didn't want to risk being late."

Lavender took out her compact and checked her hair. The wind chill had been below zero that morning, which had required her to wear a hat, and showing up here with scruffy hat head like some sort of white trash wasn't going to endear her to her son's teacher. She was pretty sure Miss Morgan already hated her for Logan being late to school so often.

Clint shuffled his feet. "How've you been?"

Lavender snapped her compact shut and thrust it into her purse. "Just dandy, thanks. You?"

Clint stretched his long legs out into the corridor, then retracted them when he saw a teacher approaching with a line of kindergartners following in single file. "I only wanted to make sure you're doing okay," he said. "I've been worried about you."

"I'm doing fine." Lavender tipped her head to the side, flipped her hair forward and scrutinized Clint from behind the blonde curtain.

He'd allowed his hair to grow longer, which made him look less like a gawky Army recruit and more like a real man. She thought he seemed sad, too, and for a moment she felt a pang of regret. They used to be so good together, so *solid*, but that was way back before life got real.

Their married life had started out happily enough. Once they'd gotten over the shock of the unplanned pregnancy and shotgun wedding, they became excited for the baby on the way. Clint got a job with the county, and his salary was enough to pay the mortgage on their modest house. They had fun pretending to be adults, setting up their new home and decorating the baby's room together. Their life wasn't a picture of harmony, but they handled things as well as a clueless young couple could be expected to.

Logan had been a placid baby, and Lavender didn't realize how easy she'd had it until the signs of ADHD started showing up when he was in the second grade. Their adorable little boy was constantly fidgeting and squirming, unable to focus or listen to directions. She'd nearly lost her mind trying to get him to sit still long enough to do his homework or eat a full meal. In contrast, Clint seemed to have a magic touch with him. He possessed a calm and gentle manner that Logan responded much better to than his mother's frazzled impatience. Lavender came to depend on Clint to intervene when Logan started bouncing off the walls, while she retreated into a fog of online shopping and chardonnay.

"I hope Logan can hold it together through this," Clint said. "You know how he can be when he's stressed."

Oh yes, she most certainly did. That was why she always had a bottle of wine chilling in the fridge, and another one on backup in the cupboard. "He seems to be getting along with his classmates better lately," Lavender said. "I guess that's a good sign."

Clint offered a wan smile. "Maybe we're doing something right for a change."

Lavender gave him a grudging smile in return. "Yeah, maybe we are."

The classroom door opened and Miss Morgan waved Lavender and Clint into her room. "It's so nice to meet you," she said, extending her hand to each of them. She was a few years younger than Lavender, and pretty in a wholesome, I-could-care-less-about-fashion-trends sort of way. With her bobbed hair and modestly-buttoned blouse, Lavender pegged her as the type of priss that she had loved to hate in high school.

Miss Morgan invited them to sit down, then opened a folder. "We're doing a unit on civilizations of the western hemisphere and Logan is very interested in the Aztecs." She showed them a pencil drawing of a terraced pyramid. "Your son has a good eye for detail. Notice the straight lines and the symmetry of the structure."

"He does like to draw," Clint said. "We've always encouraged it."

"Wonderful!" Miss Morgan's toothy smile revealed an excessive amount of her gums. She patted a hand toward Clint. "I have a little girl who loves to draw, too."

"How old is she?"

"She's four. She goes through crayons like you wouldn't believe!"

"Yeah, I remember Logan at that age," Clint said. "He went through a box of Crayolas a month."

Lavender cleared her throat to bring them back to the business at hand. Miss Morgan held up a sheet of paper covered with colorful geometric designs. "Here is another good example of your son's work."

Clint examined the drawing. "This is cool. He really used his imagination."

"Yes," Miss Morgan said, flashing him another gummy smile. "Artwork is an excellent outlet for his energy. I'm glad to see you're supportive of his interests."

Lavender tried to edge into the conversation. "I bought him a sketch book for his birthday."

"Mm hm." Miss Morgan's smile faded as she thumbed through the other the papers in the folder. "Unfortunately, Logan is performing below average on his current math and reading assignments." She showed them several worksheets that were marked up in red. "His classroom conduct has become a bit of a problem," she added with practiced diplomacy. "I'm afraid it's negatively impacting his academic progress."

Clint frowned. "Oh no. That's not good."

"His impulse control could use a little more work." Miss Morgan inclined her head in Lavender's direction. "I've sent notes home."

Lavender uncrossed, then recrossed her legs. "We're well aware of Logan's issues. We've been working on it."

"Yes," Clint said. "We have."

Miss Morgan closed the folder and placed her hands on it. No nail polish, no rings. "He started the year off very well from a behavioral standpoint, but he seems to have regressed somewhat over the past several weeks." She glanced at Clint, then looked pointedly at Lavender. "Has anything occurred at home that might be affecting his behavior?"

Meddling prude. Lavender shot a pleading look across the table to Clint: *Please don't say anything.* His eyes met hers and he gave his head an almost imperceptible shake. Turning to the teacher, he said, "Nope, no changes. Everything's normal."

"That's right," Lavender chimed in. "Everything's the same as always."

Miss Morgan nodded. "Then we'll continue to address it here in the school setting." She stood and held out her hand again, first to Clint, then to Lavender. "Thank you for coming."

Clint was out the door in an instant and Lavender had to hurry after him as he strode down the hallway. She caught up with him outside and tugged on his sleeve, and he stopped and turned to face her. "It was good of you not to blow me in back there," she said.

"I didn't think our personal life was any of her business," Clint said with a shrug. He looked composed, which Lavender wasn't feeling in the least. The guilt was hitting her hard—she'd lied to Clint on the phone last night, inflating the cost of Logan's visits to the behavioral specialist, to make sure she'd have enough money to pay the outstanding balance that she owed to her lawyer. Yet here was her stalwart husband, swallowing her lies and being a good guy, sticking up for her in front of their son's teacher.

Clint started to walk away again and Lavender ran after him, down the front steps and across the bus loop. When she was close enough, she grabbed hold of his sleeve again. "I know you think this is all my fault, Clint." An annoying lump lodged in her throat and she had to stop to catch her breath. "You're right, it is my fault. I've done so many awful things and I've been a total jerk to you. I don't blame you if you hate me." Good Lord, she was about to cry. She could hardly believe herself, shedding tears over *Clint*.

Her husband stared at her for a second, then stepped forward and circled his arms around her. Lavender hid her face in his nylon jacket, getting the front of it all wet and snotty, but he didn't seem to mind. "I'm sorry," she sobbed, trying to wipe the fabric clean with her mittens. "I'm sorry for making such a mess of things."

"It's all right," Clint said, but he sounded hopeless. Beaten.

Lavender clung to him. "Clint," she said. "Do we really need to do this?"

"I wish we didn't have to," he answered quietly, "but I don't see what else we can do. I can't—" He stepped away and shook his head sadly. "I tried, Lavender, but I can't do it anymore. This marriage has taken too much of a toll on me." He squeezed his eyes shut for a second, then opened them and looked at Lavender with the most forlorn expression she'd ever seen. "Take care of yourself, okay?" Turning abruptly, he walked away.

Lavender watched him drive off in a billow of exhaust, then trudged back to her car. She got in, covered her face with her hands, and rested her head on the cold steering wheel. What in the world was she doing? Clint was a kind and decent man, and a loving, responsible father.

She thought back to the frosty morning when they'd first brought Logan home from the hospital. Clint had carried the blanket-covered baby seat into the house first, then returned to the car to help Lavender—anxious and exhausted from her overnight transition to motherhood—across the icy driveway and up the back steps. She remembered how secure she'd felt with her husband's arm wrapped around her waist. Clint could always be counted on to look after his little family, even after Lavender had begun to openly display her resentment toward him, for pulling her into a life that was so dull and ordinary.

She hated to admit it, but her mother was right—she was blowing up a perfectly good marriage. And for what? A man who lived in a dilapidated trailer, with no higher aspirations in life than to sell submarine sandwiches? The fling she was enjoying with Burley was fun and exciting, but how far did a few rolls in the hay go when you had a child to raise with someone else?

It was too cold to sit there any longer, so Lavender started the engine and cranked the heat. If only there was someone who could tell her what to do! Her judgmental mother and her catty sisters weren't likely to be any help, or gossipy Shayna either.

Penelope, maybe? The psychic had been clear about their marriage being on the brink of destruction, but there had also been that card with the golden star on it, the one symbolizing hope and renewal. Lavender wondered if she'd misunderstood what the tarot was trying to tell her. Maybe if she tried hard enough, she and Clint might still have a chance of salvaging their relationship.

Her phone jingled and the screen showed a text from Burley: *Can't wait to see you tonight.* Chewing her lip, Lavender stared through the dirty windshield at the jagged outline of the snowbank in front of her car. She couldn't do both things. If she really wanted to save her marriage, she had to stop seeing Burley. Without responding to his text, she stuffed her phone into her purse. She needed some time to think.

CHAPTER 17

Burley was balanced at the top of a ladder trying to rig up his brand-new Sandwich King menu board when Nielsen swaggered in one Saturday morning. "Hey buddy, how's it going?" Nielsen called. "You making progress?" Propping an elbow on the counter, he pulled a Snickers bar from his coat pocket, tore off the wrapper and took a big bite.

Burley climbed down from the ladder, keeping the front counter between them. He was pissed off at Nielsen for pressuring him into doing business with the shady Bracco Brothers, and for ignoring his phone calls when he called to complain. His Sandwich King training course was due to start in a few days, and then he'd be expected to open for business. The problem was, the restaurant wasn't anywhere near being ready.

"Things aren't going so good here," Burley told Nielsen. "Those Braccos are a bunch of crooks. They keep shipping me defective equipment, and then they give me the runaround about replacing it."

Nielsen spoke around the wad of chocolate in his mouth: "My cousin never had any problems with 'em."

"Maybe he didn't, but they've given me nothing but trouble. I'm through dealing with them. I went ahead and placed a whole new order with a company in Utica that's way more professional."

"You did what?" Nielsen wadded his candy bar wrapper into a ball and plinked it toward the newly-furnished dining area. "You can't do stuff like that without consulting me," he said. "I'm the financier of this business."

"And I'm the one who's running it, like we agreed. It's up to me to make the daily operating decisions."

Nielsen wagged a thick forefinger. "No, it ain't, Burl. I can't have you blowing through my cash, then coming up short when it's time to start repaying your loan. We gotta make major decisions like this together."

Burley grabbed hold of the ladder, dragged it a few feet and repositioned it. "Together? That's a crock of shit. You've hardly shown your face around here in weeks, and you haven't responded to any of my phone messages."

"I'm busy, man. Got another big job with a deadline." Nielsen hooked his thumbs into his belt. "I'm telling you, ya gotta stick with those Braccos, they got the best deals around. I'm trying to save you money."

"Save *me* money? What the hell are you talking about? It's *our* money. We've both got skin in this game."

Nielsen narrowed his eyes. "If you expect me to help you bankroll this business, you gotta do things my way."

Burley grabbed the ladder again, shoved it a few feet forward and banged it into place. "No," he said. "We've got to purchase reliable equipment from honest people. I want this to be a quality business, not some two-bit shit shop." He placed his foot on the bottom rung of the ladder. "If you don't agree, I might have to give you your money back, and finance this place myself."

"Ha," Nielsen said. "Good luck with that."

Burley stopped mid-climb. "What do you mean?"

Nielsen laughed. "That's a good one, Burl. You mismanage my money, and then you wanna back out of our deal. Forget it, pal, it ain't that easy. We got a signed contract and I'm holding ya to it."

Burley jumped down from the ladder. Back in the day, he'd been the speedy and agile wide receiver for the Helmsburg Hawks; rounding the counter, he went at Nielsen like a shot. Nielsen, however, was a former defensive lineman; despite being forty years old, he'd kept the size and strength of his youth, and he stood his ground. Burley collided with his fist and crumpled like a ball of used cellophane. Nielsen grabbed him by the front of his shirt, hauled him to his feet and held him at arm's length. "Whaddya think you're doing, man? Biting the hand that feeds ya?"

Burley sagged against the counter and glared at his adversary. "You're an asshole," he said, wiping blood from his mouth.

"Yeah, that's what they tell me." Nielsen began backing toward the door, warily eyeing Burley in case of another sudden move. "You better get your shit together," he said with a scornful glance at the cockeyed menu board. "Clock's ticking on that interest you're gonna owe me." He shoved the heavy glass door open and walked out.

Burley swore under his breath and tried to slam the door shut behind Nielsen, but the hydraulic hinge wouldn't allow it. He kicked his new tables and chairs aside, and stomped through the dining area to his cubicle of an office in the back. The door on that room was a flimsy hollow core, so his attempt at slamming it shut didn't provide any satisfaction, either.

He dropped into his desk chair, opened a drawer and drew out the papers he'd signed at Chuck Stevens's office, and read through the loan agreement, line by line. There it was in glaring black and white, the salient detail he'd skimmed over, blinded by his impatience to bring his dream to life: payments on the loan were set to commence six months from the Sandwich King's official opening day of business, but the fifteen percent interest had begun to accrue immediately upon the signing of the agreement.

Burley had been counting on a sizeable refund from Bracco Brothers, but it was now painfully apparent that his so-called friend Nielsen had set him up for a rip-off job. The asshole was probably getting a kickback from the Braccos, and had never intended for the franchise to succeed.

Turning to his computer, Burley clicked open a spreadsheet and went over his expenditures. The numbers were distressing. When he logged into his banking website, his mood sank even further: the balance in his business account was dangerously low, and his personal checking had dwindled to a mere five hundred dollars. He hadn't planned on funneling such a large portion of his own funds into the Sandwich King, but the difficulties with the renovations and setup had pushed him to act rashly. A bank loan was out of reach now, and there was no one else he could borrow money from. His fledgling business was doomed.

Maybe he should consult an attorney. Nielsen had bamboozled him, which had to be illegal somehow, but how could he afford a lawyer when he was so close to being flat-out broke? *Fucking Nielsen*. Burley shut the computer down and locked up. He was going home and getting drunk.

• • •

Burley awoke on his couch several hours later, sat up and massaged his throbbing head. It was dark outside, and Bo and Augie were sitting beside the couch, staring at him with mournful expressions. He shuffled to the door and let them out, then went to the kitchen and chugged a tall glass of water. When the dogs barked, he let them in and dumped food into their bowls, then flopped back onto the couch with a scratchy woolen blanket pulled up to his chin. Noticing his phone sitting on the end table, he reached for it to check the time. It was ten minutes after midnight, and there were three missed calls and a text from Lavender: *Need to talk to u. Please call me*. Burley let the phone drop to the floor, then rolled over so he was facing the back of the couch and pulled the blanket over his head.

If Lavender discovered he was going broke, she'd drop him like a hot potato. He needed to figure out a way to conceal his straitened circumstances from her, but how the heck was he going to do that when she was so high maintenance? She expected him to take her out regularly to dinner and the movies, and now she'd begun talking marriage, which meant a ring and a wedding, and all that jazz. In his groggy, depressed state, the only solution Burley could come up with was to apply for another credit card to get him through the next few months, and carry a balance till the Sandwich King started making money.

• • •

Burley waited till morning to call Lavender back. "Hi honey," he said, doing his best to sound normal so she wouldn't suspect anything was wrong. "How's it going?"

Lavender sounded like she was having issues with something herself. "I need to see you," she said. "Where can we meet?"

Burley's truck was low on gas so he didn't want to have to drive too far, or end up having to buy her lunch. "How about someplace outdoors?" he suggested hopefully. "A park, maybe?"

The day was sunny and the temperature had risen into the forties, a welcome respite from the usual chill of early March, so they decided to meet at Whetstone Gulf, a beautiful state park that was an equal distance from their respective houses. Burley brought the dogs with him, to make up for neglecting them the night before, but Lavender was instantly ticked off when she saw them riding alongside him in the truck's cab. "They're always jumping on me," she complained as he was about to let them out. "They'll get my clothes dirty." Hiding his annoyance, Burley agreed to leave them behind.

He was familiar with the park's terrain because he often went duck hunting there in autumn. "Let's hike the north rim of the gorge," he suggested. "I'm sure it's started to melt up there."

Lavender cast a doubtful look at the soggy snow on the ground around them but followed Burley to the trailhead without comment. They hiked the first half mile in silence, Lavender lagging behind and Burley pausing frequently to allow her to catch up. At the one-mile point, she stopped and called for him to wait up, and he walked back to her.

"I think I'm getting blisters," she said, kneeling to retie a pair of hiking boots that looked like they'd never seen the light of day before. They continued up the trail but ten minutes later, they had to stop so Lavender could rest again. Grabbing hold of a branch, she knocked the muddy soles of her boots against a tree trunk. "I don't know why I thought coming here was a good idea," she complained, "when I fricking hate snow."

The trail grew steeper. Lavender fell further behind and finally stopped dead in her tracks. "This is too hard for me, Burley," she called to him. "I can't keep up."

"I'm sorry, honey. We can rest a minute." Burley walked back down the trail to where Lavender had one arm braced against a massive beech tree, trying to catch her breath. When he went to kiss her, she fended him off, and he drew back in puzzlement. "What's wrong?"

"Nothing."

A heaviness grew in Burley's stomach. "You said you needed to see me. Was there something you wanted to talk about?"

Lavender's gaze roved around the bare treetops, then dropped to the ground. "Yes, there's something I need to tell you." She tugged at the fingers of her gloves, pulled them off and gripped them in her hands. "Burley," she began. "I'm really sorry to tell you this. I'm not sure how I feel about things anymore."

Burley's stomach did a crazy somersault. "What things? What are you talking about?"

"I'm not sure if I want to go through with the divorce."

He stared. She couldn't be serious, not after all the whining and complaining she'd done about her dysfunctional marriage!

Lavender pulled a wad of tissues from her pocket and wiped her nose, and the words came tumbling out: "I feel so guilty all the time. I'm tired of sneaking around and making up stories for Clint, and my parents, and everybody else I know. Even Shayna. I keep telling her the legal stuff is moving along, but it's really not. I haven't told you that part yet. My lawyer says the courts are backed up and it'll take months for my divorce to go through, which means we won't be able to get married this summer like I wanted to, and I'll have to keep on living in that crappy little house, which is actually entirely *Clint's* house, I just found out, because my name isn't even on the deed, and I'll have to start working full-time for that witch Copper, who I can't *stand*, and I won't ever have enough money to buy anything or go anywhere ever again, and *God*, I hate my life right now!"

Lavender blew her nose violently and threw the wad of tissues to the ground. Using the toe of his boot, Burley covered it with a layer of wet leaves, meanwhile trying to process what she'd said. He couldn't believe she was dropping this bomb on him when everything else in his life was about to fall apart.

Lavender sniffled and wiped her teary face with her coat sleeve. "I need some time to think things over, so I don't go making a huge mistake. Clint's been good to me, even though I've been a total jerk to him." She finally looked up at Burley. "I'm really sorry baby, but I have to make sure I'm doing the right thing."

"What do you mean?" he said desperately. "Are you two getting back together?"

"Maybe. I don't know. It depends on what he says when I see him tonight."

"You're seeing him *tonight?* You gotta be kidding me. How long has this been going on?"

Lavender raised her chin. "Nothing's been *going on,* Burley. We agreed to discuss things in person before we make any permanent decisions."

Burley threw his hands in the air and began pacing back and forth. "I cannot believe this! You're going back to your husband. This is the worst possible time for you to do something like this to me, do you realize that? You could've at least told me you were thinking about it."

Lavender began to cry again. "I wasn't even thinking about it until the other day, when we went to the parent-teacher conference. Please, Burley, don't be upset with me! I don't want to make the wrong move when I've got Logan to consider."

Burley couldn't dispute that. There was a child involved here, a possible broken home. He hung his head in despair. In the space of twenty-four hours, he'd lost his business prospects and his life savings, and now he was losing his woman. He'd screwed things up royally on all fronts and there didn't seem to be anything he could do to fix it. Without saying another word to Lavender, he turned around and headed downhill, and they hiked back to the trailhead in silence.

CHAPTER 18

Burley heard nothing from Lavender over the next several days, aside from a brief text telling him he'd left a pair of gloves in her car, and she'd left them on the windowsill outside the Sandwich King. She might as well have come right out and said it—she was through with their relationship and never wanted to see him again.

Despite his worries, Burley had hardly a moment free to worry about his love life with so much Sandwich King business to tend to. His training course began and the two weeks flew by in a blur of classroom instruction at the company's headquarters in Syracuse, followed by hands-on experience at a franchise in nearby Boonville. The classwork covered the basic business concepts and management skills he'd already mastered during his years at the Mini Mart, so the course was a breeze for him.

Rochelle called to give him his results. "You did very well, Ron. Your evaluation was the highest in your group. I can come out there tomorrow for your final site inspection, and then we'll schedule your grand opening. Does ten o'clock work for you?"

Oh shit. The cost of the motel room in Syracuse, along with gas and meals, had edged Burley's financial state into precarious territory. The Sandwich King was currently stocked with a bare minimum of inventory—the best he could do at the moment, given his shortage of cash and available credit. He now had a Mastercard as well as his maxed-out Visa, and the new credit card was already nearing its limit. The only way he was going to dig himself out of his money hole was by forging ahead and opening for business. Then, with savvy management and a little luck, all his hard work would begin to pay off.

Burley took a deep breath, and psyched himself up for the grind that lay ahead. "Tomorrow's fine," he told Rochelle. "See you at ten."

Rochelle arrived early and was much more imposing in person than she'd sounded on the phone. Tall and jacked like a body builder, she had a commanding presence that threw Burley into a fit of nervous fidgeting. She strutted through the restaurant, examining the dining section, the sandwich prep area, and the newly assembled kitchen.

"You've done a nice job setting up, Ron," she said, looking pleased. "Now let's have a look at your opening inventory." Rochelle surveyed the contents of the storeroom, freezer, and walk-in cooler, and turned to Burley with a frown. "You haven't got much in stock. I assume everything's on order?"

"Yes," Burley lied. "There's a shipment coming soon." He had purchased the necessary paper and plastic products, which were relatively inexpensive, but ordering the meat, produce, and bakery items was going to be a problem because he lacked the money to pay for them.

Rochelle tapped her pen on her clipboard. "Corporate wants you to open on Friday. Are you going to be ready?"

Shit, shit, shit. Burley had intended to ask for more time while he scraped some additional cash together, but Rochelle wasn't going to play that. He'd have to sell one of the toys in his garage, and put the money toward his most urgent expenditures. "Yeah, I'll be ready," he said. "No problem."

"Excellent." Rochelle made a note on her checklist, then gave him a broad smile. "You're cleared for takeoff, Ron. I'll stop by on Friday to check in with you and take a few pictures." She extended her hand. "Best of luck to you." Burley's heart palpitated as they shook. Oh man, was he ever in a jam now. He needed to sell something to raise some cash, ASAP.

After Rochelle had left, Burley went home, walked across his sodden backyard to the detached garage, and raised the overhead door. There were his boat, snowmobile, and ATV, sitting in a haze of wintry dust. The Bass Tracker was worth the most, with its 40 horsepower Mercury engine, fish finder and trolling motor. The weather was still pretty cold, but people were starting to get spring fever and he might get five or six thousand dollars for it. Next, he looked over the Ski-Doo and the four-wheeler. He'd bought them both used several years ago and they were beat all to hell. Together, they might bring him another thousand bucks.

Burley lowered the garage door, went into the trailer and stood contemplating the gun cabinet in the corner of the living room. His collection of firearms was typical for a North Country hunter: shotgun, rifle, muzzleloader, revolver. He hated to part with any of them. After a minute or two of deep thought, he decided his best bet was to sell the boat and hang onto everything else for the time being.

Burley's flip phone was next to useless for taking photos, so he dug his digital camera out of a kitchen drawer, returned to the garage and snapped a picture of the boat. Back in the trailer, he uploaded the photo to his desktop and composed an ad for Craigslist. It pained him to post the listing, but a man had to do what a man had to do.

A potential buyer responded the next day, but said he couldn't come by until Saturday morning, which fouled up Burley's emergency cash flow plan. He called Rochelle. "I'm not feeling so well, I think I'm coming down with something," he told her. "Friday might not be the best day for my grand opening."

Rochelle was not happy. "We'll reschedule for Monday, then," she said. "I'm sure you'll be feeling better after the weekend."

Opening on Monday was impossible since there was still the trip to make to the wholesaler in Watertown for his necessary supplies, and the place wasn't open on weekends. Burley coughed a few times. "My throat really hurts," he said in a strained voice. "I think it might be covid. I don't want to take the chance of spreading something infectious to my customers. Maybe we should put it off until later in the week."

"You've got a point there," Rochelle reluctantly agreed. "I'll call the home office and explain the delay, and I want you to call me the moment you feel better. Meanwhile, make sure you update your advertising."

His advertising? Ha ha, that was a joke. All he'd been able to afford was a pile of two-color fliers he'd printed out at the UPS Store, and pasted up around town. Now he'd have to print new ones, or be a cheapskate about it and use a Magic Marker to scribble over the opening date. "Don't worry," he assured Rochelle. "I'll take care of it."

• • •

Burley ended up getting only $4800 for the Bass Tracker. The buyer was a grizzled old-timer who spent a methodical half hour pointing out the boat's various defects as he aggressively dickered Burley down in price. Forty-eight hundred was better than nothing, though. It was enough to cover the cost of his most essential supplies, and that was all that mattered.

Late Saturday afternoon, with the blessed relief of cash in his pocket, Burley decided to stop for a beer at McAvan's. As he was driving down Main Street shortly before five o'clock, he spied Lavender lowering the blinds in the front window of Mystic Moon, preparing to close up.

The boutique was kitty-corner from the IGA, so Burley pulled into the grocery store lot and parked in a space with a view across the street. The lights inside Mystic Moon went dark and a minute later, Lavender's car turned the corner onto Main. Burley watched as her taillights receded down the street, then pulled out of the parking lot and followed her.

The Impala's right-hand turn signal blinked as it approached Elm Street, which meant Lavender was heading for home. Burley's imagination got the better of him as he pictured Clint coming to spend the night with her, but after trailing her car for another a block, he turned onto a side street and stopped. Getting caught would be very bad. He'd come off looking like a stalker, which would only push Lavender further away. Swinging his truck around in a tight U-turn, he drove back down Main to McAvan's.

Sometime after midnight, after consuming an excess of $2 Natty Lights at the bar, Burley returned to Lavender's neighborhood. He was pretty well ripped when he pulled his pickup into his usual spot behind the Presbyterian church. Thoughts of Lavender rolling around in bed with her husband had been tormenting him all night, and he needed some closure. Climbing out of the truck, he pulled a dark knit hat down over his ears and started off through the silent backyards.

Most of the snow had melted, leaving bare patches of ground that were squishy with mud as Burley slipped and slid his way toward Lavender's house. Her car was in the driveway and he was relieved to see that Clint's Trailblazer wasn't parked alongside it. He crept toward the house, staying close to the high plank fence that bordered the side yard, using its shadow for concealment.

The light over the back door was off and the blinds on the living room window were drawn, but Burley could see the blue glow of the television through a gap at the bottom. He scuttled across the dark yard and hunched down in the leafless snarl of shrubbery beside the back steps, then crab-walked over to the window and pressed his forehead to the glass.

Lavender was fast asleep on the couch, a half-empty bottle of wine on the coffee table beside her, reflecting the flickering light from the TV screen. Seeing her at home—*alone!*—quieted the anxiety that had been gnawing at Burley's insides since the day of their hike. It was especially encouraging to see that Clint wasn't with her on a Saturday night. Perhaps their attempt to reconcile had failed.

Why hadn't she called, then? His anxiety revved up again as Burley considered the odds of Lavender being really and truly done with him. Maybe she'd somehow gotten wise to his money problems, and had given up on him. *Fuuuuck!* He pounded his fists on his thighs in frustration, hating the feeling of being so lost without her. Until this very moment, he hadn't realized the extent to which he'd staked his future on Lavender's love. For a fleeting moment, he considered banging on the window and waking her, or barging into the house and telling her how desperately he needed her.

But what good would that do, making a complete fool of himself? Burley's thoughts flew to Nielsen. That son of a bitch was at the root of all his problems, both financial and romantic. If it weren't for Nielsen and his swindling ways, Burley would be the proud owner of a flourishing new business, and Lavender would never have been tempted to dump him.

The guy wasn't going to get away with what he'd done, no siree! Burley clawed his way out of the shrubbery, his head still reeling from the alcohol. This might be a fine time for him to pay that dickhead Nielsen a surprise visit and hash things out between them, once and for all.

Stars shone faintly in the partially cloudy sky as Burley's pickup rolled through the subdivision behind the Walmart. The outlines of the new homes stuck up like gravestones on their bare lots, a brisk wind whistling between them. Burley killed his headlights as he turned into Nielsen's driveway, switched the engine off and jumped out of the truck.

He climbed the front steps and pressed the doorbell, and the chime echoed through the house. Burley peeked through the curtainless sidelight, and noticed that the place was sparsely furnished. Footsteps sounded inside, a light came on, and Nielsen's young wife appeared at the top of the open staircase, clad in a bathrobe. She cautiously descended the stairs and stood in the center of the empty foyer, her arms wrapped around herself. "What do you want?" she called through the closed door.

"I want to talk to Jack," Burley shouted back. "Tell him Ron Burley's here."

"Jack's not home. He's away on a job and won't be back till next week."

"Oh yeah?" Burley hollered. "Go tell him to get his ass out here."

The wife's voice became shrill: "I told you, he's not home!" She pulled her robe more tightly around her middle, emphasizing her baby bump, and when Burley saw it, his anger instantly deflated. The woman was obviously covering for her husband, but what was Burley supposed to do, stake out the house until the scumbag showed up? And then what? Coming here was a stupid move. If Nielsen had been home, he would have pummeled the crap out of Burley, and called it even.

Tipping his head back, Burley blew out an exasperated breath at the night sky. When he turned to peer through the sidelight again, he saw the pregnant wife still holding herself and watching him fearfully, which made him feel like a horrible brute. "Never mind," he called to her with an apologetic wave. "Sorry to disturb you."

CHAPTER 19

A knock on the back door roused Lavender the next morning. She had invited Clint over for dinner the evening before, but at the last minute he'd called to say that Logan was carrying on about being gypped out of his Dad weekend, so Clint had stayed home to appease him. Lavender had drunk half the bottle of wine she'd picked up for the occasion, then passed out on the couch around midnight, oblivious to her former lover skulking beneath her window like a tipsy Peeping Tom.

The knocking sounded again. Lavender got up from the couch and shuffled into the kitchen, and was surprised to see Clint standing on the back stoop. "I didn't mean to wake you," he said as he stepped inside. "I thought you'd be up by now."

Lavender pushed her hair out of her face and rubbed her eyes. "I don't have to work till noon today, so I was sleeping in."

"I left Logan with my sister so we could have some privacy to talk," Clint said. He unzipped his jacket but hesitated before taking it off. "I mean, if that's okay with you?"

Lavender's heart did a flip-flop—he'd come to tell her he wanted her back! "It's fine," she said with a casual shrug, not wishing to appear too eager. She wasn't about to overplay her hand by welcoming him home with open arms and legs. The man owed her an apology first, for his violent behavior on that night when he'd discovered the affair.

"Great," Clint said, waiting for Lavender to sit down before pulling out a chair across from her. He ran his hands through his hair, then placed them flat on the table. "Lavender," he began, "I'm really thankful we've been able to spend this time together over the past couple weeks. I've been doing a lot of thinking, and there's something important I want to say to you."

Of course there was. Lavender nodded encouragingly.

"I know we've had our differences over the years," Clint said. "We got pushed into marriage before we were ready. We didn't have a chance to grow up before we became parents and had so many responsibilities thrust on us."

Lavender bobbed her head in agreement.

"We did our best, though," Clint said, "to make it work."

She smiled. Yes, they did.

"It's been really hard at times, for both of us," Clint went on. "We've struggled through a lot together, for Logan's sake. I appreciate the efforts you've made to be a good mother to him, even when it was difficult and he pushed your patience to the limit."

Lavender bobbed her head some more. *Get to the point already.*

Clint clasped his hands. "I want you to know that I've given this a great deal of serious thought."

Here it comes, Lavender thought. The humble contrition, the plea for forgiveness, the begging for her to take him back. She folded her hands demurely in her lap, trying to suppress a smug smile.

"You've probably come to the same conclusion that I have." Clint stared down at his tightly clasped hands for a moment, then raised his eyes to Lavender's. "I think we'd both be happier if we called it quits and went our separate ways."

Lavender's jaw dropped. The impact of Clint's statement was swift and sharp, and entirely unexpected. This was *so* not the way this conversation was supposed to go!

Several shocked seconds ticked by before her brain clicked back into gear. She shoved herself away from the table, her chair legs grating on the floor with a harsh screech. "You're exactly right, Clint," she said. "I *am* going to be happier without you." Her husband looked back at her in resigned silence. "In fact," Lavender said with a careless toss of her head, "as you already know, I'm involved with someone else and it's become quite serious."

Clint cleared his throat. "As long as we're being honest here, I might as well tell you that I've been seeing someone, too."

No effing way! Clint getting it on with another woman? It simply did not compute. "Oh, really?" Lavender said with as much scorn as she could muster. "And who might the unlucky lady be?"

Clint compressed his lips as though he wouldn't deign to respond, then something seemed to come over him and he answered, "Cheryl Morgan."

"Logan's *teacher*? That is sick, Clint! Truly warped. What is *wrong* with you? You can't do that!"

"We're not officially dating yet," Clint replied calmly. "We're just talking. She's a single parent herself, and she's a very kind and understanding person. We—"

Lavender thrust a palm at him. "Spare me, okay? I don't need to hear the gory details." She turned her face away so he wouldn't see her lips trembling. "Hooray for you, Clint. I guess we're even now." She busied herself with her hair, twisting it into a loose bun that she balanced on the crown of her head with one hand, and propped her other hand carelessly at her waist. "I believe we're through here. You can go now."

Clint left without a word. Lavender peeked through the living room blinds as he got into his Trailblazer and backed it down the driveway. The moment he was gone, she whirled around, seized last night's wine bottle and flung it blindly across the room. The bottle flew into the kitchen where it whomped into the coat rack beside the back door, and dropped without breaking onto the heap of shoes and boots beneath it. Lavender clenched her fists, threw her head back and screamed up at the ceiling.

After calling in sick to work, Lavender spent the day alternately crying, cursing, and moping around the house. Her day concluded with a tearful phone conversation with Shayna that ended on a sour note. "Quit your griping," Shayna said when she'd heard enough of Lavender's complaining. "The fact is, you don't have any better options, so you'd better get over yourself and make up with Ron Burley before some other woman steps in to fill the void."

Galling as it was, Lavender had to admit her friend was right. It was over with Clint, no question about it. The man was as faithful as a golden retriever, so if he'd gone so far as to become romantically involved with another woman—never mind that BS about him and Miss Morgan "just talking"—it meant their marriage was irretrievably broken.

All of Lavender's eggs were in the Burley basket now. She needed to patch things up with him right away or risk losing him for good. Once they were back together, she'd work on persuading him to marry her as soon as possible, so she could throw it in Clint's weaselly face. Cheryl Morgan, *ha!* What a joke.

$$\bullet \quad \bullet \quad \bullet$$

Burley's cell rang as he was unlocking the door to the Sandwich King on Monday morning, and joy filled him when he saw it was Lavender calling.

"Hey baby," she said cheerily, as though everything was normal. "What've you been up to?"

"The usual," Burley answered cautiously. "Working hard, getting the restaurant ready."

"Is it going to be open soon?"

"Yeah, any day now. I'm waiting for the go-ahead."

"Oh, wow! That's awesome."

Burley was heartened by her positive reaction. "Yeah, I'm planning a big grand opening event for later this week."

"Fantastic! I'm so happy for you."

"Thanks." Burley waited a beat. "How've you been?"

"I've been missing you."

His spirits took a wild leap and he felt a spark of desire in his groin. "I've been missing you, too."

"I have the day off and Logan's going over to my mom's after school," Lavender said. "Want to meet somewhere for an early dinner, and catch up?"

Taking her out to dinner would require more money than Burley could spare at the moment. A cheap lunch date would be preferable. "I've got a lot of stuff I need to do this afternoon," he said. "Why don't we meet for lunch instead?" In his mind's eye, Burley pictured Lavender's golden hair and glowing skin. He could practically smell the essential oils. "Is Applebee's okay?"

"Yes, that's fine. I'll see you there at noon."

They met up at the new Applebee's out on Route 12, and hugged awkwardly in the parking lot. The changeable Upstate weather had turned cold and blowy again, and Lavender was dressed more sedately than usual in a pair of boot-cut jeans and a turtleneck sweater. "It's good to see you again," Burley said. His impulse was to take her by the hand and hurry her into the warmth of the restaurant, but he held himself back and allowed Lavender to lead the way instead.

After settling into a booth, they made small talk over their beverages—Diet Coke with lemon for Lavender, ice water (no charge!) for Burley. When the waitress returned to take their orders, Burley was dismayed to hear Lavender request the Bourbon Street Steak, one of the priciest items on the menu. To counterbalance the expense, he ordered the breadsticks appetizer for himself, which elicited a funny look from Lavender. "I'm not that hungry," he said, handing his menu to the waitress. "I cooked myself a big breakfast at the Sandwich King this morning."

Lavender's face lit up at the mention of his new business. "What's your grand opening going to be like? Will a lot of people be there?"

Burley beamed and told her all about it: Dwayne Tackett, Helmsburg's mayor, was going to preside over a ribbon-cutting ceremony, and the town newspaper was sending its reporter with a camera.

"It sounds very exciting," Lavender said. "I'm sure it's going to be a huge success." She reached across the table and squeezed Burley's wrist, and his neglected manhood stirred to life. Dropping his free hand to his lap, he unobtrusively made things more comfortable. He and Lavender held each other's gaze for a few seconds, and then their server appeared with their food.

Lavender's steak platter sizzled with a mouth-watering meaty fragrance and Burley regarded his breadsticks sadly. Throughout the meal, the conversation circled around the mundane happenings of Helmsburg, with no mention of their personal situation. Burley noticed Lavender's fingernails were ragged from biting, and wondered what it meant. Was she stressing over her marriage, or upset because she missed him so much? He was dying to ask where things stood between her and her husband, but he was too afraid of what the answer might be.

Lavender left half her steak untouched and declined both a take-home box and dessert. Burley was happy to skip the expense of dessert, but not taking the leftovers! He considered taking them for himself, then decided that would be tacky. As he counted out money to pay the tab, he shielded the pile of bills with his arm so Lavender couldn't see how little he'd left for the tip.

There was a smattering of wet snowflakes in the wind when they walked out to their vehicles. Using his bare hands, Burley gave Lavender's windows a quick wipe. "Looks like Old Man Winter has come back for a final round," he said.

Lavender jangled her keys on their bling ring and gestured toward her car. "C'mon, get in with me for a minute, so we can talk."

Burley opened Lavender's door for her, then walked around to the other side of the car. Before getting in, he stole a quick look at his phone; it had vibrated twice during lunch, but he hadn't dared to pull it out in the middle of their date. He saw that Rochelle had left him two voicemails, which was not a good sign. He'd have to call her back as soon as he could.

Lavender started the engine and the radio came on with a top-of-the-hour newscast. She turned the volume down and the heater up, and they sat staring at the blots of snow that had begun to accumulate on the windshield. "Burley," she said at last. "I've come to an important decision. I didn't want to talk about it inside Applebee's, so that's why I waited."

Burley flinched. She was about to lower the boom.

Lavender continued staring straight ahead, gripped her hands in her lap and took a deep breath. "I've decided I'm going through with the divorce."

Burley turned to her in amazement. "You are?"

"Yes."

"You're sure about this?"

"Yes, I'm sure."

Burley leaned over and kissed Lavender softly on the lips, then they both sat back and gazed at one another with shining eyes. The windshield became covered with a layer of snow and the light inside the car dimmed. As Lavender reached to turn on the wipers, her coat sleeve caught the volume knob on the radio and an ad for diamond engagement rings blared from the car's speakers. Slipping a sideways smile at Burley, she turned the volume back down. "Are you happy, Burley? Are you glad I'll be free soon?"

"Yes," he said. "Real glad."

Real glad, but real worried, too. He was overjoyed to have won her back, but this change of status presented a serious challenge: it was now imperative that he keep his financial troubles an absolute secret, or their rekindled romance would be history. A beautiful woman like Lavender wouldn't waste her time on a broke dude for very long.

The wiper blades needed replacing and soggy smears dragged across the glass. Burley kissed Lavender again, more deeply this time. She threw her arms around his neck and one of her ragged fingernails snagged his earlobe. It stung, but he didn't mind. She could rip his entire ear off right about now, and he wouldn't complain. "I love you," he murmured, kissing her again and again.

"I love you too," Lavender whispered back.

Burley's phone vibrated in his jeans pocket, making him jump. "Sorry," he said as he dug for it. "It's probably Sandwich King again, they've been trying to reach me all day." The call went to voicemail before he could answer, and the phone trilled a low battery warning as he flipped it open. Rochelle again.

"I'm sure you're terribly busy right now," Lavender said. "If you need to go, I understand."

"Yeah, there's something I need to take care of," Burley said. "Sorry I've gotta run. It was great seeing you again." They kissed one last time, and he promised to call her soon.

On his drive back to the Sandwich King, Burley listened to Rochelle's voicemails. She was highly irritated. "Ron," she said in her second message. "Call me back THE MINUTE you get this. I MEAN IT. Corporate's pissed about the delay. We've got to get your grand opening scheduled immediately."

There was no putting her off any longer. Burley was about to call Rochelle back when the phone rang again. "Ronald!" his mother said in surprise, as though she'd been expecting someone else to answer. "Hello there, dear. How good of you to call."

"You called me, Mom."

"Yes, yes. Good thing I got hold of you. I was getting ready to leave the IGA with my groceries, and guess what?"

Burley gripped the steering wheel. "What, Mom?"

"My car won't start!"

The phone trilled another low battery warning but Burley didn't have his charger cord with him. "What happens when you turn the key?" he asked his mother. "Does the engine crank?"

"No. It doesn't do anything at all."

Burley pushed his ball cap off his forehead and scratched his head. "Hang on, Mom. I'll be there in a few minutes."

When he turned into the IGA parking lot, his mother was standing beside the Buick in her old lady coat and crocheted hat, her shoulders speckled with snowflakes. Burley pecked her on the cheek, then slid into the driver's seat and swiftly diagnosed the problem: she'd left the gearshift in Drive. He depressed the brake pedal, shifted the car into Park and turned the key. The engine started right up.

"Hooray!" His mother clapped her hands. "You're such a smartie!"

Burley helped her into the car, then stood with his arm propped on the roof. It was getting to be time for him to tell his mother she needed to stop driving altogether, but he knew the conversation would become a battle. "You're going straight home now, right, Mom?" he said.

"Yes," his mother replied, plopping her big brown pocketbook onto the seat beside her. "Right after I stop by Helen Phipps's house, to pick up that bread pudding recipe she promised me."

Mrs. Phipps lived on the exact opposite side of town from his mother, and Burley was willing to bet she wasn't expecting a visitor this afternoon. "Are you sure you need to do that right now?" he said. "It's supposed to keep snowing and the roads might get slippery."

"Pfft! Not to worry. Bye now, dear. Thank you for your help." His mother pulled her door shut and stomped on the gas, and the Buick fishtailed out of the parking lot.

Burley got into his truck. There wasn't much left for him to do at the Sandwich King, so he might as well call it a day and go home. A mile outside of town his phone rang again: Rochelle. Dammit, he'd forgotten to call her back! When he answered, the low battery warning trilled more insistently.

"Ron!" Rochelle shouted. "Why haven't you—"

"Sorry Rochelle, my phone's about to die. Can you try me back in about fifteen minutes? I should be home and plugged in by then."

"Yes, but hurry up. We've got to get your opening scheduled or we're both going to be in trouble."

Fine, Burley thought. *Let's do this*. His reunion with Lavender had renewed his confidence and he was as ready as he'd ever be. All he could do was forge ahead and hope for the best.

The roads west of town were clear and dry, and Burley made good time getting home. He swerved into his rutted driveway, then ran inside the trailer and located his charger cord, which was buried beneath a pile of junk mail. As he was plugging the phone in, it started ringing and he flipped it open. "Hey, Rochelle," he said. "I'm home now."

"Burley?" a familiar voice said. "It's Marta."

CHAPTER 20

Burley cut Marta off. "Listen, hon, I'm expecting a really important phone call and I can't tie up the line right now."

"*You* listen," Marta said angrily. "Some friend you are, Burley! I haven't heard a single word from you in weeks. I'm calling because there's something I need to tell you."

Burley's conscience pricked him for not getting back to her about the job offer. Between the uncertainties with Lavender and the craziness of things at the Sandwich King, Marta had completely slipped his mind. He thumped into a chair. "What is it?"

"The cancer has spread."

Burley switched the phone to his other ear. "Wait, I thought you said they were treating it, and you were going to be okay."

"They are treating it, but it's in my liver and lungs now."

Just like Russ. "I'm so sorry, Marta," Burley said. "I don't know what to say."

Marta's voice was shaking. "I'm not sure how much time I have left, so I'm going to drive up to Helmsburg this weekend and see my mom and dad while I'm still able to."

"I could come down and get you if you want, so you don't have to make the drive by yourself."

"No, you don't have to do that. But could I ask you a favor, Burley?"

"Yes. Anything."

"While I'm up there, would you take me snowmobiling like you used to? Up on Tug Hill, if there's still enough snow?"

"Yeah, sure." Burley pulled his boots off and kicked them into the corner. "We're expecting some lake effect tonight so there oughtta be plenty of snow by Saturday." His phone beeped, signaling another incoming call, and he saw it was from Rochelle. "Marta," he said, "that other call's beeping in now and I've got to take it. I promise I'll call you back tonight so we can make plans, okay?"

"Okay," Marta said. "Talk to you later."

Burley switched over to the other call. "Hey, Rochelle."

Rochelle was pissed. "Where have you been, Ron? Corporate says they want your grand opening to take place on Tuesday. You don't have much choice about it at this point, so can you do it?"

Ready or not, it was time to take the plunge. "Yes," Burley said. "I can do it."

• • •

Burley felt bad for having forgotten about Marta, so he planned an extra-special day for the two of them that Saturday. After tidying the trailer and vacuuming up the clumps of dog hair, he went to the store to buy donuts and a bag of the hazelnut coffee he knew Marta liked.

What to tell Lavender had been an issue. She would have blown a gasket if she found out Marta was coming to visit, so Burley had told her he'd be tied up at the Sandwich King all weekend, getting ready for his opening day, and she was very understanding. "Take your time, baby, and do whatever you need to. I'll tell Clint he needs to keep Logan on Tuesday night, so you can come over to my house afterward and tell me how everything went."

Marta arrived at Burley's place looking even thinner than the last time. Her clothes hung loosely on her and he noticed there was no sign of her thick, dark hair beneath the knitted hat she refused to take off.

He tried to give her a hug but the dogs got in the way, barking and jumping all over her as if they'd discovered a long-lost friend.

Marta knelt down to pet Bo, the chiller one of the pair, but Augie nosed his way in and knocked her over. She laughed and pushed herself upright with her spindly arms, and rumpled Augie's ears. Burley gave her a handful of biscuits, and Marta made both dogs sit and shake obediently before rewarding them.

When the biscuits were gone, Burley helped Marta up from the floor. She brushed the dog hair off her sweater and smiled at him. "Where are we going today?"

"I thought we'd ride over to the Flat Rock Inn and do a twenty-mile loop." Burley went to the kitchen sink and ran hot water into a thermos, then dumped it out and refilled it with hot coffee. "I gave the sled a once-over last night and it's running great. The snow's fresh so we should have a nice run."

They put on their parkas and boots, and went out to the backyard where the black-and-red Ski-Doo Renegade was parked beside the garage. Burley gave Marta his extra helmet and she took her place behind him on the padded seat of the sled. The engine started with a deep purr and they set off across the yard toward the southern boundary of the property.

Crossing over to the state land, they turned onto a freshly-groomed trail lined with snowy scotch pine and hemlock, and Burley opened the throttle. The sky was bright blue and the sun cast long shadows across the trail as they zipped over the snow. Marta tightened her arms around Burley's middle and he reached his left hand back to give her leg a friendly pat.

After several miles the trail came to a T, and Burley stopped and killed the engine. They pulled their helmets off and sat with their faces tilted skyward, absorbing the late winter sunshine and the quiet grandeur of the forest. The wind whooshed softly through the treetops, and here and there along the trail a spray of snow cascaded to the ground. "It's so beautiful," Marta murmured. "I've really missed this."

They sat peacefully for a while, and then Marta began to shiver. Burley twisted around to look at her. "Are you cold?"

She shook her head. "No, I'm fine."

Another minute passed and Marta's shivering became more pronounced. Burley turned to her in concern. "Do you need to go back?" She shook her head again, but when Burley tipped her chin up with his gloved fingers, he saw her lips were tinged with blue. "You're freezing!" he said. "I'm taking you home." He restarted the sled and they took off.

Back at the trailer, Burley had to help Marta climb the wooden steps up to his door. Once inside, he wrapped her in his woolen blanket and made her lie down on the couch. He plugged in his electric space heater and turned it to its highest setting, then ran back out to the sled to retrieve the thermos. He poured two mugs of coffee and brought them into the living room, where he hesitated. Should he sit beside Marta on the couch, or by himself in the recliner? Squeezing onto the couch with her seemed a little too intimate, but sitting across the room from her might appear too aloof. He compromised by taking a seat on the floor next to her. "Are you feeling better yet?"

Marta gave him a weak smile. "Yes, I am. Sorry for making us turn back."

Burley patted her blanket-covered knees. "Never mind. We had a nice ride." He knew he needed to make his own apology, and he stared down at the mug in his hands, trying to think how to word it. "Marta," he said at last, "I just wanted to say that I feel like a total jerk, for not getting back to you after you offered me that job. My only excuse is that I've been super busy lately. I haven't had the chance to tell you yet—I quit the Mini Mart and I'm getting ready to open my own fast-food franchise."

Marta looked surprised. "Really? Which one?"

"A Sandwich King. It's been a lot of work getting it ready and I've been completely distracted, but it was really rude and inconsiderate of me not to give you an answer."

"Never mind, it doesn't matter." Marta sipped her coffee with a preoccupied look on her face, clearly not interested in hearing anymore. To fill the lull, Burley picked up the remote and turned the television on, and found a documentary about the Vietnam War playing on the History Channel.

They went without talking for a few minutes until Marta stirred and pushed the blanket off her chest. "There's been a new development that I need to tell you about, Burley. Something major."

Ah shit, here we go again, he thought. She'd already told him she was dying, so how much more major could it get?

Marta set her mug on the end table and looked at him. "Ken had a life insurance policy."

Big flipping deal, Burley thought. It seemed like everyone caved in at some point and bought life insurance—everyone except him, since he had no dependents to support. "Life insurance?" he said with a shrug. "What about it?"

"I didn't know he had it until a few months ago, when I was going through his papers. I had no idea he'd bought it, or how much it was worth. It's a huge policy." Marta hugged her knobby knees to her chest. "You're not going to believe this, but I'm a millionaire."

Burley stared. Plain old Marta Grolsch a millionaire? "Geez Louise. That's unbelievable. I guess you don't have to worry about your company anymore. You can sell off the assets and shut it down. With a million bucks in the bank, your daughter can live off the interest for the rest of her life."

Marta looked hurt. "You're not getting it, Burley! Like I told you before, that company is all she has left of her father. I can't shut it down."

A small roofing company wasn't much of a legacy, in Burley's opinion. If he was in Marta's shoes, he'd ditch the business in a heartbeat. But the bereft expression on her face reminded him—her husband hadn't been dead for very long, so her grief was still fresh. He needed to take that into account, and be more considerate of her feelings. "I know you don't want to lose your company, Marta. I wasn't thinking when I said that. You've got to do what's best for you."

He didn't feel like discussing his friend's windfall when he was on the verge of losing his ass, so he turned up the volume on the documentary. Marta wasn't done with the subject, however. She sat up straighter and her pale face became animated. "Can you believe it, Burley? I'm loaded!"

"Yeah, that's what it sounds like." Burley turned back to the television. Bombs dribbled out of an airplane and studded the Vietnamese countryside with black and white starbursts.

Marta tugged on his wrist. "Burley, listen. Look at me, will you? I want to make you a new offer, something way better than the last one."

Hmph. Burley waited.

"If you'll come work for me now," Marta said, "I'll pay you any salary you want. You name it, you got it." She pressed her hands together. "I really, really need your help, Burley. I'm getting desperate. Please say you'll agree to come work for me. It can be a temporary arrangement if you want. Come down for a few months and get things turned around for me before I'm gone, so I'll have something to leave to my daughter."

Burley was flabbergasted—any salary he wanted, with no long-term commitment! It was an incredibly generous offer that could end his financial difficulties. His mind flew in several directions at once. He could buy Lavender a diamond engagement ring, take her on a fancy honeymoon, build her a beautiful new house! And take care of his mother, too. He'd finally have the means to move her into a place where she'd be safe and have all the care she needed.

Marta's company wasn't that bad off. If he worked hard, he could whip it into shape over the summer months, drawing a hefty salary all the while, and proceed with his Sandwich King plans at the same time. He could train Dustin to run the place while he was out of town, and drive back up to Helmsburg on the weekends to keep things in order. Accepting Marta's offer could be a total game changer.

"Any salary I want?" he said. "You really mean it?"

"I was thinking around five thousand a month to start, and I'd pay you cash."

Bless Marta's little dying heart, that was sixty thousand tax-free dollars a year! Burley had to set his mug down before he spilled coffee all over the place. Sixty grand was twice what he could expect to earn from the Sandwich King. There was an added bonus to keep in mind, as well: Marta was a tough girl. She'd fight the cancer hard and might end up lingering for a year or more, so he could milk this gig for as long as possible.

Then he thought of Lavender. There was no way she'd consent to him traveling out of state every week, to work for a woman she was already suspicious of. As Burley turned this dilemma over in his mind, Marta squinted worriedly at him. "What's wrong? Is there something holding you back?"

For a second, Burley considered telling her about Lavender, then dismissed the idea. Sharing the details of his love life would only complicate matters. Lavender would squawk about the unusual arrangement, but if he emphasized the income potential and the temporary nature of the deal, he was sure she'd come around to reason.

"All right, six thousand a month," Marta said. "Plus a signing bonus of ten thousand. That's as high as I can go." She stretched her foot out from beneath the blanket and nudged Burley's leg. "Is that okay with you? Will you do it?"

It was much more than okay, it was an answer to his prayers. Burley beamed and slapped his thighs. "Yes, I'll do it."

Marta threw the blanket aside and wrapped her arms around his neck. "Thank you, thank you, Burley! I knew you'd come through for me."

She felt so bony and frail, Burley was afraid to hug her back too hard. When she released him, he helped her settle back onto her pillow. "I can't come down right away," he cautioned her. "I'm about to open the Sandwich King, and it'll take me a while to get things running smoothly and train my assistant." He tucked the blanket around Marta's shoulders. "I'm thinking April first would be a good target date, it'll give me a few weeks to get myself situated. Can you wait that long?"

"I've waited this long already, so a few more weeks won't make any difference, as long as I know you're coming."

"Don't worry, I'll be there." Burley got up and went to the kitchen to find a pen and a pad of paper. There were a ton of things he needed to do to get ready.

CHAPTER 21

The Sandwich King opened its doors for business but Lavender didn't attend the grand opening ceremony. She waited excitedly at home that night, dying to hear how things were going. The restaurant was open till nine p.m., and as the hour approached, it occurred to her that Burley would be starving after his long day, and it might be nice if she had something ready for him to eat.

Eggs, maybe. That would be easy. The ones in the fridge were three days past their expiration date, but they were all she had to offer. As she began cracking them into a bowl, Burley rapped on the back door and she hurried to let him in. "How did it go?" she said as he stepped into the kitchen.

Burley tugged his coat off and hung it over the back of a chair. "It was good, I guess."

"You must be starving." Lavender showed him the bowl of raw eggs and a baggie of chopped onions and peppers that she'd found in the freezer. "Look, I'm making you an omelet."

"Honey, you don't need to do all that. Really, I'm not hungry. I ate at work."

"It'll only take a minute." Lavender coated a frying pan with oil, dumped the runny eggs and veggies in, and turned up the gas. "Tell me all about your day. I can hardly wait to hear!"

Burley remained standing, keeping an eye on the stove over Lavender's shoulder. "Dustin did most of the prep work this morning while I got the other stuff organized. Gotta say, he catches on quick. The lunch hour was kinda slow but business picked up around four, after the county offices closed."

"Did you make a lot of money? I hope you made a *ton*." The frying pan had begun to smoke and Burley reached around Lavender to lower the flame. She grabbed a spatula, peeled half of the omelet from the pan and folded it over. The bottom was charred but raw egg was still dribbling out the sides.

Burley sat down at the table where Lavender had set out a plate and silverware, a paper napkin, and a tall glass of Diet Coke. "We did okay for the first day. I'm hoping things pick up as word starts to spread around town."

In truth, the day's business had been abysmal, and only a handful of people had shown up for the lame ribbon-cutting ceremony. Later in the afternoon, a sprinkling of customers who were more curious than hungry had shown up, and after that, foot traffic had dried up completely. Burley and Dustin had frittered away the evening, polishing equipment and rearranging the storeroom.

Lavender came over with the frying pan and dumped the omelet onto Burley's plate. Using his knife to saw off a piece, he swallowed it down, then chased it with a big gulp of the Diet Coke. "This is delicious, honey."

Lavender sat across from him. "I'm so happy you had a good first day! Sounds like you're off to a great start."

Burley speared another forkful of egg. "Do you have any hot sauce?" Lavender jumped up and fetched a bottle of Tabasco. He coated the food until it was dripping red, and resumed his methodical cutting and chewing. "There's something I want to share with you," he said when his plate was almost empty.

Lavender poured the rest of his soda into her own glass and looked at him with a happy smile. "What is it, baby?"

Burley wiped his mouth with the paper napkin. "I've been offered a job."

"Wait, what?" Lavender frowned and set her glass down. "You just opened your own restaurant. Why in the world would you be looking for another job?"

Burley dropped his napkin onto the plate, covering up the remains of the omelet. "Remember my old friend Marta who I told you about?"

Lavender's eyes narrowed. "The widow from Pennsylvania?"

"Yeah, her. She's got breast cancer."

Lavender sat back in her chair. "Oh, really."

"I'm totally serious. She's very sick. Says it's terminal."

"And what has this got to do with you?"

"She needs someone to run her company for a few months, so she can leave it to her daughter when she dies. She asked me if I would do it."

Lavender raised her hands, palms up. "I don't get it, Burley. Why does she need you to run to her rescue? Can't her family help her?"

"No, there isn't anybody. Her husband didn't have any relatives in the area and she's an only child. Her parents still live here in Helmsburg, but they're old as hell. She wants me to go down there and manage things for a while, so the business doesn't go under. It would only be temporary, and she's offered to pay me very well."

"How temporary?"

Burley scratched his head. "I'm not sure, exactly. For the summer, at least."

"The whole summer? Are you crazy?" Lavender took his plate and dropped it into the sink with a clang, then seized a dishrag and began scrubbing the table with angry swipes. "Why would you do a thing like that when you've got a brand-new business of your own to run? It sounds like a bunch of crap to me."

A sudden thought made her hand go still. This Marta woman's cancer story might be for real, but was her situation really as dire as

Burley seemed to think it was? Breast cancer was highly treatable—hardly anyone died of it anymore. Marta might be pretending to be helpless, when in reality she was a sneaky, conniving shrew who was trying to get her claws into Burley.

Lavender recalled the two weekends when Burley had gone out of town. One of them was supposedly a visit to an ancient grampa that she wasn't even sure really existed, and Burley had claimed the other one was for job-training purposes. Funny how he hadn't called her when he was away, or answered his phone when she called him. Roaming charges, her foot.

Lavender threw down the dishrag. "You've been seeing her behind my back, haven't you?"

"No!" Burley clapped his hand to his heart. "She did come up here recently, to visit her parents. We had coffee and talked about the job, but that was it. I swear to you, I'm not the least bit attracted to her, especially with her so sick. You should see how thin and weak she is, it's really bad. We're old friends and I owe her a favor, is all."

"What kind of favor?"

"It's a long story. Something that happened way back when we were teenagers."

Lavender opened her mouth to say something but Burley shushed her. "Honey, you gotta let me finish what I'm trying to tell you. She's dying and she's desperate. You won't believe what she's willing to pay me."

Lavender stamped her foot. "You can't take a job in another state when you've got a serious girlfriend right here at home. I thought we were going to get married as soon as my divorce came through. You're not thinking, Burley!"

"I am thinking, honey." Burley got up and took Lavender's hand. "I've got it all planned out, it won't be as bad as you think. I'll go down and work for her for five or six months, maybe a year at the most. I'm sure she'll be, you know, *gone* by then, and she'll be so grateful to me for helping her that she'll leave me something in her will. Then I'll convince whoever her executor is that it's in her daughter's best interest to sell the company, and I'll ask for a cut of the profits in exchange for my services. Meanwhile, Dustin will be running the Sandwich King for me, and I'll come back up here every weekend to check in on him. And see you, of course."

"Weekends, Burley? That's all I'm good for? No way, that sucks." Lavender glared at Burley. If she consented to this crazy plan, he'd be gone more than he'd be home, and that couldn't possibly bode well for their relationship. Who knew what temptations this Marta bitch might dangle in his face, down there in Pennsylvania?

Lavender realized that standing there arguing wasn't the way to handle this. Burley might become defensive and insist on doing things his own way, and she'd be left out in the cold. She couldn't take the chance of pushing him away and ending up alone.

The situation called for a change of tactics. Going over to Burley, Lavender cupped his face between her hands and switched to a wheedling tone. "Your business is going to take off, baby, and before we know it, we'll be free to do whatever we want to. Besides, I couldn't stand for you to be so far away from me for so long." She kissed him on the mouth, slipping him the tongue, and pressed her body against his.

Burley wavered for a moment, then stepped out of her arms "You've gotta understand, Lavender. I really need to do this."

He was hiding something, she was sure of it. She could tell by the way he was avoiding her eyes. Lavender fixed him with an icy look. "Why exactly do you 'really need to do this'? Give me one good reason why you should disrupt your life for someone you hardly even know anymore, because of some imaginary favor you think you owe her from a hundred years ago."

"I just need to do it, Lavender. It's complicated, see—"

Enough of this bullshit. Lavender poked her finger in Burley's face. "No, Ron. I am not going to allow you to disappear for the whole summer, to work for a sorry-ass widow who's trying to use you. Read my lips: it's not going to happen. I don't care how much money she tries to bribe you with."

"But—"

Lavender raised her palm. "It's her or me, Burley. You choose."

Burley scrubbed his forehead violently with both hands, causing his Sandwich King hat to fall off. Stooping to pick it up, he slapped it back onto his head. "All right," he said. "I won't do it."

Lavender fell on him in a flurry of kisses. "Oh baby, I knew you'd come around! Oooo, I love you so, so, so much." She slipped her hand between his legs as she kissed him, and felt him grow hard in an instant. *Typical guy.* Grabbing hold of his bright green Sandwich King shirt, she pulled him down the hall to the bedroom where they dropped onto the bed in a frenzied, pawing fit.

Lavender tugged at Burley's belt. She'd like to know more about this Marta, that was for sure. Find out the truth about her relationship with Burley. *Just friends? Yeah, right.* The belt buckle released and she started to undo his pants—annoying button fly 501s, which required some effort. She should go see Penelope for another tarot reading, she thought, and let the cards tell her if Burley really loved her or not.

Lavender yanked Burley's jeans down to his ankles and he moaned with pleasure as she went to work on him. Penelope's business card was hidden in the bottom of her jewelry box. She'd dig it out and call her in the morning.

CHAPTER 22

"Come in, come in." Penelope opened her front door wide and ushered Lavender inside. "I've got a pot of tea ready for us. Sit down and make yourself comfortable while I go get it."

Lavender seated herself in the same armchair as before, and the painted cherubs smiled down at her from their perch above the stove. She felt more comfortable being there this time, not so nervous as before. Hopefully Penelope and her mystical deck of cards would have some positive insights to reveal today, and clear away Lavender's worries about Burley and Marta.

As she waited for Penelope, Lavender's eyes were drawn to the curio cabinet beneath the stairs, and she noticed an addition on the top shelf—a large bronze angel, half-naked and obviously male, wearing a medieval-looking helmet and wielding a sword.

Penelope came in with the tea things and followed Lavender's gaze. "That's Michael the Archangel, sacred leader of the Army of God and Guardian of the Church." She went over to the cabinet, picked up the heavy statue and brought it over to Lavender. "He's also known as the Angel of Death because he carries the souls of the departed up to Heaven. See the bloody dragon writhing beneath his feet? It symbolizes Heaven's triumph in the battle against evil."

Good grief, was this woman for real? Lavender shivered and turned her eyes back to the cheerful cherubs on the wall. Penelope patted her gray curls, smoothed her dress and sat down opposite her. "Now then," she said. "How can I help you today?"

"I have a question about this man I've been seeing, but I don't have much time. I need to be back in Helmsburg by 2:00 to pick my son up from school and take him to a doctor's appointment."

"Not a problem. I'll do a three-card spread." Penelope drew the tarot deck from the drawer, handed it to Lavender to shuffle, then took it back and flipped a row of three cards onto the table. "We read these from left to right," she said. "The first one represents your current situation, the middle one is the obstacle you're facing, and the last card tells you how you should proceed."

Penelope tapped the card on the left, which was upside down. "Two of Cups." The picture showed two young lovers exchanging a pair of goblets. "It's reversed, you see. That means a breakup of some sort. Two people who no longer share the emotional connection they used to."

"Right," Lavender said. "That's me and my husband. We're getting divorced."

Penelope pointed to the next card. "Seven of Wands. It symbolizes competition, or the threat of an attack by someone who wishes to take your place. This is the obstacle you need to overcome."

Lavender slowly nodded her head. *Marta.*

The last card showed a blindfolded woman in a white robe, holding crossed swords above her head. "The Two of Swords represents a challenging situation," Penelope said, "or a path that is unclear. This card advises you to weigh your actions with care, using both your head and your heart."

This wasn't exactly enlightening, Lavender thought. Of course, she would use her head! She always did, she wasn't stupid. But wasting time weighing the pros and cons of things wouldn't answer the question of how Burley really felt about her. "Can I show you a picture?" she asked Penelope.

"Certainly. A picture often helps to clarify things."

Lavender took out her phone and swiped through her photo library until she found a selfie she'd taken with Burley on one of their movie dates. He was leaning into her, cheek to cheek, like a good boyfriend. "I wanted to ask you about this man." She used her fingers to zoom in on his face. "We've been dating for about six months and I need to know if he really loves me."

Penelope took the phone. "He looks like that country singer, what's-his-name."

"Jason Aldean?"

"That's the one." Penelope examined the photo more closely. "Does he love you," she murmured to herself.

"We've been seeing each other secretly, for obvious reasons," Lavender said. "He's the sweetest guy you've ever—"

"Shhhh." Penelope raised her hand. "I'm feeling a lot of positive energy coming from him. He's a hard worker. Loyal. A man who sticks by his friends and family." She tipped her head to one side. "Yes, he's definitely in love with you. Devoted to you, in fact, and he wants very much to be with you."

Lavender clapped her hands. "Oh, I'm so happy to hear that! I *knew* he loved me, but I wanted to be sure."

"He's got some issues, though." Penelope twirled her hand in a circle. "I'm seeing dollar bills flying through the air." She regarded Lavender with raised eyebrows. "Does that mean anything to you?"

Lavender smiled broadly. "Yes, it does. He opened a new business recently, so it must mean he's going to be making lots of money."

"Well, not necessarily. As I said, he's got issues he's dealing with, and money might be at the heart of it. Was there anything else you wanted to ask me?"

"No, that was my main question." Lavender was grinning broadly. *He loves me, he loves me!* She took her wallet out and dropped money on the table. "Thanks, Penelope! Have a wonderful day."

She raced back to Helmsburg. If she hurried, she'd have time to pop in on Burley at work before she had to pick Logan up from school. When she got to the Sandwich King, she drove around to the back of the building and parked by the rear exit door, right next to Burley's truck.

Her small hand made hardly any sound knocking on the heavy metal door so she began pounding on it with her fist. "Burley!" she called. "It's me. Open up."

The door lurched open and Dustin peered out. "I need to speak with Burley," Lavender said. "Can you tell him I'm here?" Dustin stared as though he didn't recognize her, so she pointed at herself. "I'm his friend? Lavender LeClair?"

"Hang on, I'll go tell him." The door banged shut. Lavender turned up the collar of her jacket to keep the wind out, and tapped her boot on the littered pavement. Dustin returned in half a minute and pushed the door open a few inches. "Mr. Burley is very busy and can't see you right now. May I give him a message for you?"

Self-important little shit. Behind Dustin, Lavender could see a light on in a tiny room that had to be Burley's office. "I need to talk to him," she said. "Let me in." She took a step forward but Dustin blocked her with his bulky frame.

The assertive approach wasn't going to work with this blockhead. Lavender tilted her chin and beamed a flirtatious smile at him. The chubby guys always fell to pieces when a cute girl bothered to give them the time of day. "Just for a second?" she said. "Pretty please?" She wriggled her shoulders and stuck out her chest. Lucky thing she'd worn her leather jacket today, the one with the sexy zippers all over the front of it.

Dustin stepped aside. "Okay, just for a second."

Burley was on the phone, engaged in a heated discussion with someone called Bracco. He held one finger up when he saw Lavender, then swiveled his chair around so his back was to her. "I told you, Bracco," he shouted into the phone. "I'm not paying a single dime for that order! You owe me a refund for all the defective equipment you sold me." He slammed his fist on the desk. "I'm through arguing with you about it. Quit bugging me."

Burley disconnected, and for a second it looked as if he might throw the phone across the room, then appeared to think better of it. He turned in his chair and looked at Lavender. "What is it?"

"That's how you greet your girlfriend?" Lavender draped herself over his shoulders and smooched his neck. "I was in the neighborhood so I thought I'd drop by and tell you how much I love you." Glancing over her shoulder, she spotted Dustin lurking outside the door. "Could you excuse us, please?" she said, kicking the door shut.

Burley tried to push her away. "You know you're not supposed to come here. Now Dustin's on to us."

Lavender took a step back. "He was already on to us. What's it matter, anyway? Everyone in town knows by now that Clint and I are splitting up."

"I wanted to play it cool a while longer, so no one thinks I had anything to do with it."

Lavender swatted Burley's arm. "Oh, please, who gives a crap. What was that phone call all about, anyway? You sounded angry."

"I'm pissed the hell off. Those guys that Jack Nielsen roped me into doing business with are a pack of thieves. Every day, it's someone else in that mafioso family calling me, hounding me to pay up on an order that I already cancelled. It's driving me up the flipping wall. I'm getting worried—"

Lavender looked at him curiously. "Worried about what?"

Burley stood up. "Nothing. Everything's fine. I've just got a lot of things on my mind."

Lavender put her arms around his waist and angled her pelvis into his. "I hope *I'm* one of those things. You love me, don't you?"

Burley poked his nose into her hair. "You know I do."

She started grinding against him. "You turned down that job, didn't you? The one in Pennsylvania?"

"Uh, yeah. Sure did. Told her the other day."

"That's good, baby." Lavender clamped her lips onto Burley's neck but he pushed her away.

"You'd better go," he said, "before you get me all distracted. I've got work to do."

"Okay, baby. But one more thing—Logan might be going someplace with Clint tonight, so maybe you could come over for a little you-know-what?" She batted her eyelashes at him—actually batted them—and gave him one last hip thrust. "I'll text you later and let you know for sure."

Burley walked Lavender out. The moment she was gone, Dustin appeared in the back hallway with a case of lettuce in his arms. "That chick's hot, boss. You got something going on with her?"

"No, I don't. She's married." Burley nodded his head at the lettuce. "Get that shredded, so we're ready for the dinner rush." If there even was one.

Dustin stood there looking at him, and both their faces broke into mischievous grins. "Go on, get outta here," Burley said. "And don't tell anyone."

• • •

At home that night, dreading the emotional shit show that was sure to follow when he told Marta he was reneging on the job, Burley debated whether he should telephone her or take the easy way out and send an email. He was surprised by the way he'd been able to lie so easily to Lavender, when he'd always prided himself on his honesty. Oh well, what was done, was done. It was only a tiny fib anyway, a necessary expedient to prevent undue concern on Lavender's part. It sucked though, having to turn down all that money, but Lavender's ultimatum was too much for him. She'd cast some sort of a magical love spell over him, and he couldn't do without her anymore.

A phone call would be the most appropriate way to break the news to Marta, but when Burley picked up the phone to call her, he chickened out. Going to his computer instead, he cribbed some verbiage from the internet, and fired off an email:

Dear Marta,

Thank you for the generous offer of employment with your company. Due to unforeseen circumstances, I am unable to accept the position. I appreciate your consideration and I wish you the best of luck in finding a suitable candidate.

Sincerely,

Ronald Burley

Reading it through, he felt he'd struck the right blend of polite and businesslike. He sent the message, shut the computer down and went to bed.

• • •

The next morning, Marta called him on the Sandwich King's business line. Burley sent Dustin outside with a stack of cardboard boxes to break down for recycling, so he would have privacy for the conversation he'd been hoping to avoid.

"I can't believe that email you sent me," Marta said. "It was so cold, Burley! It didn't even sound like you."

The catch in her voice made Burley's heart sink. Once again, he'd made her cry. "I was trying to be professional," he said. "I didn't mean to offend you."

"You promised you'd help me."

Had he actually promised her? He couldn't remember exactly. Man, he hated this dramatic shit! "I'm really sorry, Marta," he said. "I mean it. Something came up unexpectedly. The guy I'm supposed to be training to fill in for me here had a family emergency."

"Come on, Burley! I'm sure you can get something worked out so you can still come down in April like we planned."

Burley thought fast. "It's not that simple. See, this guy's wife was in a bad car accident." He was astonished at how easily the falsehood came to him. "She's confined to a wheelchair now, so he has to remodel their whole house to make it accessible. Gonna take a long time."

"Then hire someone else and train them instead. Running a sandwich shop can't be that complicated."

She wasn't going to give up. No matter what excuse Burley invented, Marta would have a solution to his problem. He was going to have to tell her the truth. "There's another thing," he said.

"What is it?"

"I have a girlfriend here. We've been together for a while now and I don't think it would be good for our relationship if I took a job out of state."

There was a long pause on the other end of the phone, and Burley had to literally bite his tongue to prevent himself from filling the silence with more inane lies.

Marta finally spoke. "You never told me that."

"I didn't have the chance to. We were always talking about other things."

"You slept with me. Twice."

"Um, yeah. That was a mistake."

"Sleeping with me was a *mistake?*"

"I mean it was my mistake for doing it. My bad."

"What's her name? Is she someone I know?"

"No, she's a lot younger than you." *Shit.* "I mean a little bit younger. You probably wouldn't know her."

"Her name, Burley. What's her name?"

"Lavender. Lavender LeClair."

Marta laughed out loud. "*Lavender?* For real? And what are her sisters named, Sage and Oregano? Or maybe Magenta and Pastel Pink?"

"That's not funny."

"Yeah, it is. It's a dumb name."

Burley sighed. "Look, Marta, I know I should've told you about her a lot sooner. I didn't handle this the right way."

"You used me, Burley. Again. Just like you did back in high school, when we—"

"I didn't use you!" Burley broke in. "I wasn't sure of my feelings at first. It took me a while to figure out that I really care for this woman. Once I realized that, things got serious between us pretty quick."

Marta's voice was tight with anger. "You know what, Burley? You suck. I thought you were my friend, but I guess I was completely mistaken. You're a liar and a two-timer, and I'm never going to forgive you for this. Do you hear me? Never! I don't ever want to talk to you again."

The call disconnected. *Burned that bridge,* Burley thought.

Now what? He'd been planning to use the last of the money he'd gotten from selling the boat to take Lavender out to dinner on Saturday night; but he couldn't afford to do that anymore, and he'd have to make up an excuse. The need for yet another lie weighed heavily on him, but he couldn't see any way around it.

CHAPTER 23

The cold North Country winter gradually gave way to the milder temperatures and budding greens of spring. Herds of black and white dairy cattle dotted the countryside, and the sun warmed the thousands of sparkling Adirondack ponds and lakes.

As spring progressed into the heat of summer, Lavender's divorce inched its way through the courts, and Burley finally persuaded his mother to move into the senior apartments attached to the county nursing home. Business at the Sandwich King continued to be sluggish, and the columns on Burley's balance sheet see-sawed between black and red.

The summer months passed quietly. Burley avoided spending money on Lavender by emphasizing the need for frugality as the Sandwich King became established, and frequent promises that the business was going to take off any day now. They hung out mostly at Lavender's place, when Logan was with his father.

As summer drew to a close, Jack Nielsen placed a less-than-friendly phone call Burley, to remind him of the terms of their loan agreement. "Your six months are almost up, bro," he said. "You better fuckin' pay me on time."

The first installment on the loan was due in September, and Burley didn't have the money. Besides his overhead and operating expenses, he had to pay a monthly franchise royalty to Sandwich King, which left him with barely enough to cover the minimum payments on his credit cards, and nothing to put toward the loan. "Isn't there a grace period?" he asked Nielsen. "I'm a little short at the moment, but things are going to turn the corner soon. I'm sure I'll be able to pay you next month."

"Nope. I got a baby and a new house to pay for. I can't let you slide."

"I thought we were friends. Can't you cut me some slack instead of playing hardball like this?"

"Read the contract, bozo," Nielsen said. "You miss one payment, you're in default."

• • •

Burley was back to scrounging for cash. Selling the Ski-Doo would bring enough money to keep him afloat for another month or two, but that was it. He was screwed, that's all there was to it. He was going to lose the business he'd worked so hard for, and his trailer and land along with it, since he'd put them up as collateral on the loan. He'd be forced to find a cheap room to rent, and someplace else to work. Going back to the Mini Mart wasn't an option after the way he'd stolen Dustin away.

On top of everything, it was only a matter of time before Lavender discovered he was broke. As soon as she found out, she'd kick him to the curb so quick it'd make both their heads spin.

Burley sold the Ski-Doo and paid Nielsen for September, never breathing a word about his money troubles to Lavender. As October approached, she began dropping hints about their one-year anniversary coming up, throwing him into a serious lather. He knew she'd be expecting a fancy dinner date and an expensive gift, and he wasn't going to be able to deliver.

But then, a reprieve. "I'm going to treat you this time," Lavender told him, "since you've been working so hard. Come out to the cottage on Saturday afternoon. I'm going to cook you dinner!"

Burley packed his overnight bag and set off along the back roads into a remote corner of Hogan County. After driving for thirty minutes without passing a single other vehicle, he turned onto the heavily forested Stillwater Road, traveled several more miles to where the pavement ended, then jounced over the last two miles of hard-packed dirt and rocks. At the end of the road, the deep blue water of the reservoir loomed beyond the trees, and a few hundred yards short of the rustic Stillwater Hotel, he hung a left onto the oddly-named Necessary Dam Road.

The LeClair cottage sat within a grove of ash trees at the end of a long gravel driveway that sloped down toward the lake. Burley parked his pickup on the loop in front of the cottage, got out and took in his surroundings. He'd been out here with Lavender on only two occasions before, both times at night, when he could hardly see where he was going through the dark woods. The place was more of a vacation home than a cottage, with a stately pillared porch and etched-glass front door. Burley climbed the flagstone steps and let himself in.

The ground floor contained a spacious living area straight out of a Pottery Barn catalog, a fully-equipped kitchen, and a comfortable master suite; upstairs there were two smaller bedrooms with dormered windows overlooking the front yard. Burley went into the living room where a sliding door opened onto a deck with a view of a small cove ringed with windblown pines.

Lavender met him with a kiss and pulled him into the kitchen. Burley was getting hungry already, and he was puzzled to see there weren't any pots simmering on the stove, or anything in the oven, either. When he went to look in the refrigerator, Lavender stopped him with an outstretched arm. "It's a surprise, baby. No peeking."

Burley stepped out to the deck to admire the view, which was stunning. The autumn color was nearing its peak. The glowing reds and golds of the foliage shimmered in reflection on the surface of the water, and the sunny afternoon had turned warm enough to be comfortable without a jacket. Lavender came out to join him and slipped her arm around his waist. "It's beautiful out today, isn't it? Like that day last year when we met at the soccer field."

Burley leaned over the railing and pointed at the sagging boathouse on the water's edge. "Is there anything in there?"

"I'm not sure," Lavender said. "We used to have a motorboat, but my dad got rid of it because no one ever took it out. I think there might still be an old canoe in there, though."

"Cool. Why don't we go for a paddle before dinner?"

Lavender squinched up her face. "I don't want to get wet."

"You won't get wet, I promise. I'll paddle and all you need to do is sit there and look pretty." Burley removed Lavender's arm from around his waist and tugged on her hands. "C'mon, it's a gorgeous day, hon! Let's do it. It's the last time we'll be able to get out on the water this year."

"All right," Lavender agreed. "Let me go change my shoes."

When she was ready, they walked down to the boathouse. Burley pulled the creaky wooden doors open and looked inside, and the light from a cobwebbed window revealed a dented aluminum canoe resting on a wooden rack. He inspected it, and it appeared to be in useable shape. "Let's carry it outside. You grab this end and I'll get the other. Watch your step so you don't slip off the platform into the water." They got into position at opposite ends of the boat. "Ready?" Burley said.

"Wait." Lavender wiped her hands on her jeans. "It's really dirty." Burley counted to three and she raised her end of the canoe about six inches, then let it drop. "Ugh! It's too heavy."

"Yeah, it's an oldie." Burley rapped his knuckles on the hull. "The newer fiberglass canoes are much lighter than these old aluminum ones. Let's give it another go, and put your back into it this time."

On the second try they were able to lift the canoe from the rack. Burley dragged it outside onto the grass and looked at it more closely. "It's got a few dents," he said, brushing away the sticky spiderwebs and dead bugs, "but otherwise it looks fine." He went back into the boathouse to look for the paddles.

"Those are gross," Lavender said when he returned with two wooden paddles and a pair of mildewy orange life vests. "I'm not wearing one. They smell."

Burley gave her a playful wink. "I'll wear mine so I can save you when you fall in." He draped the floppy vest around his neck and strapped it around his middle, noting with chagrin how far his waistline had expanded. Too much fast-food, too little exercise.

Working together, they carried the canoe down to the water's edge. "Look," Burley said, sweeping his arm from west to east, following the contours of the long, narrow body of the reservoir. "See how the lake is aligned with the prevailing wind? It can kick up without warning and get pretty rough out there, but we'll be fine if we stay inside the cove." He held the canoe steady while Lavender climbed in, and when she'd settled herself in the forward seat, he got in behind her and shoved them off.

The boat glided over the dark water, leaving gentle ripples in its wake. "It's pretty out here," Lavender remarked. "And so quiet."

It was peaceful being on the water, Burley thought. Away from his problems. He hadn't been in the mood to celebrate when Lavender had invited him for dinner, but now he was glad he'd come. Maybe things weren't as hopeless as he'd thought. Business at the Sandwich King just *had* to improve at some point, and everything would be okay. The holidays were coming, and that always got people into a spendy frame of mind. Meantime, he could sell more of the stuff in his garage, make his next loan payment to Nielsen, and continue limping along.

The wooded arms of the cove curved around them on both sides, and beyond its mouth they could see the choppy open water of the lake. There weren't any other boats out that afternoon, and the neighboring cottages along the shore were hidden from view by dense groves of trees. Lavender rested her paddle across the gunwales, dipped her fingers into the water, and pulled them right back. "It's freezing," she said, shaking droplets from her hand.

"It gets real cold out here when the sun goes down," Burley said. "That's why the autumn leaves have such good color this year—warm days like today, followed by chilly nights."

They continued paddling toward the mouth of the cove, then turned in a wide circle and headed back toward the cottage. When the bow of the canoe scraped the pebbly shore, Burley allowed Lavender to get out first, then dragged the boat up onto the matted grass. "Can you give me a hand putting this away, honey?"

Lavender puckered her lips. "It's too heavy, and it's got gunk all over it now. Just leave it out here, no one will care. There used to be some railroad ties that my dad always set it on." Walking toward the boathouse, she scanned the ground. "Here they are," she said, tapping something in the weeds with her foot.

Burley inverted the canoe on the heavy blocks of wood and put the paddles and life jackets away in the boathouse. The sun was low in the western sky and the late afternoon breeze had an edge to it as he and Lavender walked hand-in-hand up to the cottage.

Lavender opened a bottle of red wine and Burley hid his distaste as she poured them each a glass. He couldn't stand wine, especially this awful red shit, but Lavender kept telling him he needed to work on being more sophisticated. "Not too bad," he said after he'd forced down a mouthful. "I think I'm getting used it."

"You ought to like it," Lavender said with a sniff. "I paid enough for it, since this is a special occasion." She began setting two places at the long oak dining table. "Can you get a fire started while I get dinner going? There's wood in the rack on the front porch."

While Burley was outside, Lavender hurried to the refrigerator to get the appetizers she'd secretly ordered from Marian, the owner of the Stillwater Hotel. She opened the cardboard takeout box, and was surprised to find only a single crab cake in it, rather than the two she'd ordered. When Burley returned with an armload of firewood, she confronted him. "You ate one of the crab cakes! How could you do that, when I told you it was a surprise?"

Burley looked at her blankly. "One of the what?"

Lavender snapped a kitchen towel at him. "The stuffed crab cakes. I made a specific point of telling you to stay out of the refrigerator."

Burley dumped the wood in front of the fireplace. *What in the hell was she talking about?* He knelt and began arranging pieces of kindling on the cold grate in perfect Boy Scout fashion. "I didn't eat anything, honey. I don't know what you mean."

Lavender hissed something inaudible and went back into the kitchen. She was certain she'd picked up a full order from Marian at the restaurant. And look—there was a dribble of sauce on the side of the container, where Burley had stuck his fat hand in. She stomped back to the living room, takeout box in hand. "Why would you lie about it when I can see plain as day what you did? You're being a jerk."

Burley twisted to face her. "Honey, I did not eat a single bite of whatever's in there. I swear."

Lavender stared down at the box. "Okay, I believe you. I must have made a mistake and ordered only one."

Burley grinned at her. "Didn't you say you were making me a home-cooked meal?"

Oh hell, she was busted! Lavender balled up her towel and threw it at Burley but hit a lamp instead, causing the shade to tip at a crazy angle. They both stared at it for a second, then burst into laughter. "I give up," Lavender said. "I knew I wouldn't be able to fool you."

Burley set the lampshade back in order. Lavender rewarded him with a hug, then abruptly pulled away. "We need to drink a toast," she announced, retrieving their wine glasses from the dining table. "I was going to wait till after dinner to tell you my big news, but I can't wait any longer." She was suddenly glowing. With a stab of fear, Burley braced himself for *I'm pregnant*, then realized that wasn't likely to be the case, since she was drinking. Even Lavender had her standards.

Lavender raised her glass. "I am now officially divorced."

No, no, no! Not yet. Burley had known her divorce would be coming through any day, but he'd been hoping for more time. Now the pressure would be on him to buy her a ring and propose, but how could he, when he was on the brink of losing everything? His earlier optimism disintegrated in the face of reality. He was well and truly screwed.

"That's wonderful news, honey," he said. "I'm really happy for you."

"You're happy for *me?* How about being happy for *us?*" Lavender held her wine glass poised as though she might fling its contents at him.

Burley approached her cautiously. "I *am* happy for us. Like I said, it's wonderful news. I just wasn't expecting it so soon."

Lavender pushed him away. "What do you mean, soon? I've been waiting almost a year for this, Burley."

"It took me by surprise, that's all. It's very good news."

Lavender looked crestfallen. "I thought you'd be more excited than this. I've been dreaming all week about our wedding. I'm thinking I'd like to—"

"Wait a minute." Burley set his wine glass down and pulled Lavender onto the couch. "There's something I've been meaning tell you."

Lavender's hurt expression changed to fright. "What? What's wrong?"

Burley stood up again. He couldn't hide the truth from her any longer. It was time to come clean, and all he could do was pray that she really did love him as much as he hoped she did.

Beginning with a deep breath, he told Lavender everything. When he was done with his sorry tale, he dropped onto the couch next to her and hung his head. "I was a damn fool. All these years, I thought Nielsen was my friend, but I never should've trusted him. I guess I was so caught up in the dream of starting my own business that I didn't stop to think it through, and look what happened—I signed a contract for a loan that I have no way of repaying."

He peeked over at Lavender. She'd been remarkably quiet the whole time he was talking, her eyes fixed on the fireplace. "I apologize," he went on, "for not being straight with you all along. I was embarrassed about my situation and I hated for you to see how stupid I was."

Lavender burst into life. "Jack Nielsen is a total scumbag!" she exclaimed, jumping to her feet. "I can't believe he ripped you off like that, and still expects you to pay him back. The *balls!* Why didn't you confront him?"

"I tried to, believe me, but I could never get a hold of him. He was always out of town, off on a job somewhere. The last time I saw him, he said he'd make trouble for me if I didn't pay up, so I haven't exactly gone looking for him."

"But isn't it against the law, what he's doing? It's like extortion, or embezzlement, or something."

Burley hung his head. "No, it isn't anything like that. He set me up, yeah, but it was my fault for not being more careful about the terms of the loan. I didn't even read the whole contract. I trusted him and his lawyer, and just went ahead and signed it."

Lavender shook her fists. "He can't do a thing like this and get away with it! You should sue him, Burley. Take him to court and try to get out of it somehow."

"I wish I could, but it won't work. A contract's a contract. Besides, I don't have the money to hire a lawyer."

Lavender clapped her hands together. "I know what to do! We'll ask my lawyer to look into this, and see what she thinks."

"I just told you, I don't have the money."

"But I do."

"No, you don't."

"I don't have it right this second, but I know how I can get it," Lavender said with a crafty smile. "Clint gave me the house in the divorce settlement. I could take out a home equity loan."

"No," Burley said. "I can't allow you to do that."

"But I want to! My father gave us the down payment for the house when we got married, so there's plenty for me to borrow against. We'll file a lawsuit against Nielsen, and sue him for punitive damages, too, for your pain and suffering."

"It doesn't work that way, honey. This isn't a personal injury case."

Lavender waved a dismissive hand. "Never mind. We can still try for it."

Burley was losing control of this conversation, losing control of his life. He loved Lavender desperately, but she was trying to dictate his every move and his male pride was taking a beating. "There's no way I'm letting you pay for a lawyer for me," he said firmly. "Forget it."

Lavender's expression turned menacing. "Would you quit being so macho about it, Burley? This is a serious matter! You've got to take action, or all our plans are going to be ruined."

"Our plans—?"

"Yes, Burley, our *plans*." She enunciated like he was daft: "You know—we get married, we buy a new house, we have a baby, we live happily ever after. Remember?"

Burley didn't recall them ever discussing it quite so specifically, but this was not the time to question her.

"I wouldn't really be paying for your lawyer," Lavender went on. "I'd simply be loaning you the funds until you get out of your contract with Nielsen, and the Sandwich King starts turning a profit."

"Nope. Not happening."

Lavender growled at him, but then her hand flew up. "Wait a sec! I read this magazine article the other day, about how to solve your financial problems. You can go to a credit counselor, Burley! They review your circumstances, and then they design a plan to consolidate your debts. You end up making only one payment per month, at whatever amount you can afford."

Burley regarded Lavender in astonishment—she wasn't normally this conversant about fiscal matters. "Credit counseling?" he said. "I'm not so sure about that."

Lavender was bouncing on her toes. "What's there to be sure about? Everybody's doing it nowadays. It's the American way!"

Burley thought it over. It might be a feasible way for him to dig himself out of this hole, but it was too embarrassing to contemplate. He shook his head. "I can't do it."

Lavender narrowed her eyes. "It's that or the lawyer, Burley."

She had him by the short and curlies now. If she was going to force him to choose, he supposed the legal route was better. He'd at least have a sliver of a chance of getting his money back. "You win," he said, his shoulders slumping in resignation. "I'll go to the lawyer. But I'm only doing it on one condition—could we please put our marriage plans on hold for the time being? I can't think about anything like that until my financial issues are resolved."

Lavender threw her arms around his neck. "Sure, baby, I can wait." She kissed his cheek with a loud, wet smack. "I'll call Janice Crocker first thing on Monday and make us an appointment."

Having a plan of action brought Burley a profound sense of relief. They sat down to eat the remaining crab cake and the elaborate pasta dish that Lavender had ordered from the Stillwater Hotel, and they enjoyed a pleasant, relaxed meal. Afterward, they threw more logs on the fire and made love on top of a pile of quilts in front of the crackling hearth. When Lavender dozed off, Burley scooped her up in a bundle of blankets, carried her to the master bedroom and tucked her into the bed. "I'm going to get my bag from the truck," he whispered in her ear. "I'll be right back."

He pulled on his jeans and undershirt, and stepped out the front door. The sky was bright with stars and the crisp autumn air felt good after the heat of the fireplace. The haunting wail of a loon echoed across the cove, and another loon answered from farther out on the lake. His hands in his pockets, Burley looked up at the sky, and a feeling of calm washed over him. Lavender's love for him was solid. Things were going to work out after all.

Dew soaked his sneakers as he walked across the grass to his truck. The driver's door was getting rusty and he had to give it a good yank to get it open. The locking mechanism was broken as well, but he hadn't bothered getting it fixed when he had more pressing matters to attend to, like keeping himself solvent. He reached across the seat and grabbed his duffel bag, slammed the door hard so it would catch, then stood gazing up at the stars again, enjoying the quiet night.

A faint crunching of gravel from the far end of the driveway made him swing his head around. Black bear sightings were common in these parts and he didn't want to cross paths with one, particularly at night.

He waited a full minute, listening and peering into the darkness, but he didn't hear or see anything else.

Starting back toward the cottage, he thought he heard footfalls coming from the direction of his truck and he spun around to look. Nothing. As he began walking again, a prickly sensation at the back of his neck spurred him up the steps to the porch, where he turned again and surveyed the inky yard. Who could be out there? Not a neighbor, when all the other cottages in the vicinity were closed for the winter. Clint, maybe? The finalization of the divorce might have triggered a burst of anger at his ex-wife. Perhaps he'd followed her out here tonight, to see what she was up to. Or could it be Nielsen, trying to scare Burley into paying up? Nielsen was enough of a butthole to pull a stunt like this.

Then Burley saw it—or thought he saw it. A dark figure standing at the edge of the woods. But the harder he looked, the less sure he was that anyone was really there at all. He looked away for a second, then back again, and the shadowy figure was gone.

CHAPTER 24

Lavender drove Burley out to Janice Crocker's office later that week. The lawyer was dressed in her usual cargo pants, and one of the hip pockets appeared to be stuffed full of hundred-dollar bills. She leaned on her overflowing desk and listened intently as Burley explained his predicament.

"I know all about that Nielsen clan," Janice said when Burley had finished. "They're all the same—sweet-talking liars and cheats. Like half my clients." Slapping her thigh, she brayed like a donkey.

Janice hadn't invited them to sit down, so Burley stood beside Lavender in the middle of the room, shifting from foot to foot. "Do I have any legal recourse? I put my property up as collateral for the loan, and Nielsen's threatening to take it if I don't make my next payment."

Janice kept her eyes on Burley, ignoring Lavender. "Have you explained your situation to him, and asked if he's willing to work with you?"

"I talked to him yesterday and offered to let him assume ownership of the Sandwich King, but he said hell no. He's got his own electrical contracting business, so he's not interested in running a franchise."

"Unfortunately," Janice said, "you have a signed contract, which is generally not subject to modification. There are certain circumstances that might allow you to get out of the loan, such as fraud or misrepresentation, but neither of those seems to be applicable here. To put it bluntly, you don't have a case."

"Wait," Lavender piped up. "I did some research on the internet. Nielsen's signature on the contract wasn't notarized. Wouldn't that invalidate it?"

Janice smirked. "Sorry, no."

"What about the misrepresentation thing?" Burley said. "As a condition of the loan, Nielsen insisted that I purchase my restaurant equipment from this shady outfit in Syracuse called Bracco Brothers. I'd bet you anything he was getting a kickback from them."

Janice sniggered. "A name like that, they're probably all mobbed up and planning to whack you."

Neither Burley nor Lavender cracked a smile. Janice stepped out from behind her desk and looked pointedly at the door, but Burley didn't move. "There's got to be something you can do to help me," he said. "Otherwise, I'm ruined."

Janice threw up her hands. "It's a long shot, but we could argue that Nielsen coerced you into agreeing to certain terms in the contract."

"Okay," Burley said uncertainly. "That sounds hopeful?"

"Nah. It won't really get us anywhere. But if you insist on trying, I'll give it a shot."

Lavender stepped forward. "You mean you'll represent us?"

Janice curled her lip and indicated Burley with a nod of her head. "I will represent *him,* and I'll be needing a retainer."

Burley pulled out the five hundred dollars that Lavender had given him on the drive over; Janice took the wad of money and stuffed it into a different pocket of her cargo pants. "I'll be in touch."

When they got out to the parking lot, Burley hesitated before getting into Lavender's car. "Wait here a minute," he said. "I forgot something." Going back inside, he poked his head through Janice's doorway. "Can I ask you one last question?"

The lawyer looked up from her computer. "What is it?"

"If there isn't any legal remedy, then what do I do?"

"You might consider filing for bankruptcy, to prevent losing your home."

It felt like Burley's stomach had dropped out. *Bankruptcy.* Things couldn't get any worse than that.

• • •

Burley sold his ATV but it didn't bring enough money for him to cover his next loan payment. "I'm gonna sue your ass for defaulting on that note," Nielsen threatened over the phone. "You better get ready to move out."

"Can't you give me a little more time?" Burley pleaded. "Business is picking up. I'm sure I'll have the money in a few more weeks."

"No can do, bro. Like I told ya before, this is business. I'll see you in court."

• • •

Nielsen promptly followed up on his threat. The contract gave him the right to demand immediate payment of the entire principal plus interest, and the lawsuit he filed demanded immediate possession of Burley's trailer and land.

Burley called Janice Crocker in a panic. "I'm not going to sugarcoat things," she said. "It doesn't look good for you. But let me see what I can do."

She phoned him back the next day. "I spoke with Jack Nielsen's attorney Chuck Stevens and told him I was going to contact the state attorney general about the business practices of that Bracco outfit. If Nielsen is in cahoots with them, it might compel him to agree to a deal."

"Good," Burley said. "That might work."

"Don't get your hopes up. Sit tight till you hear back from me."

Janice called back a week later. "They won't play ball. Stevens says his client is adamant that the financial agreement between the two of you was entirely transparent and aboveboard, with no coercion whatsoever. A hearing has been scheduled in municipal court at one o'clock on November eighteenth, with Judge Stanwell."

Burley swore. Judge Stanwell was Hunter Stanwell, his egotistical high school nemesis. It was over, he was going down big time. Goodbye Sandwich King, goodbye home, goodbye Lavender.

The day before the hearing, Burley arrived at work early, having been unable to sleep all night. When he logged into his email, he found a message from an address he didn't recognize. Clicking it open, he read:

> *Dear Ron,*
> *My name is Lyla, I'm your friend Marta's niece. I came up from Baltimore to help take care of her daughter because her cancer spread faster than we expected and she's under hospice care now. My aunt told me you're an old friend of hers and she says there's something very important she needs to tell you. I know it would make her very happy to see you one last time. Could you please come as soon as you can?*
> *Thanks,*
> *Lyla*

Hospice. That meant Marta was close to the end. Burley sat there with his face in his hands, letting the sad reality sink in: his childhood friend and sometime lover was dying.

Several minutes passed before he could shake himself out of his gloom. If Marta had something important to tell him, it must mean that she wasn't mad at him about the job anymore. That was a comfort, at least. She was seeking closure and wanted to forgive him in person. She'd been raised by fundamentalists who believed in eternal damnation and the torments of hell, so she was probably afraid of departing this earthly life without squaring things up with the Almighty first.

Burley wasn't too psyched about making the long drive down to Granger when his future was hanging by a nut hair, but it was his friend's last dying wish, after all. He had to go. He typed a quick reply:

Dear Lyla,

I'm sorry to hear about your aunt. Please tell her I'm coming. I have some business to take care of tomorrow but I promise I'll drive down on Saturday.

Ron

The hearing took place in the white-columned Hogan County Courthouse. Burley arrived half an hour early and parked himself on the long wooden bench in the lobby, anxiously waiting for his lawyer to arrive. He'd made a point of asking Lavender not to come, knowing full well that his case was hopeless. He couldn't bear for her to witness his downfall.

At a quarter to one, Janice Crocker came charging through the double doors, briefcase swinging. She flashed her ID at the security guard and came clumping across the echoey marble foyer in a going-to-court ensemble of blazer, slacks, and scuffed loafers.

Burley stood to offer her a seat but Janice waved him off. "I talked to Chuck Stevens this morning. I pushed hard for a settlement but they won't budge." She glanced around. "Where's your girlfriend?"

"I told her not to come."

"Good." Janice clomped toward the courtroom and Burley followed her. She pushed the heavy doors open, strode up the center aisle and led him to a pair of seats at the front of the room. Balancing her battered briefcase on her knees, she clicked it open and began shuffling through a sheaf of papers. A minute later, Nielsen and his attorney entered the courtroom. Stevens exchanged a polite nod with Janice, and he and his client sat down on the other side the aisle.

The court was called to order as Judge Stanwell entered from a side door. The skinny around town was that years ago, Hunter had barely squeaked through a downstate law school, then struggled for a foothold in the cutthroat legal world of Manhattan. After several unproductive years, he'd quietly returned to Helmsburg, where his father used his political connections to get his son elected to a local judgeship.

Stanwell seated himself behind the bench and scanned the documents laid out before him. If he was aware of his former classmate sitting before him in the front row, he didn't acknowledge it.

A variety of cases were presented: shoplifting, trespassing, traffic violations, a landlord/tenant dispute. Stanwell listened to each case with a bored expression, and disposed of the cases swiftly. When *Nielsen vs. Burley* was called, the judge cocked eyebrow, and his glance traveled briefly in Burley's direction.

Nielsen was called first as a witness, and he answered Janice's questions with a smug self-assurance that set Burley's teeth on edge. Then Burley was called, and on cross-examination, Chuck Stevens asked him if he'd sought quotes from any vendors other than the Braccos. "No, I didn't," he admitted, with a despairing look at his own lawyer, whose eyes were now glued to her notes. "It never occurred to me to do that."

When the attorneys had finished their back-and-forth, Judge Stanwell bestirred himself. "Mr. Burley," he intoned, peering down from the bench. "You have alleged coercion on Mr. Nielsen's part, but you clearly didn't perform your due diligence. If you were foolish enough not to seek additional estimates before purchasing your restaurant equipment from Bracco Brothers, this court isn't going to bail you out. My ruling is in favor of the plaintiff." He smacked his gavel. "Next case, please."

Burley was stunned, and it took a hard jab in the arm from Janice to get him to rise from his seat. She steered him out of the courtroom and into a quiet corner of the lobby where she addressed him in a calm voice. "Don't freak out yet. Nielsen can't collect on the judgment right away. He'll have to file for a lien first, then initiate a foreclosure action to get possession of your property. All of that could take months. In the meantime, I'll look into filing for Chapter 7." Burley nodded in mute resignation. His life had taken an unpleasant and humiliating turn.

As he trudged out to his pickup truck, Burley's cellphone buzzed with a text from Lavender: *How did it go?* Prior to the hearing, he'd answered her questions about his case in evasive terms, and had avoided telling her how hopeless things looked. Now that it was a done deal, he couldn't face her. He texted back: *Will call u later.* It was sure to piss her off, but too fucking bad. He needed to go home and think hard about his predicament, and try to figure out a way out of it.

• • •

Back home in his trailer, Burley sat on his couch for hours, lost in a deep funk and ignoring Lavender's repeated phone calls. When her texts became frantic—*WHERE R U?!!! WHAT'S WRONG?!!!*—he finally broke down and called her back.

"Fucking A, Burley!" Lavender spluttered when he told her the outcome of the case. "That is *horrible.* What are you going to do?"

Her pointed use of "you" rather than "we" made his spirits sink even lower than they already were. He was losing her. "I don't know," he said.

"You need to *do* something, Burley! You can't sit there moping about it."

"I'm not moping," he said, unconvincingly. "I just need some time to figure this out."

"Fine." Lavender's tone became chilly and distant. "I'll talk to you later." Burley fell back onto the couch with his arm flung across his face, and remained there for hours, mired in misery.

At midnight, he attempted to rouse himself. His future depended on him making a success of the Sandwich King, so he needed to show up for work in the morning. Going into his bedroom, he discovered he had no clean shirts to wear because he'd forgotten to do laundry this week. Scrounging around on the closet floor, he found a shirt that might be serviceable if he hung it up to get wrinkles out. As he was reaching for a hanger, he remembered something that had slipped his mind: he was supposed to drive down to Pennsylvania tomorrow, to see poor dying Marta.

Burley stabbed the hanger into the neck of the rumpled shirt and slapped it onto the closet rail. Visiting someone who was on the cusp of death was the absolute last thing he felt capable of doing at this moment, and he didn't think he could stomach it. He'd shoot the niece a quick email, saying something had come up at the last minute, and he couldn't make the trip.

But after thinking about it more, he realized that blowing town for the weekend would be a good way to avoid the humiliation of facing Lavender. It would buy him some time to formulate a plan for dealing with his troubles, and Dustin could cover for him at the Sandwich King while he was away. The idea brought immediate clarity to his jumbled thoughts. Forget canceling the trip—he was definitely going.

• • •

Burley had been on the road for over an hour when Dustin called the next morning. "There's a problem at the shop," his faithful employee said. "The whole place is flooded. Looks like something's leaking in the kitchen. You want me to call a plumber?"

Burley cursed out loud. Another water leak! A plumber would cost him money he didn't have, and he'd be forced to borrow from Lavender, which was untenable. "No, don't call anybody yet," he told Dustin. "Wait till I get there and have a look at the damage. Put a sign on the door saying there's been an emergency and we're closed until further notice." At the next exit, he veered off the interstate, looped around and got back on going in the opposite direction.

• • •

Back at the Sandwich King, Burley and Dustin sloshed around in a puddle of water for over an hour before determining that the leak was coming from somewhere within the wall behind the dishwasher. They hacked through the sheetrock, exposing a confusing array of aged pipes. Burley wiped his sweaty forehead with his sleeve. "I'm not tackling this job. I'll only screw it up and make it worse."

"You'd better call Winkler," Dustin said. "He's the best plumber in town."

The fee for a service call was seventy-five dollars. "That's just for me to come out and assess the job," Winkler told Burley over the phone. "Can't say how much the whole job will come to, depends on the extent of the work. Might be a simple fix, might not."

Burley rubbed his temples, feeling like his world was caving in on him. "I understand," he said. "How soon can you get here?"

It took the rest of the day for Winkler to repair the leak, and the total for the work came to over three hundred dollars. Burley dropped the bill into the wire basket on his desk and went back to mopping up. What a fucking calamity. He'd lost an entire Saturday's revenue, and he wasn't sure how he was going to pay for the repairs. Wringing the mop out, he rolled the metal bucket across the kitchen and started on a new section of wet floor. Dustin stayed with him into the evening, helping to clean up and put the kitchen back in order. By nine o'clock, they were both worn out and went home.

As Burley was getting ready for bed later that night, he remembered his promise about going to Marta. *Screw it*, he thought. He was too tired and discouraged to deal with that mess right now. It wasn't like Marta was going to drop dead at any second, anyway. His brother Russ had been under hospice care at the end of his life too, and he'd lingered for weeks.

The Sandwich King was closed on Sundays, so Burley spent the next day vegging out in front of the TV and worrying about the state of things with Lavender, whom he hadn't spoken to since Friday. To his surprise, an unforeseen attitude of obstinacy had begun to bloom in him. If Lavender couldn't accept him as he was, flaws and all, then the hell with her.

Back at work on Monday, Burley had plenty more cleaning and catch-up work to do, so it wasn't until Tuesday that he got around to checking his email. He scrolled through the first several messages in his inbox, which were mostly invoices from vendors, but the next email in the queue was from Lyla Grolsch. Opening it, the first sentence gave him a jolt:

Dear Ron,

I wanted to let you know that my aunt passed away on Saturday night.

Burley smacked himself on the forehead. While he'd been wallowing in his own troubles, Marta's imminent death had gone clean out of his head. What kind of friend was he, to forget a thing like that? He cringed as he read the rest of Lyla's message:

I told her you had promised to come but she was too weak to hang on any longer. She was asking for you right up to the end.

Tears filled Burley's eyes. Marta had been languishing on her deathbed and he'd forgotten all about her. What a complete and utter jerk he was. A heartless dick. The least he could do now was to pay his respects by going to her funeral.

Lyla hadn't mentioned anything in her email about when the service would be held, and Burley felt it would be inconsiderate to bother her with questions when she had enough to deal with already. He did a Google search for newspapers in Marta's town, and found a website for a daily called the *Granger Sentinel*. It was a small-town paper, so it didn't take long for him to scan the obituaries, but there was no entry for Marta Grolsch. He searched the previous day's edition as well, but still didn't find anything. Clicking back to Lyla's email, he hit the Reply button and typed:

I'm sorry to hear about your aunt's passing. Something came up here so I wasn't able to come on Saturday like I said. Sorry about that too. I hate to bother you but would you mind sending me the details for her funeral?

Lyla's reply came within seconds:

Her funeral was yesterday.

Aargh! Burley smacked his forehead again. He couldn't catch a break. He'd had good intentions, but Lyla didn't know that, and it wasn't the sort of thing you could explain in an email. Forget it, then. He'd run over to Kinney Drugs on his lunch break, pick up a sympathy card, and drop it in the mail to her first thing tomorrow. It was a lame gesture but it was something, at least.

Two days later, he was checking his email again when he saw another message from Lyla:

Dear Ron,
I was cleaning out my aunt's desk this morning and I found an envelope with your name on it. Right before she died, she said she had something very important to give to you. I think this envelope must be what she was talking about. It's from a law firm and there's a handwritten note attached to it that says it has to be delivered to you in person. Can you come and get it? Please let me know as soon as you can.

Burley read the email a second time, and bolted upright so fast that his desk chair almost flew out from under him.

Money. It had to be! Marta had told him she was a millionaire. She must have left him a portion of the money that she'd tempted him with so many times, to prove she'd forgiven him for turning down her job offer, and for being in love with someone else. Burley hurriedly pedaled his chair back to the desk and typed a reply as fast as he could:

I'll come as soon as I can.

CHAPTER 25

Since he was basically broke, Burley needed to lay his hands on some quick cash to pay for the gas to get down to Pennsylvania. "Hey, Dustin!" he called from his office. "Can you come here?"

Dustin materialized in the doorway, a pair of crinkly food service gloves clinging to his hands. "What's up, boss?"

There was no sense advertising the fact that he was about to go chasing after a dead woman's money, so Burley gave his employee the first plausible story he could think of: "My mother has an urgent medical issue that I need to go take care of, and I'll be gone the rest of the day. Think you can handle things on your own here?"

"Sure, boss. No prob."

"Good." Burley removed his coat from the hook behind the door and pulled it on. "We're expecting bad weather tonight, so you can close early if it's dead."

"Got it," Dustin said. "You'll be back in the morning?"

Burley hesitated. He'd have to drive all night, but he could do it. Had to do it, since he couldn't spare the money for a motel room, and no way was he going to spend the night in Marta's death house with her stoic niece and orphaned child. "Yeah, I'll see you in the morning," he said. "Bright and early."

Burley went home, unlocked the glass door of his gun cabinet and surveyed his collection of firearms. There was a Smith & Wesson .22 revolver that he used for small game and plinking out back, a Remington 12-gauge shotgun for duck hunting and trap shooting, a Knight .50 caliber muzzleloader that his dad had given him for his eighteenth birthday, and a Winchester .30-06 deer rifle that had belonged to his brother Russ.

The gun he treasured the most for sentimental reasons was the Winchester. Taking it out of the cabinet, Burley turned it over in his hands. It was a fine piece of craftsmanship, with a 24-inch barrel and a satin wood finish. It was worth more than the other guns, but he wasn't sure he could part with it.

As Burley regarded the contents of the cabinet, he was shocked by the realization that he hadn't taken any of the guns out since he'd become involved with Lavender. Between work and all the running around he'd had to do to keep their affair a secret, there hadn't been any free time left for hunting or shooting. And once he and Lavender were married—which depended on Marta's presumed generosity—he had a funny feeling she wouldn't approve of him disappearing into the woods for long hunting weekends with his pals, like he used to do. Might as well sell everything and put the money to more productive use. He could replace the pieces after he received the inheritance from Marta, and got himself back on his feet.

Burley removed the pistol, shotgun and muzzleloader from the cabinet and laid them out on the rug, but when his hand fell on Russ's rifle, he stopped. Selling it would be a sin. He didn't really believe in the supernatural, but if there actually *was* such a thing as ghosts, he was certain his brother would come back from the beyond and haunt him mercilessly for the sacrilege.

It was quite a valuable gun though, and selling it would net him a nice chunk of badly needed cash. Burley stared at it, trying to make up his mind. *No*, he finally decided. He couldn't do it. Not yet, anyway.

He loaded the other firearms into his truck and drove to a small gun shop he knew of, out on the Number Four Road. The owner was a staunch Second Amendment defender who scrutinized Burley's offerings with a practiced eye, and tallied their value. "I'll give you $850 for the lot."

It wasn't the number Burley had been hoping for, but it was enough to cover the plan that was taking shape in his mind. "I'll take it," he said.

With the cash safely stashed in his wallet, he got back into his truck and tried calling Lavender, but his phone showed a No Service message, which wasn't an unusual occurrence this far into the Adirondacks. Heading back into Helmsburg, he stopped for gas at the Mini Mart. As he was waiting for his tank to fill, he dialed Lavender again, and got a recording: *Your call cannot be completed at this time.* When he redialed, the recording played again. *Weird.* He'd never had trouble getting a signal in the middle of town before.

Burley drummed his fingers on the steering wheel, trying to figure out what the problem was, and then it hit him—he hadn't had the money to pay his last phone bill, so his service had been cut off. *Fuck it*, he thought. He didn't use his cellphone that much, anyway. All his Sandwich King business was conducted over the landline in the office, so not having a cell wouldn't make a difference to anyone except Lavender, and he'd be seeing her very soon.

Burley was going to ask her to marry him. He knew it would be wiser to wait and see exactly how much money Marta had left him, but an overwhelming sense of urgency had taken hold of him. Lavender was slipping away, he was sure of it. He could hear it in her voice and feel it in his bones. If he didn't take the leap and propose to her immediately, he was certain he'd lose her forever.

Pulling out of the gas station, Burley drove across town and turned onto Route 26 north. There was a pawn shop up in Carthage where he could buy an engagement ring on the cheap. He was counting on Lavender not being able to tell a real diamond from a fake, and a cubic zirconia was all he could afford with his limited funds. She likely wouldn't notice the difference anyway, since his proposal would be sweetened by the astounding news that he was about to become a rich man.

The least expensive of the rings on display at the pawn shop was a small lab-created stone in a 10-karat white gold setting, for $175. The price was right but the setting looked cheap, which wouldn't fly with Lavender. One step up from that was a smallish cubic zirconia set in 14-karat yellow gold, for $299. Burley dithered for a minute before deciding to go with the costlier ring, to play it safe. The tattooed girl behind the counter placed it in a green velvet box and offered him her congratulations.

When he got back into his truck, Burley automatically pulled out his phone to call Lavender, but—*duh!*—the call wouldn't connect. He tossed the useless phone to the floor, and turned on the radio for the weather forecast. "According to the National Weather Service," the announcer said, "a massive Canadian low pressure system is tracking southward. As temperatures drop, we can expect storm conditions to descend upon Central New York this afternoon, with significant snowfall occurring in regions south of the Thruway." Burley groaned. It was too early in the season for this kind of weather! He'd have to get on the road as soon as possible, and try to outrun it.

As he drove back into Helmsburg, Burley passed the IGA on Main Street, where the parking lot was filled with shoppers busily stocking up for the storm. Parking in the alley behind Mystic Moon, he entered the boutique through the back door. A red-haired woman in a paisley caftan instantly appeared and barred his way. "This is not a public entrance."

Burley had a hazy recollection that her name was something metallic like Cobalt or Chromium. To avoid a mistake, he fudged. "Hello, Ma'am," he said politely. "Please pardon the interruption. I need to speak with Lavender for a minute, it's very important."

The woman smelled strongly of things that grew in the forest. Giving Burley a withering look, she hollered to Lavender that her boyfriend was there, making it sound like he was a vagrant she'd caught skulking around in the alley.

Lavender approached with a puzzled look. "We need to talk," Burley whispered. "In private. Get your coat so we can go outside."

They went out to the alley and stood in the fenced nook beside the trash cans, where they were partially sheltered from the rising wind. Even though it was rapidly getting colder out, Burley could feel nervous sweat rolling down his back. "Listen honey," he said, taking Lavender's hand. "I've got some bad news to tell you, but some really good news, too."

Lavender looked at him in alarm. "What happened?"

"I'll give you the good news first. Marta is dead." Burley shuffled his feet. "I guess that's not *good* news, exactly. What I mean is, I got an email from her niece, who found an envelope with my name on it in her aunt's desk. Marta was loaded, Lavender! She got millions of dollars from her dead husband's life insurance, and I'm pretty sure she left me some of that money when she died. The bad news is that I need to drive down to Pennsylvania right away."

Lavender's expression was stuck somewhere between disbelief and elation. "How much money?"

"I don't know, but it's probably a lot."

"What do you mean by a lot?"

"It could be a hundred grand, or more."

Lavender's eyes went wide and her mouth gaped. "Oh! Wow, that's incredible! What did you—"

Burley shushed her. "I don't have time to tell you the whole story, I gotta get on the road before this storm hits. I promise I'll explain everything after I get back tomorrow." Pulling her close, he kissed Lavender hard on the lips. The ring in his coat pocket felt like it was going to burn a hole through the heavy fabric, but a sudden flash of fear made Burley lose his nerve. Was he really worthy of a woman as lovely as Lavender, or was it all just a ridiculous dream? An uncultured oaf like him would never be able to hold onto her love. Turning abruptly, he started to jog toward his truck.

"Burley, wait!"

He stopped in his tracks and turned around. Lavender was shivering from the cold and had her hands shoved into her armpits, but she was looking intently at him. "I love you," she said.

There was something in her face that hadn't been there before—an emotion deeper and more genuine than her usual breezy declarations of love. Burley ran back to her and they stared into each other's eyes as the wind whipped their bare heads. Something had changed, he could feel it. All of a sudden, their love felt more real than ever before. His bad luck had finally turned, transforming their relationship into something solid and indestructible.

Looking around, Burley took in the bare alleyway and the filthy garbage cans. This was no place for a romantic proposal, but he didn't have any time to spare. Getting down on one knee in the deepening snow, he pulled the ring out of his pocket and held it up. "Lavender," he said in a voice strengthened by newfound confidence. "I love you with all my heart. Will you marry me?"

Lavender's eyes zeroed in on the ring like a heat-seeking missile and her hands flew to her mouth. "Oh my God, Burley!" she shrieked. "*Yes!*"

Lavender's head was spinning as she watched Burley drive off. She was going to be a bride! Again! She'd do it up right this time, too. None of that Does-my-dress-still-fit, I-hope-they-can't-tell-I'm-pregnant business with *this* wedding. With all the inheritance money coming his way, Burley could fly her and Shayna to New York City for a girls' weekend. She could shop for a wedding dress at Bloomingdale's, and buy lots and lots of shoes.

A gust of wind blasted through the alley and knocked over the boutique's trash can, but Lavender was too cold to be bothered picking it up. She hurried back inside, hung her coat up in the hallway, and went into the shop. Copper was occupied with a shipment of ceramic statues that she was unpacking and arranging on the shelves in the front window. She looked at Lavender over the rims of her eyeglasses—a vivid emerald today, to complement her brassy hair. "What was that all about?"

Lavender put her nose in the air, unwilling to share her news with her nosy boss. "Nothing much. There was just something he wanted to tell me."

"Isn't that what phones are for?" The drapey sleeves on Copper's caftan kept getting in her way and she shook them back in annoyance. "I'd like you to finish up here. I've got calls I need to return."

Lavender pulled a wad of wrapping off an iridescent dove and held it up to the light. "This one's pretty."

Copper grabbed her left hand. "What's this?"

Lavender pulled her hand away. "It's an engagement ring."

"Oh my," Copper said. "What did he do, pop the question in the back alley? How classy."

"For your information, he proposed to me last weekend," Lavender lied. "At the Mirror Lake Inn, in Lake Placid. Not that it's any of your business."

"The fast-food business must be more lucrative than I thought." Copper shook out her sleeves again. "Make sure you put the most expensive pieces on the middle shelf, so they're at the customer's eye level." She whisked off to the back room, leaving a eucalyptus-scented cloud hanging in the air.

Lavender removed another parcel from the shipping carton and undid the bubble wrap, revealing a pink-cheeked little angel with flowing hair and glittering wings. Hallmarky stuff didn't normally appeal to her, but the figurine looked so sweet and innocent, unlike those spooky angels that Penelope had in her odd-shaped house out there in the middle of the woods.

As she placed the little angel in the center of the shelf, Lavender wondered if she ought to get another tarot reading. Even though Marta was dead now, there was something about her attachment to Burley that wasn't sitting right. He'd insisted they were nothing more than childhood friends, so how did that result in Marta leaving him money in her will? They couldn't have been very close, with Marta married and living in another state for so many years. Plus, Burley had rejected her job offer when she was dying and desperate, which would have crushed any friendliness between them. There was something seriously messed up about all this.

After making sure Copper was occupied in her office, Lavender scrolled through her contacts on her phone until she found Penelope's number. "I need a reading right away," she said in a low voice when the psychic answered her call.

"Oh, it's you," Penelope said. "I've got an hour free later this afternoon, but you'd better not drive all the way out here with that storm coming."

"I guess not," Lavender agreed. "Can you do it over the phone?"

"I don't usually like to do that. It's too hard to get a feel for the energy."

Screw the energy, she needed answers! "Can't you do it for me just this once?" Lavender pleaded. "It's really important. There's something I need to know right away."

Penelope sighed. "All right, call me around four."

Using her old standby of menstrual cramps, Lavender asked to leave work early that afternoon. Copper was irritated but gave her consent, and at three o'clock, Lavender grabbed her things and walked out to her car. Several inches of snow had fallen and the Impala required a thorough brushing-off before Lavender could back it out of its parking space. She drove east on Main Street for a block in case busybody Copper was watching from the window, then circled back west on the side streets and cut over to Hickey Road. There was something she needed to look for in Burley's trailer before her phone reading with Penelope.

Nubby paw prints were frozen into the mud on the wooden steps at Burley's front door, and he'd left the place unlocked as usual. When

Lavender stepped inside, Bo and Augie bounded up from their stinky beds; she fended them off with the toe of her boot and a sharp *No*. Going into the bedroom, she closed the door so the dogs couldn't follow her. Dirty clothing was scattered across the floor and the funk of bedsheets in need of a wash reminded her of why she refused to ever spend the night there.

The louvered doors of Burley's closet were standing open. Lavender turned on the light and scanned the shelves, which held a collection of ball caps, a carton of light bulbs, and several assorted boxes of ammunition. She knelt and peered into the recesses of the closet, and spotted a cardboard box with *High School Stuff* scribbled on the side of it in magic marker.

Lavender dragged the box out into the bedroom and rummaged through bits of memorabilia and old notebooks until she found a yearbook at the bottom. It was from the 1997-1998 school year, ten years before she'd graduated from dinky, asbestos-riddled Helmsburg Central School. Grades K through 12 all in one building, with teachers who looked like they'd been hired back when Donny & Marie were still a thing.

Lavender flipped through the yearbook. The senior portraits were a hoot—spiky haircuts on the boys, clumsy Rachel shags on the girls. She turned to the B's, and found Ronald Burley looking athletic and handsome, sporting a wisp of a mustache on his upper lip. Lavender brushed the picture with her fingertips. Her sweet Burley. Using her iPhone, she zoomed in and snapped a photo.

She turned more pages and scanned the G's until she found Marta Grolsch. Lavender sat back on her heels and studied the woman's picture. Marta was prettier than she'd expected, with dark hair, intelligent eyes and a soft, shy smile. *Rest in peace, bitch*. Lavender snapped another photo and continued flipping through the book, and paused when she came to a two-page spread of prom pictures.

The photos were low quality and she had to examine them closely before she was able to pick out the happy couple—Burley rocking a fitted tuxedo, Marta unexpectedly busty in spaghetti straps. They were avoiding each other's pelvis as they danced to Faith Hill's *This Kiss*, according to the caption. *Uck*. Lavender snapped another photo, then ripped the entire page out and stuffed it into her purse.

The sky was ominously dark when she got home. Lavender went inside and smoothed out the wrinkled prom picture on the kitchen table. It irked her to see Burley holding another woman, six feet under or not. She wadded the page into a ball and threw it in the trash, then texted Penelope the three photos she'd taken.

It was going on four o'clock now, so Lavender took a bottle of white wine out of the fridge, poured herself a big glass over ice, and dialed the psychic's number. "Thanks for agreeing to do this over the phone," she said when Penelope answered. "I was afraid to go out with that snowstorm coming."

"Phone readings aren't ideal," Penelope said, "but I'll do my best,"

•   •   •

The conversation left Lavender cold with fear. According to Penelope's mysterious visions, Marta was a psycho who wasn't actually dead, and Burley was in some kind of danger. She needed to warn him! But when she dialed his number, the call wouldn't go through. It was all too freaking insane for her brain to comprehend. Lavender clutched the phone in her trembling hands, and stared out the living room window as the wind picked up and the swirling snow began to come down harder.

CHAPTER 26

The afternoon light was fading when Burley turned his pickup into the parking lot of Marta's office building. He tried to tamp down his excitement, reminding himself that Lyla was in mourning and it wouldn't be fitting for him to appear too eager to collect the money.

As he walked toward the office, he noticed the windows were dark and there was a handwritten note taped to the door. Pulling it free, he read:

Sorry I'm not here to meet you, problem at job site. Tried to call but couldn't get through. Please wait if you can. Bob Johnson from next door will let you in.
—Lyla

The building next door housed a cluttered machine shop, and old Mr. Johnson looked to be a good ten years past his expiration date, with thick eyeglasses and hearing aids in need of a battery change. He squinted up at the leaden sky as he unlocked Marta's office. "Looks like you brought that storm with ya," he said, holding the heavy glass door open for Burley. "Gonna be a big one, fer sure."

The front room looked the same as before, with its drab walls and shabby furniture. The door to Marta's small office was ajar and Burley spotted another note taped to the telephone on the desk: *If you see a call from 555-2368 please answer (it's me). Help yourself to coffee.*

There was no telling when Lyla might return, but Burley was determined to wait all night if he had to. A copy of the *Granger Sentinel* lay on the desk; pulling the chair out, he adjusted the seat so he could lean back comfortably and paged through the newspaper. It took only a few minutes to skim the latest news, which was mostly about a variety of mud snail that had infested the local trout streams. He scanned the editorial page and the sports section, then tossed the paper aside with an impatient flick of his wrist.

Burley yawned and rubbed his face. Five long hours on the road coming down, five more going back in the dark. He got up and poked his fingers through the slats of the dusty venetian blinds on the window. No sign of snow yet. The threatening forecast would probably turn out to be a lot of overblown hype. If it continued to look like the storm was holding off, he'd push through and go home tonight, after he got what he needed from Lyla. Might be a good idea to try and catch a catnap while he waited. Returning to the desk chair, Burley tilted it back even further, and within minutes he was snoring.

When he awoke sometime later, he couldn't remember where he was for a second. The room had grown dark, so he got up and turned on the overhead light, and stood blinking in the sudden brightness. The clock on the wall showed twenty minutes past five. In need of something to clear his sleepy head, he went over to the Keurig machine on the table in the corner. A small bowl held a few K-cups of something called Sumatra, which he'd never had before. He brewed himself a cup, and found an open carton of creamer in the little refrigerator next to the table. He hadn't stopped to eat on the drive down, and he suddenly realized he was starving. To blunt his hunger, he poured a generous amount of creamer into his coffee, then stirred in several spoonfuls of sugar.

The telephone on the desk rang. The incoming number was Lyla's, so he lifted the receiver. "Hello? This is Ron Burley."

The connection was staticky and he couldn't hear her very well because of the noise in the background. "There's been an accident!" Lyla shouted. More static and garbled words, something about an ambulance and the police. "Hang on," she said. "Let me go someplace quieter." The noise faded, and then she came back on the line. "I can't leave here till this is cleared up." Her voice sounded echoey, like she was in a tunnel. "I'm really sorry. I know you came all this way because I asked you to, and I don't want to keep you waiting all night. The envelope's in the middle drawer of my aunt's desk. It's locked, but the key is in the Phillies mug on the—" The static cut in again; Burley couldn't make out the rest of what she was saying, and then the line went dead.

He replaced the receiver and turned in a circle, scanning the room. *Phillies mug, Phillies mug!* Ah—there it was, on the shelf above the printer. He grabbed it and dumped out its contents, and spotted a small gold key in the mound of rubber bands and paper clips. Going over to Marta's desk, he unlocked the middle drawer and pulled it open, and found a 9 x 12 manila envelope inside. *Ron Burley* was printed on it in Marta's handwriting, and the name of a law firm with a Philadelphia address was stamped in the upper left-hand corner.

He was right, Marta had remembered him in her will! Raising his eyes heavenward, Burley thanked his departed friend for rescuing him from ruin. He was about to tear the envelope open when a knock sounded on the outer door, and a moment later Bob Johnson poked his grizzled head through the doorway. "Sorry, mister, but I gotta lock up here and git home while the roads are still clear."

"Right," Burley said. "Give me a second while I grab another coffee for the road." He brewed another cup and pressed a plastic lid onto it, pulled his coat on and tucked the envelope securely under his arm.

Snowflakes were trickling down as Burley hurried out to his truck. His dome light didn't work anymore, so he had to drive out of the dark parking lot and find a streetlight to park under. He opened the envelope and drew out a formal-looking letter from the law firm of Caselli, Brogan & Sterne, and as he began reading, his eyeballs almost popped out of his skull: Marta Marie Grolsch, being of sound mind and under no constraint or undue influence, had bequeathed to Ronald Charles Burley the unbelievable sum of one million dollars.

Sweet Jesus. Tears stung Burley's eyes. His oldest, most loyal friend in the world had come through for him in the end. He skimmed the next paragraph, which instructed him to present himself to the law firm for verification of his identity, and to arrange for the transfer of the funds. The rest of the letter was a blur of legalese that he'd have to reread later because it had begun snowing harder and his windows were getting covered, blocking out the light.

Burley turned the radio on, hoping to catch a weather update, but it was all commercials. The prudent move would be to find a cheap motel to hunker down in until the storm passed over, but that meant he'd have to put off sharing his stupendous news with Lavender, since his phone was useless. He checked his watch, saw it was a quarter to six. If he left right now and the weather held, he'd get back to Helmsburg around eleven, which wouldn't be too late of an hour for him to turn up on Lavender's doorstep.

He decided to chance it. If the roads got bad, he'd pull over somewhere and wait it out. Burley slid the letter back into the envelope and put the truck into gear.

CHAPTER 27

The car in the far corner of the parking lot had been sitting there with its engine running for the past hour, its exhaust fumes condensing in the gathering darkness. Burley didn't appear to take notice of it as he came out of the building and hustled to his truck. The woman in the car watched him until he'd driven off, then got out of her vehicle and ran across the parking lot.

She unlocked the glass door of the office, went into the smaller room in the back and flipped on the lights. The room was as neat as she'd left it earlier, except for the newspaper splayed on the desk and the upended Phillies mug. Going straight to the Keurig machine in the corner, she dropped the used K-cups into a large Ziploc bag, then set a Styrofoam cup on the drip tray and ran eight ounces of fresh water through the machine. She took the cup of water into the bathroom, poured the contents into the toilet and flushed it away, then placed the empty cup in the Ziploc along with the used K-cups.

She brushed the mound of rubberbands and paper clips back into the Phillies mug and replaced it on the shelf, then took the newspaper from the desk, folded it twice and stuffed it into the Ziploc, which she then sealed. After one last look around the room, she turned the lights off and locked the front door behind her.

Returning to her car, the woman drove out of the parking lot and onto the main road, and traveled half a mile to a Sheetz convenience store. She drove around to the back of the building, lowered her window and tossed the Ziploc into a dumpster, then raised the window and turned up the volume on the radio, which was tuned to a local station. A weather bulletin came on with an urgent winter storm warning, and Marta smiled to herself as she drove away.

CHAPTER 28

Burley skidded through the empty streets of Granger until he spotted the sign for Route 15 and began heading north. His coffee had gone cold already but he drank it anyway, to fortify himself for the long trip. Spinning the radio dial, he found a country station and hummed along to a Brooks & Dunn song, tapping his fingers in time on the steering wheel.

Twenty minutes into the drive, he started to feel sleepy again, which was surprising after his nap and the two cups of coffee. That Sumatra crap from Marta's office was probably decaf. He wished he'd looked to see if there was any regular.

It was snowing like mad now, and Burley could feel the pickup sliding even though he'd put his snow tires on a week ago. His mind became muddled, as if his thoughts were churning through mud. His blood sugar must have gotten too low from not eating all day. He'd heard of that happening to people. Better stop someplace and get something to eat.

A few miles down the road, his headlights picked out a sign for a roadside diner in a town called Liberty. It would be a good place to get a sandwich and more coffee, and use the restroom. Burley turned off the highway and came to an intersection, and through the pouring snow he saw a neon red *Restaurant* sign glowing on the opposite corner.

The diner's parking lot was full of thrumming eighteen wheelers waiting out the storm, and he had to circle around twice before finding a place to park. He cut the engine and picked up the manila envelope lying on the seat next to him. The letter it contained was precious and he needed to safeguard it, but the envelope was too big to stuff into his coat pocket, and he didn't want to bring it inside with him either, when he'd need his hands free to use the john.

Burley climbed out of the truck and reached behind the seat for the release lever. He angled the seatback forward, and dropped the envelope safely behind it. He wasn't concerned that the driver's door didn't lock anymore—no one would be out looking for things to steal on a night like this, especially from a beaten-up old truck like his.

The restaurant was crowded with truckers. The windows had steamed over and the place smelled deliciously of fried onions. Burley's stomach growled and he was tempted to slide onto the vacant stool at the end of the counter and order himself a hamburger platter, but thoughts of Lavender waiting at home held him back. He went up to the register and ordered a ham sandwich and jumbo coffee to go, then watched the harried waitress filling his cup from the big urn behind the counter. He rubbed his eyes with his knuckles. Boy, he was tired. Maybe that catnap hadn't been such a good idea after all, since it had left him feeling so lethargic. The waitress handed Burley his coffee, and had to ask twice if he wanted cream and sugar. When his sandwich came, he fished a few bills and loose change from his pocket, laid the money on the counter and walked out.

It was dumping snow now, and the pickup was covered. Burley scraped it off with his long-handled brush, then cautiously made his way back onto the highway. Visibility was poor. He remembered this stretch of road from his previous trips to Pennsylvania—a series of long, twisting curves that cut across the mountainsides, high above the river valley. After traveling several slow miles, a sheer rock cut loomed up along the shoulder and seemed to break the wind a bit, and it looked like the road here had been recently plowed. Burley relaxed his grip on the steering wheel and wished again for his cellphone. He'd love to be talking to Lavender right now, telling her about his incredible reversal of fortune, and he tried to imagine the look on her face when he told her.

If only he could keep his eyes open! Burley rolled his shoulders to loosen them up and turned the radio louder. A torrent of snowflakes flew at him in the beam of the headlights, creating a hypnotizing whirl. He tried to eat his sandwich but the smell of it nauseated him and he thought he was going to vomit. Rolling his window down, he stuck his head out, but the sharp flakes stung his eyes and blinded him. Too late, he realized he was on an overpass that was coated with ice. The truck went into a skid and he overcorrected, causing it to fishtail violently. He was out of control.

The road curved to the left but the truck wasn't responding properly, and Burley was unable to make it go in the right direction. He watched in mute horror as the forest came rushing at him, then felt the truck become airborne as it smashed through the guardrail and hurtled over the edge of the cliff. There was a scream of twisting metal, and he felt his bones snapping as the pickup rolled down the steep ravine and landed on its side on the frozen riverbank.

CHAPTER 29

Lavender pushed a spoonful of pureed green beans between Burley's lips and waited as he methodically chewed and swallowed, his eyes staring blankly at the wall. Why was he *chewing?* The food was soft as frigging mush. A greenish thread of saliva leaked from the corner of his mouth and dribbled down his chin, and she sighed and wiped it away with a napkin.

She still couldn't get over what had happened. On the night of the accident, an alert snowplow driver had spotted the broken section of guardrail that Burley's pickup had smashed through, and reported it to the Pennsylvania State Police. When a rescue team pulled him from his mangled vehicle, Burley was near death and had to be helicoptered to the level 1 trauma center at Upstate Medical in Syracuse. The authorities in Syracuse contacted the sheriff's office in Helmsburg, and after some delay, Lavender received the shocking news that her betrothed was in the ICU with a severe head injury and multiple broken bones.

After racing to the hospital, she'd wept at Burley's bedside as the neurologist told her the diagnosis: a grade 2 diffuse axonal injury. Whatever the hell that meant. A shearing injury, the doctor had explained, showing Lavender a plastic model of someone's head. As Burley's truck careened down the mountainside, his brain had ricocheted around in his skull, tearing the nerve fibers apart and inflicting irreversible damage.

He was in a coma for three weeks, and when he eventually regained consciousness, he was transferred to the Hogan County skilled nursing facility for rehabilitation. What exactly they were planning to rehabilitate was a mystery to Lavender, given his dire prognosis. The probability of death was high, and permanent brain damage was expected, notably paralysis and severe cognitive impairment. The only physical activity Burley was currently capable of was sitting propped up in a wheelchair, and mustering a lopsided smile when Lavender walked into his room. That, and endlessly chewing his goddamned puree.

Lavender scooped up another dollop of colorless meat and waved the spoon back and forth in front of Burley's face. His eyes tracked the movement for a second or two, then went back to staring at the wall. She threw the spoon down on the meal tray and shoved it away, fell back in her chair and crossed her arms. This sucked.

Her life had taken a total one-eighty. In the days immediately following the accident, she'd held out hope that Burley would make a full recovery, but as the weeks went by, reality had gradually set in. Her darling had become a vegetable, and she'd been reduced to a handmaiden, feeding him his gruel and wiping snot from his nose. He couldn't talk to her, or kiss her, or even hug her back when she wrapped her arms around his slumped shoulders and tried to squeeze some life into him.

Lavender lifted her left hand to gaze at her engagement ring, and tears filled her eyes. They'd had so much to look forward to, so many things to plan for their new life together! But everything was ruined now, all because of that scheming woman who had reeled Burley in with the promise of money—money they'd never, ever see now, since the key to getting hold of it was locked inside his damaged head.

At first, Lavender had thought it would be a simple task to track down Marta's niece, but that soon proved to be a dead end. Burley hadn't told her the niece's name, or even what town Marta had lived in— he'd only said it was somewhere in Pennsylvania. An internet search for

Marta Grolsch hadn't turned up anyone by that name in the entire state, and the number for the single Grolsch listing in the Hogan County phone directory had been disconnected. Lavender recalled Burley mentioning at one time that Marta's business had something to do with construction, but it was such a broad category that she'd given up in frustration after an entire day of fruitless phone calls.

Lavender continued to sulk until the sound of approaching footsteps interrupted her dejected train of thought. Someone knocked gently on the open door. "Excuse me?" a male voice said.

She twisted around in her chair. "Can I help you?"

The visitor stepped into the room, then stopped and stared at Burley slumped in his wheelchair. Turning toward Lavender, he became aware of the meal tray and the uneaten food. "Sorry, am I interrupting? I can wait till you've finished."

For a split second, the man's appearance unnerved her—he looked so much like Burley! Lavender studied him with curiosity. He was attractive and well-dressed, and there was an air of prosperity about him. She uncrossed her arms. "No, we're done."

"Please forgive me for showing up unannounced like this." The man extended his hand. "I'm Richard Burley, Ron's brother."

Aha! The rebellious younger brother who skipped town years ago. " Nice to meet you. I'm Lavender."

"Oh yes, Ron's fiancée. It's a pleasure to finally meet you."

Lavender was busily absorbing details: smart haircut, cashmere V-neck, spiffy shoes. An upper-class version of his brother. She smiled and gestured toward Burley's empty bed. "Please have a seat."

Richard cast another a glance at his brother. Burley raised his eyes for a moment, then sank back into his stupor. Richard smoothed the bedspread with his hand and gingerly seated himself. "I would have come right away but I was on a cruise in the Virgin Islands," he said with a regretful expression. "I was incommunicado for several weeks, and wasn't able to get here any sooner."

Like it mattered. There wasn't anything he could have done for his brother, anyway. Lavender eyed him some more. "How did you find out about the accident?"

"An uncle in Watertown called and filled me in on the particulars." Richard looked closely at his brother. "Can he talk at all?"

"No, but he does seem to recognize certain people. This kid who worked for him was here the other day, and he made eye contact for a minute." Lavender had crossed paths with Dustin a few times, when he'd come to visit his former boss. After Burley's accident, the Sandwich King had been permanently closed and Dustin had gone back to work at the Mini Mart.

Richard got up, placed his hands on his knees and spoke loudly into Burley's face: "HELLO RON. IT'S YOUR BROTHER RICHARD."

"You don't have to yell," Lavender said. "The nurse says he can hear just fine."

Burley rotated his head in Richard's direction. His face remained blank but there was a faint glint of recognition in his eyes. Richard frowned and sat down again. "Poor son of a gun. His life will never be the same."

"Ya think?" Lavender blurted, then caught herself. This was no time for snark. "Sorry," she said. "We were going to be married this summer."

"Yes, I heard. I'm so sorry. You must still be in shock from all this."

"I am. It's been a very difficult adjustment." Lavender looked at Burley, who appeared to be dozing off. "Such a sweet guy," she said, patting his inert hand. "I loved him so much."

Richard touched her lightly on the arm. "I'm sure you did, and I'm sure he loved you."

Lavender took note of Richard's manicured fingernails and expensive wristwatch. No wedding band, but that didn't guarantee he was single. She needed to fish a little more. "You were in the Virgin Islands?" she said. "How interesting." She hadn't a clue where they were, but Richard's mention of them provided a convenient opening for her to dig for more info. "Did you and your wife enjoy your cruise?"

"I'm not married, actually. I went with three of the agents on my team. I'm a real estate broker and the cruise was a reward for them being the top producers in our region this year."

"My goodness! That sounds so glamorous."

"Yes, it was. We went with Celebrity. Every aspect of the trip was positively top-notch."

"I've always wanted to go on a cruise," Lavender said. "Maybe one day I'll get my wish."

Richard's teeth were gleaming white when he smiled. "Maybe you will."

Burley had opened his eyes again. When Lavender turned to look at him, his gaze locked with hers for a moment, then his eyelids drooped and he was asleep again.

A pair of nursing assistants appeared in the doorway. "We're here to put him to bed," one of them said. "If you wouldn't mind stepping out of the room for a minute."

Lavender jumped to her feet, glad for an excuse to get the hell out of there. "Come right in. We were getting ready to go."

The aides rolled a Hoyer lift into the room and Richard followed Lavender out. "I would enjoy chatting with you some more," he said as they started down the hallway together. "I was going to walk over to the assisted living wing and visit with my mother for a few minutes, but I'll be free after that. Would you care to join me for dinner?"

Lavender marveled at way the universe sometimes dropped things into your lap when you were least expecting it. She smiled at Richard. "I'd love to."

They came to the main corridor and paused. "I can pick you up at seven," Richard said, "if you're comfortable with that."

"That would be great." Lavender took out her phone. "Why don't you give me your number, and I'll text you my address." They exchanged their contact information, and parted with a friendly wave.

As Lavender turned toward the lobby, she almost crashed into someone who was coming around the corner at the same time. "Watch out!" she snapped, then pulled back in surprise as she recognized the homely face and bobbed hair of Cheryl Morgan. Clint was following close behind her, holding the hand of an equally plain little girl.

Lavender glared at him. She'd seen very little of Clint since their divorce was finalized, and had learned through Logan that he'd moved in with the insipid Miss Morgan, and a spring wedding was in the works. It galled her to see their happy little trio when her darling Burley was down the hall drooling on his pillow, dead to the world. "What are you doing here?" she said to Clint, ignoring his companions.

"We came to see Cheryl's grandmother. She's recovering from a stroke."

"How nice." Lavender started to walk around them, but Clint put his hand on her arm as she passed. "I was sorry to hear about the accident," he said quietly. "I hope you're doing okay."

"I'm fine," Lavender replied brightly. "Now, if you'll excuse me, I need to be on my way."

•　•　•　•

Richard picked Lavender up for dinner in a two-door Chevy Spark. "This was the only car Hertz had left at the airport," he said as he opened her door for her. "Syracuse is playing Georgetown at home this weekend, so there must have been a run on rental cars."

He took her for an expensive dinner at the Surf 'N Turf, Helmsburg's finest (and only) seafood and steakhouse. Lavender had been there a few times when her parents were picking up the tab, but never with Burley. To impress her date, she'd worn a low-cut wrap dress and styled her hair in a fetching up-do; Richard himself was looking fine in a pair of slim-fit chinos and a soft black sweater that had to be cashmere. Extremely pleased with his appearance, Lavender casually slipped her arm into his as the elegant hostess showed them to a candlelit table for two.

The restaurant had a sumptuous look, with dark wood paneling and paintings of horses and foxhounds on the walls. Richard ordered a bottle of pinot noir and filled Lavender in on his backstory: "I dropped out of school in the middle of my senior year, and left home three days later. Told my family I was never coming back. I hitchhiked to Florida and got a job as a gofer for a large property management company. The owner recognized my potential and convinced me to get my GED, and then I started studying for my real estate license. I worked hard and hauled myself up the career ladder, and eventually became a broker, specializing in high-end properties in the greater Miami area."

Lavender was duly impressed. "That must be very exciting."

"Indeed it is. I deal almost exclusively with famous actors, musicians, and professional athletes."

The waiter brought their appetizers and refilled their wine glasses. "Did you ever miss home?" Lavender asked.

Richard chuckled. "No, not really. Once you've acquired a taste for Florida sunshine, it's hard to return to the northern climate."

"You and Ron must not have seen each other very often."

"We were close growing up, but we grew apart as adults. I suppose that was to be expected, given the distance between us and the very different career paths we chose to follow."

Their entrees arrived and the conversation lagged as they savored their lobster tails and filet mignons, and drank more wine. "Enough about me," Richard said between bites. "I'd like to hear more about you and Ron. It will do my heart good to hear about the happier times in my brother's life. How did you the two of you meet?"

Smiling sweetly, Lavender related the story of how she and Burley had met, omitting the minor detail of her having been married at the time. "How romantic," Richard said. "He was a lucky man to have met an enchanting woman like you." He raised his glass for a toast. "To Ron."

Lavender drank deeply, gazing back at Richard over her wineglass. The sting of seeing Clint with his Lifetime Movie replacement family hadn't faded yet. It wasn't fair that her ex had found happiness when her future had been snatched right out from under her. Maybe Richard was the antidote. He was more handsome, more sophisticated, and much better off financially than his older brother, not to mention having the ability to walk, talk, and feed himself. A guy like him would be a real catch.

Richard began chattering about the attractions of Miami, and ordered another bottle of wine. Lavender was feeling pleasantly tipsy. They finished their meals and the waiter returned with the dessert menu. "They have my favorite, creme brulee," Richard said. "Would you care to share a dish of it with me?"

"I *love* creme brulee." Even though Lavender normally turned down dessert, if Richard was offering it, she was accepting. When the dish arrived, she dipped her spoon in and let the creamy goodness slide across her tongue. Tingles of lust were stirring inside her, fueled by the glass of sauterne that arrived with the dessert. It had been a long time.

Richard set his spoon down. "There's something I've been wondering about." He dabbed his lips with a linen napkin and set it aside. "Why was my brother in Pennsylvania?"

It took a second for Lavender to wrench her thoughts from the sexual fantasy unfolding inside her head. "He had a friend down there who died," she said. "A woman he knew since they were kids. You might know her—Marta Grolsch?"

Richard nodded. "Yes, I remember Marta. They were best friends for years. How did she come to pass away so young?"

"She had cancer."

"I'm sorry to hear that. Ron had driven down for her funeral, I take it?"

Why did he want to dwell on depressing stuff like this? Lavender sucked down more wine before answering. She was sliding past tipsy now, heading for drunk. "No, he missed the funeral, but Marta's niece emailed him and said there was an envelope she needed to give to him."

Richard raised his eyebrows. "An envelope?"

"Yeah, he was convinced she'd left him some money."

"So, he was on his way home with the envelope when the accident occurred?"

"I guess so," Lavender said. The wine was really loosening her up, which was a good thing; otherwise, she might not have the nerve for what she was fantasizing about doing with Richard tonight. A pang of guilt surfaced but she brushed it away. Burley's condition was hopeless, so why shouldn't she take advantage of what was right here in front of her? She deserved a bit of comfort after the hell she'd been through over the past several weeks.

"Where is it now?" Richard was staring at her, and Lavender felt his knee press against hers beneath the table, interrupting her X-rated thoughts.

"Where is what?" she said.

"The envelope. What became of it? Was it recovered after the accident?"

The guy must think he was on CSI or something. She had no idea what had become of the stupid envelope. "I don't know," she said. "It's gone. The truck was totaled and they towed it to a junkyard somewhere in the boonies. All the state police found in it was his cellphone. They passed it on to me, and I pitched it. It didn't work anymore because he hadn't paid his bill. It was only a cheap flip phone, anyway."

Richard frowned. "Was my brother having financial difficulties?"

Lavender snorted. "Oh yeah, he was in debt in a big way. We hired a lawyer but it didn't help, so he was counting on that bequeathment or whatever you call it, to dig himself out of the hole."

Richard placed his hands on the tabletop. "He was anticipating a significant amount of money, then?"

"Hell, yeah. So much money that he took off in the middle of a snowstorm in that piece of shit truck of his, and—" A lump clogged Lavender's throat. Hapless, gentle Burley. He wasn't dead yet, but she already missed him. "Do you mind if we don't talk about this anymore?" She snatched her napkin from her lap and threw it onto the table.

"Certainly," Richard said. "Please forgive me if I've been insensitive."

Lavender had had enough conflicting emotion for one night. "I'd really like to go home now, if you don't mind."

After signaling for the check, Richard handed over a credit card, but the waiter returned a minute later with an embarrassed look on his face. "I'm sorry, sir," he said in a low voice. "Your card was declined."

Richard looked deeply insulted. "There must be some mistake." He thumbed through his wallet and produced another card, which he handed imperiously to the waiter.

Once the bill was settled, they returned to the hostess stand, where a girl appeared with Lavender's coat. As Richard helped her into it, she was swept into the heady fragrance of his cologne. The fantasies returned with a riotous vengeance and she felt herself getting hot. She was craving an escape from the shock and sadness of the past weeks, a release that would blot out the pain of her loss. Taking a pair of black leather gloves from her pocket, she drew them on with a provocative look at Richard that screamed *Take me to bed.* As they stepped outside into the starry night, he drew her close and kissed her.

CHAPTER 30

Marta followed Richard's rental car from the restaurant to Lavender's house, and watched them rush inside. They were so keen to get to the bedroom that she was easily able to slip unnoticed into the house after them. She hid in the boy's room, plugging her ears to the obscene moaning and grunting, and the interminable thumping of the headboard against the wall.

When the commotion had quieted down, Marta ventured out of her hiding place and went into the kitchen. The overhead light was still on from when the lovebirds had blown through in their sex-crazed frenzy; she turned it off and activated the flashlight on her phone, and shined it around the room. It was a cute place, if you were into 1970s kitsch. It reminded her of the house she and Ken had moved into when they were newlyweds.

• • •

Fresh out of college, and totally into each other. Marta agreed to stay in Pennsylvania so they could get married, and life had been a dream come true at first. Kenny's degree was in business, so when his cousin died, he was fully prepared to assume ownership of the roofing company. It wasn't a glamorous operation but Ken was proud of it, and Marta was more than willing to do her part by helping out around the office. They were happy back then, weren't they? Building their future together. They put off having kids and poured all their energy into growing the business.

Several years passed, and then the arguments started. Marta felt it was time they started thinking about having children, but Ken said he wasn't ready, and what was the rush? He was burdened with work and had no time to spare for a family. Another year went by, fraught with tension and strained emotions. When Ken finally grew weary of her pleading and agreed to try for a baby, Marta learned she wasn't able to conceive due to the premature failure of her ovaries.

The news crushed her. As a woman, she'd suddenly been rendered inadequate. Damaged. It triggered something ugly in her psyche, and she became intensely afraid that her husband was going to abandon her for being useless. She knew her fears weren't logical, but her feelings seemed to have a life of their own, and they sometimes overwhelmed her.

• • •

A noise from the bedroom startled Marta back to the present. Ducking behind the breakfast bar, she held her breath and listened, but all was quiet. She knew she ought to leave, but she had a feeling she should stay and see what Richard would do in the morning. She remembered what a cunning, manipulative little prick he'd been growing up, and she suspected the intervening years hadn't changed him a bit. Returning to the boy's room, she took his pillow and blanket, and crawled underneath the bed.

CHAPTER 31

Lavender awoke to the squeak of her shower turning on and the dull ache of a hangover pulsing inside her head. She groaned and rolled over, wondering if Burley had put the coffee on yet.

The sound of a male voice singing the opening lines of *Freebird* jolted her wide awake. Clutching the comforter to her bare chest, she sat up and saw a pair of chinos and a cashmere sweater folded neatly on the armchair in the corner, and realized it wasn't Ron Burley in her bathroom, washing away the sticky remnants of a night of love, it was his much better-endowed and far more talented brother Richard.

Guilt hit her hard—she'd slept with her fiancé's *brother!* It was wrong on so many levels. She pulled the comforter up to her chin and squeezed her eyes shut. *Please let this be a drunken dream.*

But what a night it had been! The snippets of it that she could remember, at least. She'd never known how inventive sex could be. Flopping back onto the pillows, she stretched her arms over her head and let out a long, satisfied yawn.

The shower turned off and Richard came out of the bathroom with a towel tucked low on his waist and his lustrous hair slicked back from his forehead. His skin was a smooth tanning-booth bronze, and his sexy radiance evaporated Lavender's cloud of shame. The fact that they'd spent the night together wasn't a bad thing, necessarily. With Richard's similar looks, it was almost like he was an extension of his brother. Burley wouldn't want her to be sad and lonely forever, would he? He'd want her to move on and be happy. Richard's sudden appearance in her life might be the universe's way of evening things up.

Lavender wriggled her shoulders to make the comforter slip down off her breasts and crooked a finger at Richard. He grinned but didn't jump back into bed with her; instead, he reached for his boxer briefs and undershirt, and proceeded to get dressed.

"What's your hurry?" Lavender said. "Got something you need to do this morning?"

Richard bent down and kissed her. "Yes," he said, tucking a strand of her hair behind her ear. "There's something we both need to do."

Lavender gripped her pounding head. "Can you get me a couple Tylenol first? I can hardly think straight with this headache." Richard went into the bathroom, shook two tablets out of a bottle in the medicine cabinet, and brought them to her with a glass of water. "Okay, what is it that we need to do?" Lavender said when she'd washed the pills down.

"We need to find that envelope."

Lavender squinted in confusion, and then it clicked. "Oh, you mean the one that Bur... I mean, the one Ron was going to get from Marta's niece?"

Richard picked up his sweater and shook the creases out of it. "Yes. We've got to find it." He pulled the sweater over his head and checked himself in the mirror. "I know my brother. He wouldn't have driven all that way to pick up an envelope from a stranger unless he was certain it contained something of great value."

It occurred to Lavender that Richard couldn't have known his brother very well, on account of being gone for the past fifteen years; but this was no time to quibble. "You're right," she said. "He was smarter than that."

"Exactly. If Marta did in fact leave him some money when she died, we have an obligation to act on his behalf to secure those funds. With his extensive injuries, he's going to have a pressing need for them, to pay for his long-term medical care."

Lavender nodded. "Definitely."

"Assuming there *is* money involved here. Which we don't know."

"Right. We don't know."

"But if there is, we need to act, and soon."

They stared at each other for a few seconds. Lavender ran her fingers along the satiny edge of the comforter. "What do we do?"

Richard began to pace. "First, we need to get in touch with Marta's niece and tell her what happened to Ron on his drive home. She might not know about the accident, since it happened in the middle of nowhere. Then we'll ask her what was in that missing envelope. If there was a check in it, she could perhaps stop payment on it, and send him a new one."

"But I don't have a phone number for her," Lavender said. "Or for Marta, either. I tried looking it up, but it isn't listed. I don't even know what town she lived in, or what the name of her company is."

"What about email? You said the niece emailed Ron."

"She did, but I don't have her email address." Lavender thought for a second. Burley had always left his email account open so he wouldn't have to remember his password. She smiled at Richard. "I know how to get it, though. We can go over to your brother's place and look it up on his computer."

Richard stopped pacing, darted his hand out and tweaked the covers off Lavender's naked body, making her squeal. "Get moving, woman!" He swatted her butt cheek. "We've got things to do."

They drove out to Burley's trailer. The dogs had been farmed out to a neighbor, after having a crapfest all over the place in the days after the accident. "Mind if I look around?" Richard asked.

"Go ahead." Lavender dropped her coat and purse onto the coach. She didn't want to be here anymore, this part of her life was over. She tapped her foot impatiently as Richard made a quick circuit of his brother's dingy rooms, poking his nose into closets and drawers. He circled back to the small living room and paused in front of the gun cabinet, which now held only the Winchester rifle. "What did he do with all his guns? He used to have a whole collection of them."

Lavender came to stand beside him. "I have no idea. I never really noticed what was in there."

Richard opened the cabinet and removed the rifle. "I remember this. It used to belong to my brother Russ." He put the gun to his shoulder and aimed it out the window at the Chevy Spark in the snowy driveway, then lowered it and returned it to the cabinet. "I never got into hunting the way my brothers did. Didn't quite see the point of it." He looked around. "Is there a desk or something, where he keeps his important papers?"

Lavender went to the kitchen and pointed at one of the cupboards. "He kept all his bills and things in there."

Richard opened the cupboard and riffled through a handful of file folders, but then he set them down. "It isn't my place to be going through his things. I'm his brother, but you're his fiancée. I think it's more appropriate if you do it."

Lavender shrugged. "I don't mind, really. Let's do it together." They each took a folder and opened it.

"One thing, though," Richard said in an offhand way. "I think we should make sure we find his bank account information and any other important documents, such as his birth certificate and social security card, and bring them to your house for safekeeping."

"Good idea." Lavender located the documents, put them in a separate folder and tucked it into her purse. "I already have his driver's license and insurance card," she said. "The nurse gave them to me when he was transferred to the nursing home."

"Very good," Richard said. "Now let's have a look at his email." They sat down at the computer, and it was a simple matter for Lavender to access Burley's email.

The messages from Lyla were at the top of his inbox. Lavender read them out loud with Richard hanging over her shoulder. When they got to the one about Lyla finding the envelope with Burley's name on it, Richard let out a low whistle. "It's got to have something to do with her will." He stroked his chin, thinking hard. "Yes, it's almost certainly money," he said after a moment, and his serious expression broke into a grin.

Lavender grinned back at him. "What do we do next?"

Richard leaned over her, one hand on his hip, the other braced on the table. "We write back to her, but we have to be careful how we word it. If she finds out he's been badly injured and can't even walk or talk, she might think we're trying to take advantage of the situation, when we're actually trying to help him. So, here's what I think we should do: you write the email as if it's coming from Ron. Tell her you got into a little fender bender on your way home from Pennsylvania and somehow misplaced the envelope, then ask her if she could she possibly replace whatever was in it, and mail it to you."

Lavender looked doubtful. "A month later, I'm telling her this?"

Richard waved his hand. "You could say you broke your hand in the accident, and it took you a while to recover to where you could type on the computer again."

"What if I say it was a broken shoulder, and I had to have surgery? That makes it sound more serious and believable."

Richard kissed the top of Lavender's head. "Damn, you're good. Beautiful *and* smart."

· · ·

They returned to the trailer every day for a week to check Burley's email, but no reply came from Lyla. "It seems strange that she hasn't responded," Lavender said as they lounged in her bed after making love one evening. Logan had started spending most nights with his father now, and Richard was enjoying the benefits of the arrangement. "You'd think she'd want to make sure her aunt's last wishes were carried out."

"Maybe she feels she's already done her duty," Richard said, "and she doesn't want to deal with it anymore." He laced his hands behind his head and sank into thought.

Lavender propped her chin on her hand and silently admired him. He was so darned handsome, so amazingly physically fit. Unlike his brother. In the months before the accident, Burley had really started to let himself go. The extra pounds and lack of energy were undoubtedly due to the stress he'd been under, but that was no excuse for not keeping yourself looking attractive for your girlfriend. Lavender laid her hand on Richard's smooth chest, felt the powerful beating of his heart. It was wonderful to be with him, he made her feel so safe and secure. They already felt like an established couple, spending every free moment together. Burley had been a good man, but when his brother held her in his arms, Lavender was certain she'd finally found the true man of her dreams.

Richard stirred from his musings. "I think I know what our next step is. I'll bet the police in Pennsylvania didn't bother to do a thorough check of Ron's truck since it was totally wrecked. If they found any important documents, they would have already contacted his next of kin. We've got to make some phone calls and find out what junkyard the truck was towed to after the accident. Then we'll go down there, locate the truck, and search through it until we find that envelope."

Lavender gazed at Richard, her eyes shining with admiration. "You're a genius," she said, scooting closer for a kiss. Next thing she knew, they were back at it.

CHAPTER 32

Crane's Auto Salvage in the township of Guthrie, Pennsylvania, was a multi-acre labyrinth of vehicle carcasses. Lavender and Richard walked into the pole barn that served as an office, and the proprietor eyed them curiously as they paid the $2 entrance fee. "We're looking for a 1998 Ford Ranger that was towed here about six weeks ago," Richard said. "Can you tell us where we might find it?"

The man consulted his computer. "It's in row eighteen. Go about halfway down the center road and you'll see all the Ford trucks on your left. You brought your own tools, didn't you?"

Richard held up the crowbar and flashlight they'd purchased at a Tractor Supply on their way to the junkyard. Lavender followed him outside and they picked their way across the sprawling lot, past assorted makes and models of cars and trucks in various states of scavenging. Some of the vehicles lacked doors or a hood, others were missing the entire engine block. They came to row number eighteen and walked to the end of it, where the remains of Burley's rusted blue pickup rested next to a frozen drainage ditch.

The roof of the truck was caved in and driver's door was hanging ajar, and for a few awful seconds, Lavender pictured it tumbling down the mountainside with Burley trapped inside, and had to shake her head hard to dispel the horrible image. She hung back while Richard checked the glove compartment and center console, but both were empty. He squatted down and felt beneath the driver's seat, and found only an empty Pepsi can that he tossed aside. Walking around to the passenger's side, he pulled on the door; it was stuck fast and he had to use the crowbar to pry it open. Nothing under that seat, either. He grabbed hold of the seatback and tried to tilt it forward, but it was jammed in place. Using the crowbar again, he wrenched the seat free and peered behind it.

"Give me the flashlight!" he said. "I think I see something."

Lavender handed it over and crowded in behind him. "What is it, what do you see?"

Richard leaned into the cab and stretched his arm as far as he could behind the seat, then pulled back and raised his arm in triumph, a manila envelope in his hand.

"You found it!" Lavender shrieked, and threw her arms around him, laughing and exclaiming. "Open it, open it!"

The afternoon shadows were lengthening and the temperature had begun to drop. "Let's wait till we're in the car," Richard said, "so we'll have privacy." He tucked the envelope inside his coat and they hurried back across the muddy lot and through the barn, where the owner nodded absently at them when he saw they were empty-handed.

When they were back in their car, Richard passed the envelope to Lavender. "I think you should open it."

Lavender slid her finger beneath the flap, loosened it and drew out the letter. She read the first paragraph and turned to Richard in astonishment. "She left him a million dollars. A freaking *million*."

• • •

They stopped at a Hardee's for double cheeseburgers, and ate their meal in silence as the discovery of Burley's enormous inheritance sank in. "Here's what we'll do," Richard said at last, crumpling his empty burger wrapper. "We'll drive back to Helmsburg and get my brother's ID and bank account information, then I'll fly to Philadelphia, go to the law firm, and present myself as Ronald Burley to the attorneys."

Lavender was aghast. "You're going to steal his identity?"

"What else are we supposed to do? In his present condition, he can't very well walk into a lawyer's office and collect the money himself, can he?"

"Obviously not," Lavender said. "But isn't there some other way to do this, that isn't illegal?"

Richard leaned across the table and lowered his voice. "We've got a golden opportunity here, Lavender. My brother needs money to cover his medical bills, but not the entire million dollars. Think about it. We can put a portion of it away for him, to make sure he's taken care of, but he'll never be able to spend the rest. After all the effort you and I have made on his behalf, I think we deserve a piece of the pie." He nodded his head at Lavender. "You, especially. Think of how you stood by him through his financial difficulties, and then the accident. You've been so loyal and patient. It says a lot about you." He caressed the back of her left hand, which still held her engagement ring. She really needed to take that thing off.

Lavender stared down at Richard's tanned hand covering hers. It was so strong and masculine. Feeling his eyes on her, she looked up. A lock of his dark hair had fallen over his handsome brow and she had to stop her herself from brushing it back. "You make a good point," she said. "We do have to help him because it's the right thing to do, but we should consider our own needs, too. It only makes sense."

"Yes," Richard said. "It does make sense. Ron's needs will be our first priority, naturally. I have an attorney friend who can act as his legal guardian. We'll make absolutely sure he's being properly cared for before we even begin to think about ourselves."

Lavender liked how Richard kept saying "we," as if they were a team. It felt good to be treated like an equal partner for a change, instead of having to be the one calling the shots. The whole time she and Burley were dating, she'd always had to tell him what to do and how to do it. Sure, he'd paid for their occasional dinner dates and movie tickets, but that was small beans compared to the finer things in life that his brother appeared to be well acquainted with. Richard was an assertive, take-charge man who didn't require the constant instruction and badgering that his brother had.

"I agree with everything you're saying," Lavender said. "What's our next step?"

Richard explained the rest of his plan: after the million dollars was deposited in Burley's bank account, he'd fly home to Miami, where he would consult the list of high profile contacts he'd acquired through his real estate dealings. He'd find someone who could set up a secret offshore account, then transfer the bulk of the money into it, leaving enough behind in Burley's account to cover his medical needs.

"And then," Richard said, taking Lavender's hands, "you and I will disappear into the Caribbean."

"Wait a minute." Lavender pushed her cold french fries aside. "You don't expect me to run off with you and leave my son behind, do you?"

Richard looked surprised. "I thought that was what you wanted. You've been complaining to me this whole time about what a difficult child he is, and how much you hate living in Helmsburg."

"Logan is difficult," Lavender conceded, "but I can't just abandon him. And what will my ex-husband think if I up and disappear? I'm sure he'll be suspicious. He might even get the police involved, and our whole plan will unravel."

"You wouldn't be leaving forever. You could say you're taking an extended vacation in the islands, to recover from the trauma of Ron's accident."

"And then what?"

"And then," Richard said, leaning across the table to kiss her, "you decide you're madly in love with me. You call your ex and tell him you've met someone, and you've decided to stay. You'll have more than enough money to fly back and forth to see your son whenever you want to."

The possibility of trading the cold, grey Adirondack winters for piña coladas and white sand beaches gave Lavender a heady thrill. It might actually work. She'd divide her time between Helmsburg and the Caribbean, and Logan could come visit on his school breaks.

But still. "It's really tempting," she said, "but I can't do it. It's too much to drop on a ten-year-old kid."

"You need to look at this a different way." Richard's eyes sparkled as he grasped Lavender's hands. "We'll be building a new life together, for all three of us. I already love Logan like he's my own son, and I'd want to have him with us as often as possible. We'll use the money to spoil him with surfing lessons and scuba gear, maybe even buy him his own sailboat. He'll be loving life down there!"

Lavender weighed this for a moment. Clint's small-town offerings would pale in comparison. Moving to the tropics would be an impressive way of making it up to Logan for her years of sloppy parenting, and a potent means of sticking it to her ex. "How soon would this have to happen?" she asked.

"As soon as possible." Richard turned grave. "Time is of the essence here, Lavender. The sooner we put things in motion, the safer we are."

• • •

The next day, Lavender handed Burley's identification and banking information over to Richard, so he could book a flight to Philadelphia in his brother's name. The plan was for Lavender to lie low in Helmsburg until Richard sent word that the money had been secured and he was on his way to Florida; then she'd catch a flight out of Syracuse, and meet up with him again in Miami.

Secrecy was crucial. "You'll need to keep your travel plans as quiet as possible," Richard warned her, "so no one starts asking questions. Tell your family you're going away with your girlfriends for a few days, and be vague about the details. We don't want anyone getting wise to what we're doing, and reporting us to the police."

While Richard was busy making his travel arrangements, Lavender returned to Burley's trailer to pick up the clothing his brother would need for his subterfuge at the law firm. The weather had turned warmer overnight, and a layer of dirty snow covered the yard like a soggy blanket. Lavender pushed the front door open and stood still for a moment. It felt creepy being alone in the silent trailer. She went straight to the bedroom and found a pair of jeans in a dresser drawer and a clean flannel shirt hanging in the closet. Folding the clothing under her arm, she went back out to the living room.

Something seemed out of place. Lavender scanned the room, but nothing caught her eye until she came to the gun cabinet. It was empty. That was strange—she clearly remembered her first visit here with Richard, when he had removed the Winchester rifle, played around with it for a minute, then put it back.

What the hell had become of it? Right away, she thought of the unlocked front door. By now, it was common knowledge that Burley was stuck in a nursing home, so some opportunistic jerk had probably come out here and stolen the gun. It was a good thing they'd had the foresight to take Burley's important papers away with them. Lavender took a quick look around the trailer to make sure she hadn't overlooked anything else, and made sure the door was locked when she left this time.

She returned to her house, where Richard was packing his things. His flight to Philadelphia didn't leave until the next day, but he'd booked a room in a motel near the Syracuse airport for the night, thinking it would be safer to make his final preparations in a location other than Helmsburg.

When he was ready, Richard set off in the Spark and Lavender followed him in the Impala. They returned the rental car at the airport, then drove to a dismal Rodeway Inn off the Thruway. Richard checked in and paid cash up front, then went out to find a barber shop while Lavender waited in the room. When he returned, his beautifully thick hair had been shorn to match his brother's plain country style.

Lavender gave him the clothing she'd taken from Burley's bedroom. Richard changed into the flannel shirt and jeans, and put on the Carhartt coat and work boots that Lavender had removed from

Burley's closet at the nursing home. He turned from side to side in front of the mirror. "How do I look?"

Lavender caught her breath. "Good. You look just like him."

"Don't forget," Richard said, coming over to hug her. "We're doing this for Ron."

• • •

The next day, they said goodbye to each other at the motel. Richard gave Lavender last-minute instructions: "Try to stay out of sight for the next few days. If you need groceries, stop at a store around here where no one knows you, then go home and stay put until you hear from me. Don't try to call me, I'll call you. We don't want to leave an electronic trail."

It was getting a little too real. Lavender plucked nervously at Richard's sleeve. "I'm not sure I'm ready to go through with this. Can't we wait another day, and go over all the details one more time, so we don't screw anything up?"

"No." Richard shook his head in irritation. "We have to move fast, before he dies. That would spoil everything."

The sordidness of it all cut through Lavender like an icy wind, and the harsh words rang in her ears: *Before he dies. Before Burley dies.*

CHAPTER 33

Heeding Richard's warning to keep a low profile, Lavender stopped for groceries at a Tops Friendly Market near the airport. Her shopping list was short: coffee, bagels, a few cans of soup. At the checkout, she was about to swipe her credit card, then thought better of it and paid with cash. Walking out to the car with her plastic grocery bags in her hands, she looked over her shoulder to make sure no one was following her.

As she continued the ninety-minute drive home through a light rain, Lavender passed the turnoff for the road leading to Old Forge, and suddenly thought of the stream of dollar bills that Penelope had claimed she'd seen flying through the air. Did the money even exist, or was Marta toying with them from beyond the grave? On an impulse, she swung the car into a sharp U-turn, and her tires sent up a slushy spray as she sped in the direction of the psychic's house on Birdsong Lane.

Penelope didn't seem surprised when she answered her door. "Hello there," she said, sounding a touch less welcoming than she had in the past. "You look like you could use a cup of tea." Lavender settled into her usual armchair and tried to compose herself with cleansing breaths. Penelope brought the tea things and filled both their cups, then seated herself in the other chair. "What can I help you with today?"

"Remember those photos I texted to you, when we did the phone session a while ago? I need to know more about that woman, Marta."

Penelope held her hand out. "Let me see her picture again."

Lavender pulled the photo up on her phone and handed it over. "I want to know what she was planning to do with all her money before she died."

Penelope scrutinized the photo, then looked up at Lavender. "As I told you before, I don't believe she's dead, and she doesn't have cancer, either."

"But her niece said she was dead! She emailed Burley and told him he'd missed her funeral."

"Her niece, you say? I'm not feeling any vibrations coming in around a niece." Penelope closed her eyes and her brow crimped in concentration. "There's no niece, or any other children. She's barren." Her eyes opened again. "She hasn't got a pot to piss in, either. Don't be fooled by those stories she's been telling, about having loads of money. You'd better be careful. I'm telling you, she's looney tunes."

Lavender clutched the arms of her chair. Richard was on his way to Philadelphia to meet with—*who?* Batshit crazy Marta, and her make-believe niece? He was about to walk smack into the middle of something that was seriously messed up. She jumped to her feet, spilling her tea on the rug. "He's in trouble," she said. "I've got to do something."

"Ron is fine," Penelope said. "He's safe where he is."

"No, no, not Ron. I meant, um… someone else. A friend. It's complicated."

Penelope looked amused. "I'm sure it is."

"It's a long story. I don't have time to go into it now."

Penelope *tsked* and shook her head. "You're such a young soul, and you're not learning anything as you go along."

Lavender groped for her car keys in her purse. "I have to go."

"That's fine, dear. You can PayPal me later."

The moment she was in her car, Lavender dialed Richard's number, but the call went to voicemail. Checking the time, she realized his flight had departed already. She hung up without leaving a message, hoping he wouldn't get mad at her for calling when he'd specifically told her not to. Her heart was hammering and she felt sick with fear, but there wasn't anything she could do until Richard arrived in Philadelphia and called her back. She started the car and headed for home.

CHAPTER 34

Marta parked around the corner from Lavender's house and waited for dusk to fall, then used a credit card to jimmy the back door. Moving through the empty house, she entered the master bedroom. She was afraid she'd missed her chance and her quarry had skipped town already, but when she threw the closet door open, Lavender's clothes were still there.

The fools had played right into her hands. After she had followed Lavender and Richard back here after their first date, she'd spent an uncomfortable night under the boy's bed while they banged away in the next room, but her patience was rewarded in the morning when she overheard them talking about going to Pennsylvania to find Burley's truck. It was ridiculously easy to predict what their next move would be, once they got their hands on the envelope. She was certain that Richard, still the same greedy bastard she remembered from her youthful summers on Fourth Lake, would try to claim the money for himself; and lovestruck, dipshit Lavender would undoubtedly agree to be his accomplice.

Marta stretched out on Lavender's unmade bed that smelled of Downy April Fresh and sex, and remembered how it used to be with Ken. The chemistry between them was intense, and they'd made a pastime out of getting it on in unusual places. But after the discovery that she couldn't have children, the spontaneity they'd once reveled in had shriveled to sporadic, passionless encounters that eventually disappeared altogether. The young daughter she'd bragged about to Burley was purely imaginary, a pretty scrap of window dressing she'd invented to salve her wounded ego.

Her marriage became volatile. As the days went by, Ken added to his litany of complaints about her—inappropriate anger, unpredictable mood swings, frightening impulsiveness—and she'd lashed out viciously at him in self-defense. Her natural tendency toward sarcasm became bitter and hurtful, as though she was deliberately trying to push him away.

Her erratic behavior spiraled for endless, exhausting weeks that stretched into months, and then a full year. Ken dragged her to a marriage counselor, who was deeply concerned by what he heard, and referred Marta to a psychiatrist for intensive therapy. But by then it was too late. Ken was done. He'd traveled too far down this godawful road with her and he couldn't take anymore.

Marta had idolized her husband, but Ken had turned cold and uncaring, and couldn't get away from her fast enough. He packed his bags and vanished one day while she was at the drug store, picking up the medication that her new doctor had prescribed. To avoid the mortification of being exposed as an abandoned wife, she told her elderly parents back in Helmsburg that her husband had died unexpectedly of an undiagnosed heart defect, and to honor the wishes of his family, the funeral service would be private.

Their split was excruciating. She was angry with Ken, so angry! The coward had bailed on her before she even had a chance to get well. A husband was supposed to stick by his wife's side, help her through the pain of the rough patches. When the aftershocks of the divorce subsided somewhat, Marta found her mind floating back to tranquil memories of her childhood and adolescence, and the happy times she'd shared with her old friend Burley. He crept into her dreams, lingered at the edge of her thoughts. She convinced herself that he was The One, the man she should have been with all along. Their teenage romance had budded too soon, before Burley was mature enough to recognize his destiny standing right in front of him.

A year ago, she'd made her second play for him by dangling money and easy sex in his face, and when that didn't work, she tried guilt-tripping him with the elaborate cancer hoax. She'd always been slender, so it didn't take long to drop a few more pounds by taking laxatives and drinking quantities of green tea. On the nights before she saw Burley, she'd purposely deprived herself of sleep, to enhance the bags under her eyes and the pallor of her skin. She really *was* freezing on that snowmobile ride they'd taken together, thanks to starving herself and getting her weight down to a dangerous level. She'd even shaved her own head.

But her plan didn't have a chance of succeeding, thanks to that married hussy who had snared Burley with her slutty ways. They both deserved to suffer—Burley for leading Marta on once again, then cruelly rejecting her, and Lavender for stealing him away.

The sound of a car engine interrupted Marta's thoughts. She jumped up from the bed, ran to the kitchen and peeked through the blinds. Behind the cold curtain of rain falling outside, the taillights of the Impala glowed red in the driveway. She needed to hide, quick. Opening the door to the cellar, she hurried down the stairs.

CHAPTER 35

It was dark out when Lavender got home, and the light drizzle had turned to a cold, steady rain. She ducked her head and ran inside. Kicking her shoes off, she sat down at the kitchen table and tried to make sense of her situation. Everything had happened so fast—Burley's accident, Richard's arrival, finding the letter from the law firm. It was all so bewildering.

She thought some more about Penelope's assertion that Marta was neither deceased nor a millionaire. How could it possibly be true, when Burley had seen with his own eyes how ill she was with cancer? And how would Marta have gotten hold of that letter from the law firm? It had looked completely genuine and official.

There was a good chance Penelope had been wrong about everything. Take that nonsense about Burley's explosive temper, for instance. As far as Lavender knew, he'd never raised a hand at anyone in his life, not even that prick Nielsen, who deserved to be punched in the teeth. Penelope wasn't God, after all; she was just a dotty old grandma with a weird hobby, and that hogwash she'd spewed about Marta not being dead was just too crazy to be true.

The key to it all was Richard. He wouldn't have been fooled by the letter if it was a fake-he was much too intelligent to fall for something like that. Lavender needed to have faith in him, and forget about everything else. His ploy at the law firm was going to go off without a hitch, and they'd soon be reunited in Miami.

She slapped the table with both hands. That's it, she was done worrying. She'd wait for Richard's call, and get herself ready to leave in the meantime. Taking her phone out to make sure she hadn't missed a text from him, she saw a missed call from Copper that must have come in as she was passing through a dead spot on her way back from Syracuse.

Copper had left a testy voicemail, demanding to know why Lavender hadn't shown up for work at noon. *Oops.* So much for not attracting anyone's attention. She was about to call back with a made-up excuse, then thought the hell with it. In a few more days she'd be gone from this sleepy town and on her way to a sun-drenched Caribbean island with the handsome, clever new boyfriend that she was fast becoming positively infatuated with.

Time to start packing. Lavender opened the door to the cellar and pulled the string on the bare lightbulb, illuminating the unfinished walls of the narrow stairwell. The wooden steps creaked beneath her feet as she made her way down, past the opaque black rectangle of a dusty casement window. Stretching up on her toes, she yanked the string on a second light, exposing a cement floor littered with plastic storage bins, outgrown kiddie toys and pieces of broken furniture. The shadowy corners of the cellar creeped her out. She grabbed her rolling suitcase from the shelf beneath the staircase and bumped it up the steps, leaving the light burning below.

Lavender wheeled the suitcase into her bedroom and began going through the dresser. Clint's side of it was empty except for one drawer that Lavender's collection of bras and panties had spilled over into. Her sweaters could stay where they were in the bottom of the dresser, but all her tees, tanks and shorts needed to be packed. She piled the summery clothing onto the bed along with her bikinis and her swim cover-up, then went to the closet and gathered an armful of gauzy blouses, sundresses and capri pants. Turquoise waters and sandy beaches called to her as she sorted through her clothes. No more heavy fabrics, no more dark colors!

When she was finished, Lavender shoved several pairs of shoes into the overloaded suitcase on top of her haphazardly folded clothing, then kneeled on it and tugged the zipper closed. A last-minute thought prompted her to pack a small overnight bag of warmer clothing and toiletries, to get her through the next few days. She rolled her luggage out to the kitchen and set it by the back door, laying over the top of it the heavy winter coat that she planned on stuffing into a trash can the moment she arrived in Miami.

Traveling light was necessary for a quick getaway, but she wanted to be sure she hadn't forgotten anything. Lavender wandered around the silent house, turning on lights and peeking into closets. In Logan's room, she paused to look at the pictures and pennants on the walls. He'd grown up so much in the past year! The colorful Minecraft and Mario Kart posters that he used to love had been replaced by sinister images of Hogwarts Castle and the Desolation of Smaug, and his bookshelf was crowded with fat volumes of *Harry Potter* and *The Lord of the Rings*, books he was proud of owning but struggled to read.

Overcome with emotion, Lavender sank onto the bed. When Logan was born, she'd resented his intrusion in her life. It wasn't his fault that he was unplanned and unwanted—by his mother, at least. Clint had been excited about becoming a father, once he'd recovered from the initial shock. He'd been more than willing to marry Lavender, and had gamely thrown himself into the responsibility of supporting his new family.

Clint had a natural gift for parenting, while Lavender was more like a reluctant babysitter. Leaving Logan behind with Clint and Cheryl would be the best thing for the boy, Lavender thought. He'd get the love and attention she'd never been capable of giving him. Richard's desire to be a stepfather to him was wonderfully touching and generous, but Logan's place was right here at home in Helmsburg.

Logan's favorite Hogwarts T-shirt was draped over the bedpost, a memento of his last overnight visit with his mother. Lavender held it to her nose, and memories flooded her mind—some happy, others not so much. Her conscience prodded her and she wondered if she should swing by Clint's house to see her son before she left. It might be better to tell him about her moving plans now, instead of waiting till after she was gone. But that would require explaining herself to Clint as well, which wasn't an option. He was certain to make a fuss about her moving so far away, which might put her and Richard's scheme in jeopardy.

Lavender folded the T-shirt and left it on the bed, then returned to the kitchen where she paced beneath the glare of the overhead light. The ice maker in the freezer dumped its load of cubes with a crash that made her jump, and her feet slowed to a halt. There was another sound, something barely audible over the hum of the refrigerator. She stood still and listened, and there it was again—a creak, followed by a faint shuffling. Her pulse quickened and goosebumps rose on her arms. The logical part of her brain told her that no one could be in the house when she'd walked through every room only minutes ago, but what about the cellar? Someone could be hiding down there, waiting for night and the chance to strike. Scenes from *Friday the 13th* flashed through her mind, and she suddenly felt like she couldn't breathe.

She had to get out of here! She pulled on her boots, grabbed her purse, coat, and the luggage, shot out the back door and ran through the rain to her car. After throwing the bags into the backseat, she jumped in the front and locked the doors, then took several deep yoga breaths and told herself she was safe, there was no need to panic anymore.

But where to go now? None of her choices were very enticing. Her parents' house was out of the question. After Burley's accident, Mr. and Mrs. LeClair had put two and two together about the affair that had ruined their daughter's marriage, and Lavender's involvement with Richard had only made matters worse. Another option was to drive down to Syracuse tonight, but the idea of holing up in a skeevy airport motel all by herself gave her the willies.

Maybe she should go to Shayna's house. Her girlfriend would be full of probing questions that Lavender couldn't really answer at the moment, but at least Shayna understood the reality of failed marriages and rebound relationships.

To Shayna's it was. Lavender took a final look at the place she'd called home for the past ten years—her entire adult life, in fact. She'd left the lights on when she ran out to the car, and the brightly-lit windows looked warm and cheerful, as though a happy family lived there.

Well, goodbye to all that. Her tedious life in Helmsburg was over and done with, except for one last thing she needed to do before she left forever. She started the engine and shifted the car into reverse, and as she was backing down the driveway past the house, she could have sworn she saw someone standing in the kitchen.

CHAPTER 36

The rain let up a bit as Lavender zoomed out of her neighborhood. The clock on her dashboard showed twenty-five minutes past seven; if she hurried, she'd be able to catch a glimpse of Logan as he came out of his trumpet lesson at 7:30.

She turned onto Main Street and slowed to a stop as the traffic light near the Mini Mart blinked from yellow to red. When the light changed to green, she hooked a quick left and parked around the corner from the apartment building where her son's music teacher lived. Keeping a wary eye out for Clint's Trailblazer, Lavender darted across the street and stood in the shadows beneath the arching branches of a leafless maple tree, where she had a clear view of the building's front entrance.

At precisely 7:29, the Trailblazer pulled up to the curb and Lavender shrank back into the darkness. Two minutes later, Logan emerged from the building with his trumpet case dangling from his hand. As Clint climbed out of his vehicle to greet his son, Logan switched to a run and crashed into his dad with a bear hug around the waist. The scene caused a lump to form in Lavender's throat, and her eyes filled with tears. She almost called out to them, but the poignance of the father-and-son moment held her back. Swallowing her tears, she continued watching from her place in the shadows until they'd driven away. *Her baby boy.* She hoped he wouldn't miss his mama too much after she was gone.

The route to Shayna's house went past the nursing home. As Lavender neared the one-story brick building, she pictured her luckless Burley trying to sleep with the head of his bed raised thirty degrees to prevent him from choking on his own spit, and a wave of remorse washed over her. *Oh heck,* she thought. What harm could come from a super-quick visit, to give him a kiss and say goodbye? She veered into the nursing home's driveway, and parked around the side of the building where the lighting wasn't so bright.

Visiting hours ended at 7:45, so there wasn't much time before the nurses came marching through the place, herding everyone out. Lavender breezed past the unmanned reception desk and hurried down the deserted main corridor, wrinkling her nose at the pervasive odor of Lysol. It wasn't an attractive facility, but at least they made an effort to keep it clean.

As she turned the corner onto Burley's hallway, she thought she heard someone coming and glanced over her shoulder, but saw only the tall linen cart stacked with towels and incontinence pads. A nursing assistant spoke to the resident in the next room, saying she'd be right back with the bedtime snacks. Lavender ducked behind the linen cart and waited until the young woman had disappeared down the hall, then darted into Burley's room.

He was still sitting up in his wheelchair. *Wheel of Fortune* was playing on a television mounted high on the wall, a strategic location that prevented the bedridden residents from playing with the channel buttons when the daytime staff wanted to catch the latest episode of *General Hospital* or *Dr. Phil.* Lavender turned the TV off, pulled a chair over and sat down next to Burley, and reached out to pat his stubbled cheek. His eyes traveled jerkily from the blank television screen to her face, and one corner of his mouth twitched up.

She took hold of his hand. It felt warm and familiar, and she rubbed her fingertips across his calloused palm. He'd always been such a hard worker, so reliable and industrious. Maybe that tenacity would see him through the discomforts he'd have to endure here in this lonely place, for however many more days remained in his life. Lavender wiped her brimming eyes, pressed her cheek to Burley's, and looped her arm around his neck. "I'll always love you," she whispered.

The tears welled over as she realized she couldn't bear the weight of her conscience any longer. "I'm so sorry, Burley," she sobbed. "I wish things could have turned out different." Words continued to tumble out as though she had no control over her tongue. "After the accident, I didn't know what I was going to do without you, but then Richard showed up and it seemed as if he'd come to take your place—in a good way, I mean. Don't feel bad. He's your brother and I care for him just as much as I cared for you. It's like I've been given a second chance at love. You're really sick now, and there's no way you could ever do anything with all that money Marta left you, so Richard and I are going to use it to make a fresh start for ourselves."

Lavender covered the side of Burley's face with kisses. "Oh sweetie, this is so hard for me. I'm leaving soon, to meet up with your brother, and I couldn't go away without saying goodbye to you."

A harsh choking sound rose from deep in Burley's throat. Lavender jerked her head back in alarm, and saw the color rising in his face, turning it from a sickly gray to purple. Scrambling for the call button on the bedrail, she pressed it frantically.

Something inside Burley snapped as a surreal power surged through his frozen limbs. He clamped his hands onto the tray table in front of him and hurled it to the floor. A primeval roar issued from the depths of his chest, and his useless legs came to life as he rose from the wheelchair, straining his arms toward Lavender. She ran to the door screaming for help, and collided head-on with Dustin.

A nurse came running right behind him. She charged into the room, the stethoscope around her neck swinging wildly. Using both hands, she pushed hard on Burley's chest, and he dropped into the wheelchair with a thud. With one hand splayed on Burley's chest to steady him, the nurse turned on Lavender. "*Get out of here*." She stabbed her free hand toward the door. "Get out. You can't come in here upsetting a patient like this." Lavender sputtered something in response, but the nurse raised her chin and showed her the palm of her hand. "Go, before I call security."

Lavender snatched up her purse and ran from the room with Dustin following close behind. "Hey, wait up!" he shouted. She almost ignored him and kept going, then realized some damage control might be necessary here, in case Dustin had overheard what she'd confessed to Burley.

Lavender stopped and turned around, and Dustin lumbered up to her, panting. When he'd worked for Burley, she'd always thought his attitude had bordered on servile, but something about him was different now. A hard glint shone in his eye, and his face was tight with anger. He came closer, stepping into Lavender's space. "I heard you in there," he said, his voice accusing. "I heard every single bit of what you said, about stealing his money and running off with his brother." Dustin's features twisted in disgust as he gripped his Mini Mart visor in his fist and shook it at her. "How could you do that to him, after all the suffering he's been through?"

Lavender spun around and made a break for the fire exit. Within thirty seconds, she was in her car and racing away from the nursing home with the pedal down. The *nerve* of that fatass! Who did he think he was, confronting her like that? It wasn't her fault that Burley had gone out in the middle of a blizzard and crashed his truck! And what she had decided to do with her life in the aftermath of the accident was no one else's damned business.

Realizing that she was speeding in the opposite direction from Shayna's house, Lavender slowed down and pulled over to the side of the road, and waited for her heart to stop racing. She thought of Richard at his Philadelphia hotel, prepping for the crime he was going to commit tomorrow. The need to get hold of him was doubly urgent now that their cover was blown.

But when Lavender dialed his number, he still didn't pick up. She tried to compose a text message explaining what had happened, but with her hands shaking so badly, she had to resort to typing CALL ME in all caps.

Another car approached from behind and slowed down as it went around her. Lavender knew she needed to keep moving in order not to attract attention, but where could she go? Dustin was onto her, and possibly that nasty nurse as well, so staying in town was out of the question. The only place she could think of was the cottage. The thought of driving by herself down that the dark forest road made her stomach knot up, but the remote location seemed like the most sensible choice. The Stillwater Hotel was close by, at least. She could get some dinner there, and a bottle of wine to take the edge off the coming night that it looked like she was going to have to spend alone.

CHAPTER 37

Richard was beyond annoyed when he finally landed in Philadelphia. His direct flight out of Syracuse had been cancelled due to mechanical problems, and he'd been rerouted with a connection through Detroit, of all places. It defied geographical logic. He didn't get to Philly until seven, then had to take a smelly taxi downtown to his hotel, because for some unknown reason there weren't any Ubers available. Checking his phone on the cab ride, he saw the missed call from Lavender earlier that afternoon, which irritated him even more. He'd specifically told her not to contact him. If the dumb broad wasn't more careful, she was going to screw up his whole plan.

In expectation of his coming riches, Richard would have liked to treat himself to a city view room at the Westin Philadelphia, but the constraints of his present circumstances dictated the more economical choice of the DoubleTree. He commended himself for the excellent job he'd done, convincing Lavender that he was a hotshot man of means. She didn't need to know the truth, which was that after years of effort, he was still only a low-level agent struggling for his commissions—a very small fish in the extremely large pond of Miami real estate. The opulent Virgin Islands cruise he'd boasted about to Lavender had actually been a three-night cheapie trip that he'd won in an office raffle.

After dumping his luggage in his room (standard, with a view of the parking lot), he went back downstairs to the hotel bar and ordered a Jack and ginger with lime. As the bartender was mixing the drink, Richard's phone lit up and he glanced at the screen: Lavender. *What the fuck?* Now he was truly pissed. The chick was cute as hell and ball-busting sexy, but he'd known from the start that he'd be better off going it alone. Lavender had served her purpose by helping him find the envelope and providing him with his brother's identification and other crucial documents, but now it was time to cut her loose. He pressed Decline and signaled to the bartender for a menu.

CHAPTER 38

The rain started to come down harder, then turned into a wintry mix as Lavender sped out of town. It was hard to see in the dark and she almost missed the turn for Stillwater Road, and her heart began to hammer again as the forest closed in around her. The trees looked ghostly in the narrow span of her headlights, and pools of snow still covered the ground in places. When the pavement ended, Lavender bumped along the poorly-graded dirt track, steering around large rocks and attempting to avoid the deepest ruts. The Impala wasn't made for this kind of driving, and its springs screeched in protest.

A pair of headlights popped up in the rearview mirror, then disappeared as Lavender rounded a bend. There was a washout ahead that had narrowed a section of the roadway to a single car's width, and she slowed to a crawl and held her breath as she navigated the tight space, praying her wheels wouldn't slip over the muddy edge and land the car in a ditch. When the road opened up again, she exhaled in relief, but then the mysterious headlights reappeared, sending her frayed nerves into high alert. She told herself that most of the lakeside cottages were shut up for the winter, so whoever was following her was most likely a guest heading back to their cozy room at the Stillwater Hotel.

The car's tires met pavement again, and soon Lavender could see the lights of the rustic chalet-style hotel, and the carved wooden sign reading *WHERE THE ROAD ENDS AND A GOOD TIME BEGINS*. There was a black SUV parked directly in front of the restaurant entrance; she pulled up next to it, stepped out into an icy puddle, and sloshed to the door.

Inside, it was warm and dry. The only other customers there were a boisterous party of four seated at one of the tables in the pine-paneled dining room. The room was festooned with Christmas garland and white twinkle lights, and a stately grandfather clock stood in the center of one wall. The longtime owner, Mother Marian, was behind the bar, restocking the beer fridge. When she saw Lavender walk in, she smiled and greeted her by name. "Awfully wet out there tonight," she said in her Rockland County accent. "Where's your fella? I hope you didn't drive out here by yourself."

Bringing Marian up to speed about Burley's accident would invite too many questions, so Lavender drummed up a quick lie. "He's working overtime this week," she said with a casual wave of her hand, "so I thought I'd get away by myself for a few days, to check on things at the cottage and make sure it's ready for winter."

Marian set a case of Bud on the bar. "Your family doesn't seem to use that place very much," she commented as she transferred beer bottles to the fridge. "Have you considered offering it as a vacation rental? You could get top dollar for a nice waterfront property like that."

Lavender climbed onto one of the heavy wooden barstools. "Actually, we're thinking about selling it. A real estate agent is coming to look at it tomorrow." Her ability to concoct a smooth cover story pleased her, although she didn't like having to lie to Marian, who was good people.

"Would you like a glass of wine?" Marian asked.

Would she ever. "Yes, please. Red, if you've got a bottle open."

Marian winked. "You know we do." She set a wine glass on the shellacked bar top and took a bottle of cabernet from the shelf behind her. "Not the best time of year to be putting anything on the market," she said as she poured. "Might be better to wait till spring."

Lavender swallowed a large mouthful of wine before replying. "You're right. I think we will."

Marian resumed her restocking. The small bar area was snug and welcoming. A narrow window on the back wall opened into the kitchen, and the shelves above it were crammed with an assortment of wine and liquor bottles. The walls were covered with pictures of snowmobilers, hikers, hunters, and fisherman, and at the far end of the bar, a collection of police, fire and EMS insignia from all over New York state surrounded photographs of the burning Twin Towers and President George W. Bush.

Lavender checked her phone—still nothing from Richard. The people in the dining room howled at a joke and pounded on the table, making their plates and glassware rattle. Lavender ordered a hamburger, which was handed through the narrow window by someone in the kitchen. As she chatted with Marian about the restaurant's autumn wine-pairing dinner, a woman in a gray raincoat and matching hat came in through the side entrance and called to them, asking where the ladies' room was. "It's there on your left," Marian called back. She set a stack of receipts on the bar and began tallying them up as Lavender paged through a copy of the *Adirondack Express*. Something that sounded like a bin full of silverware crashed to the floor in the kitchen, and Marian poked her head through the little window. "You okay in there, Dewey?" When no response came from the kitchen, she shrugged and went back to her receipts.

The rowdy group of diners finished their meal and came into the bar to pay their bill, then left in high spirits and peals of laughter. Lavender checked her phone again. It was nearing ten o'clock, and Marian probably wanted to close up. She threw the newspaper aside. "Can I get a bottle of wine to go?"

Marian looked up. "Only one? You might want a couple bottles if you're staying for a few days." Lavender considered for a moment. If Richard called her sooner than expected, she might have to leave at a moment's notice, but she didn't want to take the chance of arousing Marian's suspicions. "Yeah," she said. "Better make it two."

Marian hollered for Dewey again, and when he appeared she sent him down to the cellar for the wine. The bottles he returned with were speckled with dust. Alcohol to go was only allowed in New York if the customer also purchased food to go with it, but Stillwater made its own rules. Marian wiped the wine bottles clean and presented them to Lavender in a brown paper bag. "We can settle up later. Have a good night."

Lavender pulled up the hood of her jacket, tucked the bag into the crook of her arm and went out to her car, which was the only one left on the premises. The glass of wine and quiet conversation with Marian had calmed her, and she was relieved to see the icy rain had let up for the moment, which would make the short but dark drive down to the cottage a little easier.

As she turned into the gravel driveway, the cottage was practically invisible in the midst of the surrounding trees. Parking at angle so that her headlights were pointing directly at the front steps, Lavender got out and located the house key in its lame hiding place underneath an empty flower pot. She unlocked the door and flipped the porch lights on, then went inside and walked through the downstairs rooms, hitting switches and turning on lamps until the place was lit up like a Christmas tree. Returning to the car, she retrieved her overnight bag and the two bottles of wine. After making sure the front door was locked and dead bolted, she checked the sliding door in the living room as well. Everything was secure. She found a corkscrew in the kitchen drawer, opened one of the wine bottles, and poured herself an overflowing glass.

CHAPTER 39

From her vantage point in the unlit parking area down by the Stillwater boat launch, Marta watched Lavender get into her car and turn north onto Necessary Dam Road. Leaving her headlights off, Marta drove up the hill past the hotel and restaurant, then made a right-hand turn and followed the Impala's taillights down the winding road.

An online search had revealed which cottage belonged to the LeClair family, so Marta knew where to stop before she got to it. The cloud cover was breaking up and the faint light of a waning moon helped her to discern the outlines of a dirt track leading the neighboring property. She steered the car into it and cut the engine.

Marta eased her door open, got out and listened intently for a minute. The night air was cold and still, filled with a whiff of frost and the rank odor of decaying leaves. Reaching into the front seat, she removed her canvas backpack and the Winchester rifle she'd stolen from Burley's trailer. She hooked the backpack over her shoulders and tucked the rifle beneath her raincoat, pushed the car door closed with a gentle click, and began walking along the road, taking care to stay in the deep shadows beneath the trees.

Several yards from the end of the LeClairs' driveway, Marta stepped off the road and moved toward the cottage, using a hedgerow along the border of the property for concealment. The porch light was on, casting a shimmery glow over the ice-coated grass in the yard, and she had to pick her way carefully to avoid slipping and dropping the rifle. She could see Lavender moving from room to room inside the cottage, turning on the lights.

Marta crouched down behind an overgrown holly bush a few feet from the porch. When Lavender went back out to her car to get the rest of her things, Marta made her move. She sprinted up the steps and through the front door, then dashed upstairs and ducked into one of the empty bedrooms.

CHAPTER 40

Lavender's previous visits to the cottage with Burley had been mostly enjoyable, sex-saturated occasions, but tonight the place had a strangely menacing feel to it. Turning the TV on for company, she flipped through the channels until she found a reality show to watch, and turned the volume up loud, to drown out any mysterious background noises.

For a little while, the petty grievances of the Real Housewives of wherever helped to divert her, but as she got deeper into the wine, Lavender waxed maudlin as memories of Burley crowded her thoughts. She took her phone out and swiped through dozens of selfies of the two of them, amazed at how strong the bond between them had remained, through all the difficulties of her divorce and Burley's money problems.

Tears wet her cheeks as she relived the moment when Burley slipped the diamond ring onto her finger and gave her a final kiss before they were parted forever. Pausing her mind-movie, Lavender corrected herself—technically, it hadn't been their final parting, since she'd been with him at the nursing home only hours ago. But then again, she rationalized, time spent with a man whose brain had turned into a turnip didn't count.

Lavender stared at her engagement ring. It was time to let go. She set her wine glass down, twisted the ring off and held it up to the light. "Goodbye, Burley," she murmured, and the tears came afresh as she zipped the ring into the inner pocket of her purse.

As midnight approached, she told herself it was time to stop this pathetic weeping. Pushing herself up from the couch, she was taken aback when she saw the two wine bottles on the end table—one completely empty, the other down by half. She hadn't meant to drink *that* much. Come to think of it, she didn't even remember opening the second bottle. Staggering to the kitchen, she dropped the empty one into the garbage can. The cork for the other bottle was nowhere to be seen, so she shoved a paper towel into its neck and left it on the counter for tomorrow.

Lavender weaved her way to the master bedroom, where she pawed through the dresser until she found one of her mother's long cotton nightgowns to change into, then lurched into the bathroom. The floor tilted and she banged her hip on the door frame. Fumbling with the toothpaste, she squeezed a gob onto her toothbrush and aimed it at her mouth. *Richard,* she thought as she scrubbed red wine from her teeth. He was probably pissed at her for calling and texting him so many times, but she needed to hear his voice, reassuring her that everything was going to work out. What harm could one more little phone call do?

Lavender stumbled back to the bedroom, found her phone and redialed Richard's number, but once again, there was no answer. She collapsed onto the bed and immediately passed out, the phone still clutched in her hand.

CHAPTER 41

After he'd eaten dinner and downed a second drink, Richard returned to his hotel room and began to go over his preparations for the morning. He had a nine o'clock appointment with Joseph Caselli, one of the attorneys whose name was on the law firm's letterhead. After double-checking his wallet for his brother's driver's license and social security card, he unlocked his briefcase and took out the folder containing the letter about the inheritance, along with Ron's birth certificate and most recent bank account statement.

He set his suitcase on top of one of the beds, unzipped it and removed the country boy getup of blue jeans, flannel shirt and Carhartt coat. He arranged the clothing neatly on the bedspread, and placed his brother's worn pair of work boots by the door. Next, he set the alarm on his phone for six a.m., to give himself plenty of time to shower, dress, and get into character, and then he called down to the front desk to request a wake-up call as a backup. Satisfied with his arrangements, he turned the television to a random movie in progress, and prepared for bed.

His eagerness to get on with things prevented him from sleeping, and he clicked restlessly from one late-night television show to the next. Around midnight, his phone lit up with another incoming call Lavender. *Ignorant fool,* he thought. *Enough already.* If she kept this up, he might have to block her number.

CHAPTER 42

Burley was still lying awake at midnight, due to a painful pounding in his head. The eleven-to-seven nurse had made her rounds shortly after coming on duty, but he wasn't able to communicate his discomfort to her as she made a cursory check of his room.

Lavender's treachery dominated his thoughts as he struggled to make sense of what she had confessed. She'd hooked up with his *brother*, of all people, and was planning to steal his money to boot! It was too unbelievable. As the night wore on, he continued to fume, and his blood pressure began to creep silently upward.

CHAPTER 43

As the jaunty *Real Housewives* theme music started up for the fourth time, Marta tiptoed out of the upstairs bedroom and peeked down the stairwell. She'd checked on Lavender periodically throughout the evening; each time, the little wench had been curled up on the couch, glugging wine and blubbering over pictures on her phone.

The couch was empty now, and there were noises coming from the master bedroom. Marta crept down the stairs and waited in the living room, peeking around the corner toward the bedroom every minute or two until she was certain Lavender was passed out for the night. All the lights were still on, which she was afraid might attract attention if someone happened to drive by in the middle of the night. She padded through the rooms, flipping switches until the entire cottage lay in darkness, then felt her way back up the stairs.

In the small bedroom where she'd been hiding, Marta turned on the bedside lamp and draped her hoodie over the shade to dim the light. The room held two twin-sized beds; the rifle was lying on one of them alongside the backpack, which contained bottled water and protein bars, a box of ammunition and a pair of latex gloves. Marta picked up the gun, loaded a round into the chamber and set the safety, then stuffed a handful of cartridges into the pocket of her raincoat that was hanging on the back of the bedroom door. She ate one of the protein bars, drank some water and made a quick trip to the bathroom, then stretched out on the other bed, still fully dressed. Everything was going perfectly, and she smiled at the craftiness of her plan.

It had all started so long ago, on that summer night when Burley had shown up at the bowling alley with his giddy new girlfriend. Marta knew she needed to get a grip on herself and get over her crush on him, but she couldn't help feeling that Burley had no right to hook up with someone else so soon after dumping her. She had to get back at him for rubbing it in her face.

The slashed tire was only meant to be an inconvenience that would prevent him from taking the girlfriend home. She'd had no intention of doing anything worse. But the feel of the knife slicing through rubber had set something off in her. A white-hot fury took hold, and it was like she'd lost her mind. Burley needed to suffer for the pain he'd caused her. Crawling behind the front wheels, she'd slashed at the brake lines until they bled, thinking the truck would eventually wind up crashed in a ditch, or wrapped around a tree.

But then she saw Hunter Stanwell leading drunken Donna out to his car, and Burley running to the girl's defense. Hidden behind a nearby car, Marta had watched in disbelief as Hunter lied to the sheriff's deputy. *Holy Jesus*, she thought as Burley was frisked and handcuffed. *He's going to jail.* The unfairness of it infuriated her. Burley was a good guy! He was kind and generous, always willing to lend someone a hand. He didn't deserve to have his reputation destroyed by false accusations. It was too late to undo the damage to his truck, but she could at least go down to the police station and set the record straight.

She was terrified Burley would figure out what she'd done, and prayed he would blame the townies. His decision not to report the vandalism was a huge relief, and it put Marta in the clear. The night's unfortunate events left her resolved to swallow her anger and hurt, and prove to Burley that there were no hard feelings on her part. They could still be friends.

Yet here she was twenty years later, and still not over it. The laced coffee was meant to kill Burley, but the maiming that resulted was even better. For the remainder of his miserable life, he'd be at the mercy of everyone around him. He'd never again know joy, or love, or the simplest pleasures of life.

And of course, there was Lavender to get even with as well. Marta laughed out loud. That bitch wasn't going to walk away from this. She was going to pay, too.

CHAPTER 44

Lavender woke at dawn with a pounding head and some serious cottonmouth. She found an expired bottle of Bayer aspirin in the bathroom, swallowed four tablets, and slouched out to the kitchen to put on a pot of coffee.

The weather had cleared overnight and the early morning sun cast a golden glow on the mist rising from the cove. When the coffee finished brewing, she wrapped herself in a striped blanket, pushed her bare feet into a pair of her mother's slippers, opened the sliding door and stepped out onto the deck. A few breaths of the brisk December air would do her throbbing head a world of good. The thermometer tacked to the railing registered thirty-six degrees, which was chilly but tolerable if she didn't stay out too long. Lavender settled herself in one of the bright blue Adirondack chairs with the blanket tucked snugly around her shoulders, and took in the panorama of water and blue sky.

As the aspirin and coffee kicked in, her head started to feel a little better, but the teary mood of the preceding evening returned with the sober realization that she might never see this place again. Setting her mug down on the small wooden table beside her, she began to reminisce.

Her parents had purchased the cottage when she was in the ninth grade, so it was full of memories from her teenage years, when she and her girlfriends used to sneak out there on the weekends, to party and hook up with their boyfriends. It had been such a happy, carefree time of her life—until she got pregnant with Logan, and everything changed.

If only she could go back and do it all differently. Lavender sipped her coffee, gazing out at the dark water in the center of the lake, until the sound of the door sliding along its track jerked her from her thoughts. Turning her head, she stared in horror at the slender woman standing a few feet from her, holding a rifle in her hands. "Get up," the woman said, motioning with the gun.

There was something oddly familiar about her, but Lavender was too frightened to think of what it was. The woman tipped her bare, shorn head toward the sliding door, indicating where she wanted Lavender to go. Lavender pushed herself out of the Adirondack chair and did as she was told. When she was standing in the middle of the living room with the striped blanket still wrapped around her shoulders, the woman lowered the gun. "You know who I am, don't you?"

"N-no," Lavender stammered. She studied the woman more closely, and all of a sudden it clicked. "Oh my God," she said. "You're Marta."

A slow smile spread across Marta's face. "That's right. And you're stupid.

Lavender retorted without thinking: "Fuck you, bitch."

The rifle jerked up as Marta aimed it dead at the center of Lavender's chest. "Drop the blanket," she ordered. "Go to the bedroom and start packing your things. I'll be right behind you.

CHAPTER 45

Richard rose promptly at six the next morning, a burst of energy coursing through his limbs. He was psyched for the challenge that lay ahead today, and was pumped for the role he was about to play. The money was going to transform his life.

After he'd shaved and showered, he took his time with the hotel blow-dryer, using it to mold his hair into a subdued style to match the photo on his brother's driver's license. When he was done, he put on the flannel shirt and buttoned it up. The jeans were a little too big for his trim waist, but Lavender had provided him with Ron's leather belt, which he cinched up an additional notch. Hand-brushing the sides of his hair, he nodded in satisfaction at his reflection in the mirror.

Too excited to eat breakfast, he settled for a cup of coffee that he brewed in the room. As he drank it, he half-listened to a morning news program on TV, and paged through the complimentary copy of *USA Today* that had been slipped under his door during the night. When he was finished skimming the paper, he opened the Google Maps app on his phone and reviewed his route to the law firm. It was a seventeen-minute walk, so if he left the hotel at 8:30, he'd arrive with time to spare. Right now, it was 8:00 on the nose. Thirty minutes till go time.

CHAPTER 46

When the nursing assistant came to check Burley's vital signs that morning, the throbbing in his head had become even more painful and insistent. The young woman lifted his lifeless arm, wrapped the stiff blood pressure cuff around it, and placed the bell of her stethoscope on the inside of his elbow. Her eyes locked on the pressure gauge as the air released from the cuff with a soft wheeze. Tugging the arms of the stethoscope from her ears, she dropped it on the bed and ran for the nurse.

CHAPTER 47

Lavender moved toward the bedroom, her legs wobbling like they were about to give out. When she reached the doorway, she turned to look back at Marta.

"Go on," Marta said with the rifle still aimed at Lavender's chest. "Start packing."

In the bedroom, Lavender cast her eyes around in a panic, searching for her phone so she could call 911. Her clothes were strewn on the floor where she'd discarded them last night. She knelt and pawed through them, but the phone wasn't there. Gathering her things with shaking hands, she stuffed them into her overnight bag, then looked up at Marta. "Why are you doing this?"

Marta regarded her with loathing. "You deliberately kept Burley away from me when you knew I needed him."

"You did not need him." Lavender stared back in defiance. "I know you lied about having cancer. It was just a ploy to get him to feel sorry for you."

Marta barked a short, evil laugh. "I did what I had to do, and now I'm going to make you wish you'd never met him."

Lavender recoiled in terror, clasping the overnight bag to her chest like a shield. "What are you going to do to me?"

Marta ignored the question. "Follow me," she said, backing down the hall. When they reached the living room, she instructed Lavender to leave her bag by the front door. "If you try to make a run for it, I'll blow your head off."

Lavender dropped the overnight bag on the throw rug in the entryway. "My purse," she whimpered. "I need my purse."

"It's right there on the couch, dumbass, where you left it when you were wasted last night." Marta reached for the purse with one hand, and tossed it onto the floor next to the overnight bag. "Don't touch it."

Lavender started to cry. "Please, please don't hurt me. I never meant to upset you, I swear. I just—"

"Shut up." Marta backed up a few steps, leaving room for Lavender to pass in front of her. "Go," she said. "Outside."

The sliding door was wide open and a cold breeze was blowing in, ruffling the long white curtains that framed it. Lavender stepped over the threshold, then looked down at the cotton nightgown she was wearing. She turned pleadingly to Marta. "It's freezing out here."

Marta smiled. "I know."

"Can't I at least put my boots on?"

Marta rolled her eyes. "God, you're such a fucking girl. Okay, get your frigging boots."

Lavender grabbed her Uggs from the floor beside the couch, where she'd kicked them off the night before. When she'd pulled them on, Marta pressed the muzzle of the rifle between her shoulder blades and forced her back outside. They crossed the deck, went down the steps, and began walking toward the water.

CHAPTER 48

Richard stepped off the elevator into the lobby of the law firm of Caselli, Brogan & Sterne, and strode up to the polished woman seated behind the reception desk. "Good morning," he said smoothly. "My name is Ronald Burley. I have a nine o'clock appointment with Mr. Caselli."

The receptionist consulted her computer monitor. "Very good, Mr. Burley. Please follow me." She escorted Richard down the hall to a small conference room and invited him to have a seat. "I'll tell Mr. Caselli you're here," she said, and closed the door as she left.

Richard crossed his legs and jiggled his foot nervously. The view from the windows was of another high-rise office building, where people in power suits were talking on telephones and staring at bluish computer screens. He checked his watch and drummed his fingers on the polished mahogany table. A minute later, the door clicked open and a slender thirtyish man in a clipped beard and dark suit walked in. "Good morning, Mr. Burley," he said, extending his hand. "I'm Colin Hargraves, assistant to Mr. Caselli."

Colin pulled out a chair and sat down. "I've reviewed the notes from your initial inquiry, and I understand you're here about an inheritance matter. How can we be of assistance today?"

Richard opened his briefcase, removed the letter from the folder and slid it across the table. "A close friend of mine named Marta Grolsch passed away recently, and she apparently bequeathed a portion of her estate to me in her will. I'm here to make the necessary arrangements for the transfer of the funds."

Colin took the letter and read it, glanced up at Richard, then looked back down at the letter and read it through again. A thin line formed between his brows and he scratched his bearded chin.

Richard folded his hands in his lap to suppress the urge to fidget, and watched as Colin placed the document on the conference table, rubbed his thumb across the letterhead, and brushed away some invisible dust. "If you would please excuse me," Colin said, "I'd like to consult with Mr. Caselli for a moment."

Richard leaned forward in his seat. "Is there something else you're in need of? I have my identification right here." He pulled his wallet from his back pocket, extracted his brother's driver's license and tossed it onto the table. "I would be happy to provide you with additional documentation, if you require it."

Colin placed two fingers on the driver's license and rotated it so he could look at the photo. "That won't be necessary, your license is sufficient. I'll go make a copy of it for our files."

"Certainly." Richard gave him a polite smile, then leaned back in his chair and casually re-crossed his legs, to show the little twerp how at ease he was. Nothing to see here, dude. Just keep things moving and give me my money.

CHAPTER 49

Lavender gripped her arms around her middle, shivering uncontrollably as she walked down the slope toward the lake, with Marta on her heels. That flaky Penelope had been right after all—the woman was indeed sick in the head. She cursed herself for not taking the psychic's warning seriously.

When they were within a few feet of the pebbly shore, Lavender stopped and looked around at Marta, and her voice was shrill with fear: "What do you want me to do?"

Marta cocked an elbow toward the canoe resting on a pair of railroad ties. "Drag that boat down to the water and get into it."

Lavender's eyes widened. "Wait, what? I can't do that, it's too cold! Look at me, I'm in a *nightgown*."

"You think I give a shit?" Marta tightened her grip on the rifle. "Do what I said."

Lavender stepped into the snowy weeds, gripped the edge of the canoe with both hands, and heaved it sideways off the railroad ties. She grabbed hold of one end and lugged the heavy craft down to the water's edge, with Marta watching closely and keeping the rifle trained on her the whole time. When the canoe was in the water, Marta spoke. "Get in," she said, "and take the paddle."

Looking around, Lavender saw one of the old wooden paddles lying on the ground. She stooped to pick it up, then climbed clumsily into the canoe, the hem of her nightgown trailing in the water. Marta placed her foot on the stern and gave the boat a violent shove. The aluminum hull grated against the stones and drifted away from the shore.

"Start paddling, and don't stop," Marta called. "I'll have my sights on you the whole time, so don't even think about turning back."

Lavender gripped the paddle in her cold hands and dipped it into the frigid water. The morning sun had begun to burn the mist off the lake, but there were bits of ice floating in the shallow nooks along the shore. It was petrifying, knowing there was a gun pointed at her back, but also a relief to be getting away from that madwoman. The farther Lavender paddled, the less terrified she felt. At least the nutjob hadn't shot her on the spot. Marta probably just wanted to scare the crap out of her, in revenge for being edged out of their cozy little love triangle with Burley. She couldn't be crazy enough to commit a murder out here in the open.

Twisting around to look back, Lavender saw Marta still standing on the shore, the rifle raised to her shoulder. *Shit,* she thought. *She actually expects me to paddle all the way out into the lake.* She scanned the surrounding waters, searching in vain for another boat she could call out to for help, but the lake was deserted. Looking back once more toward the shore, the only sign of life was the curtains fluttering in the wide-open sliding door of the cottage.

All she could do was keep paddling out of the cove, then follow the shoreline down to the Stillwater Hotel, where she could summon help. Lavender plunged her paddle in deeper and repositioned her feet to get better leverage. A splashing sound made her look down, and she was shocked to see several inches of water swirling over the tops of her boots. When she bent down to see where the water was coming from, she discovered with horror that there was a long gap in the seam at the bottom of the canoe.

Seized with fear, Lavender began scooping the water out with her bare hands, but her fingers were soon too cold and stiff to be of any use.

Casting around for something to use as a bailer, she thought of her boots. As she leaned over to pull one of the Uggs off, her frozen hands lost their grip and she tumbled backwards, causing the canoe to tip dangerously onto its side, then capsize.

The icy water shocked her senses. Lavender flailed her arms and tried to grab hold of the paddle, but it floated out of her grasp. Clawing the water with her hands, she struggled to keep her head above the surface, but the cotton nightgown had wrapped itself around her legs and the heavy fabric was dragging her down.

The overturned canoe floated away. The mist had burned off completely by now, revealing the rocky arm of the cove in the distance. If she made a concerted effort, she might be able to swim to land. It didn't look that far away.

But her arms and legs were going numb, and her body felt heavy, so heavy. She was exhausted. Treading water took too much effort and she couldn't do it anymore, she needed to rest. Just for a minute, then she'd swim to shore. Lavender closed her eyes and felt the water creeping up over her chin to her mouth, and then her nose. She was sinking, sinking. Grainy images flashed before her eyes: *Logan. Her mother and father. Burley*. The morning sunshine grew dim, then disappeared as the water closed over her head.

CHAPTER 50

Richard waited for several minutes, growing first impatient, then nervous, then outright panicked and ready to bolt. He got up and stuck his head out of the conference room door, and saw a maze of cubicles and people bent over their desks. No one seemed to be paying any attention to him, so he put his head down and hurried along the corridor.

The receptionist's head shot up as he passed. "Sir?" she called out. "Wait a moment, please." Richard rushed past her and jabbed the Down button for the elevator. Out of the corner of his eye, he saw the woman on her feet behind her desk, telephone to her ear. "Sir," she called again. "Please wait, Mr. Caselli would like to speak with you."

The elevator wasn't coming. Richard turned in a frantic circle, searching for an escape route. Over to his left he spotted a sign for the stairwell, but before he could make a run for it, the elevator doors whirred open and two uniformed police officers were staring him down. He backed away but the receptionist was behind him now, blocking his move. One of the cops grabbed his arm as the other one brandished a pair of handcuffs.

CHAPTER 51

The pounding in Burley's head intensified. A wave of nausea rose from his gut and he vomited on himself. A sharp pain jagged through his head as the aneurysm at the base of his skull ruptured with a silent *poom*, leaking blood into the surrounding brain tissue. His vision blurred for a moment, and then everything faded to black.

CHAPTER 52

When the ripples on the water had disappeared, Marta lowered the rifle. She drew Lavender's phone from her coat pocket and threw it as far as she could into the lake, then turned and walked back up to the cottage. She removed the latex gloves from her backpack and put them on, then retrieved Lavender's wine glass from the living room and the coffee mug from the table on the deck, washed and dried them thoroughly, and put them away in the cupboard. The grounds from the coffee maker went into an oversized Ziploc bag, along with the wine bottles and the missing corks she'd found on the floor. She ran her fingers along the top edges of the bag to seal it, and placed it in the backpack.

In the master suite, she plumped up the pillows and remade the bed, and hoped Mrs. LeClair wouldn't miss her hideous Little House on the Prairie nightgown, which was now wrapped around her daughter's body at the bottom of the lake. She then went into the bathroom, where she tidied the unused towels and wiped a dollop of toothpaste off the counter with a Kleenex that she flushed down the toilet.

The Impala was still parked in the driveway. Marta carried Lavender's overnight bag and purse out to it, and pulled the car into the garage. It was far from being an ideal hiding place, but it would buy her time before the police came searching in earnest. She lowered the overhead door and returned to the house for one last check.

The cottage looked as orderly and unused as it had when she and Lavender had arrived the night before. Smiling with satisfaction, Marta slipped out through the sliding door and disappeared into the dark forest.

THE END

ACKNOWLEDGEMENTS

Many thanks to my Rochester, New York critique group: Len Messineo, Ralph Uttaro and Ted Obourn. Your insightful comments and candid (and often very funny!) feedback via countless Zoom meetings were an indispensable part of my writing process. Thanks also to my Florida writers group, graciously hosted by Kyle Ann Robertson. I'm so glad to have connected with all of you here in the Sunshine State. A special thank you goes to my immensely talented developmental editor, Rowan Humphries, for her enthusiasm, spot-on commentary, and invaluable millennial perspective. Another special thank you goes to Brendan, for providing entertaining conversation and silly dog stories when my writing brain was in need of diversion. And last, a shout-out to my Emery Runners, whose friendship has sustained me on my long writing journey. Miss you guys!

ABOUT THE AUTHOR

Regina is a registered nurse-turned-writer who was raised in beautiful upstate New York, where she spent many happy years exploring the winding back roads and scenic hiking trails of the Adirondack mountain region. She recently traded the snowy northern winters for the tropical breezes of the Sunshine State, where her favorite pastimes are kayaking among the mangroves, strolling the gorgeous beaches, and attempting to teach tricks to her boisterous corgi. Connect with her on her website at: www.reginabuttner.com

ABOUT THE AUTHOR

NOTE FROM THE AUTHOR

Word-of-mouth is crucial for any author to succeed. If you enjoyed
Down a Bad Road, please leave a review online—anywhere you are
able. Even if it's just a sentence or two. It would make all the difference
and would be very much appreciated.

Thanks!
Regina Buttner

We hope you enjoyed reading this title from:

BLACK ❧ ROSE
writing™

www.blackrosewriting.com

Subscribe to our mailing list – *The Rosevine* – and receive **FREE** books, daily deals, and stay current with news about upcoming releases and our hottest authors.
Scan the QR code below to sign up.

Already a subscriber? Please accept a sincere thank you for being a fan of Black Rose Writing authors.

View other Black Rose Writing titles at
www.blackrosewriting.com/books and use promo code
PRINT to receive a **20% discount** when purchasing.